MW01135877

PRAISE FOR
LESLIE GRAY STREETER

"*Family & Other Calamities* is vintage Leslie Gray Streeter: hilariously funny, and with a powerful emotional punch. It's a deep study in the gifts we get from the people we love the most, even when we don't always like them."

—Jen Lancaster, *New York Times* bestselling author of *Housemoms*

"Leslie Streeter's dialogue is delightful. Even when the good times slam into bad times, her heroine holds on to her sense of humor and you won't want to leave her side. As a bonus, this novel offers deep wisdom about being a journalist, so not only will you laugh—and be moved—but you will also learn how to be a better writer."

—Nell Scovell, author of *Just the Funny Parts*

"At the core of this story about the journey of grieving and healing is a story of family, friends, and failure that will resonate with anyone. It's frank, messy, and wryly funny in turns."

—Mikki Kendall, *New York Times* bestselling author

"*Family & Other Calamities* delivers exactly what I want when I sit down to read a novel. It has genuinely memorable characters, a fresh voice that kept me reading, lines that made me laugh out loud, and scenes that brought me to tears."

—James Patterson, #1 *New York Times* bestselling author

"*Family & Other Calamities* is about love in many forms—family, friendship, and standing up for what is yours. Dawn Roberts is a funny and charming character you will want to root for. Streeter's signature humor and charisma shine bright in this bighearted debut."

—Karin Slaughter, *New York Times* and
#1 international bestselling author

"A compelling story of truth, justice, and the American way. Leslie Streeter understands both the news business and the heartbreak business."

—Josh Mankiewicz, correspondent for *Dateline NBC*

"A vividly imagined tale of family drama and workplace betrayal, filled with gallows humor and heart. With her snappy dialogue and impeccably flawed characters, Streeter proves she has her finger on the pulse of messy, heartbroken Gen Xers. You'll binge Dawn's story like it was your favorite show."

—Geraldine DeRuiter, James Beard
Award—winning author and blogger

FAMILY
&
OTHER
CALAMITIES

FAMILY & OTHER CALAMITIES

a novel

LESLIE GRAY STREETER

LAKE UNION
PUBLISHING

Published by Lake Union Publishing, Seattle

www.apub.com

Amazon, the Amazon logo, and Lake Union Publishing are trademarks of Amazon.com, Inc., or its affiliates.

EU product safety contact:
Amazon Media EU S. à r.l.
38, avenue John F. Kennedy, L-1855 Luxembourg
amazonpublishing-gpsr@amazon.com

ISBN-13: 9781662527616 (hardcover)
ISBN-13: 9781662527623 (paperback)
ISBN-13: 9781662527630 (digital)

Cover design by Jarrod Taylor
Cover image: © nastyrekh / Shutterstock

Printed in the United States of America

First edition

To Ida B. Wells, all the truth tellers that came after, and those to come.

Chapter 1

GOD BLESS SAM DONALDSON

1981

"Who's that, Daddy?"

I'm swinging back and forth in one of the very 1970s imitation Eames chairs in our Baltimore dining room. I've been trying to hide the remaining bits of cold mashed potatoes under my napkin so I can get up and go listen to Michael Jackson's *Off the Wall* album on my little Donny & Marie record player. It's really my parents' album that I snuck to my room, so I'm hiding it, just like these nasty mashed potatoes.

My daddy looks over his shoulder to the little black-and-white TV sitting on the counter. On the tiny screen is a shot of the White House. President Ronald Reagan is trying to walk past a group of men in suits and trench coats without talking to them, but they don't seem to be letting him. I'm ten, so I don't know a lot about this politics stuff, but I've gotten the feeling from the way my parents talk about the president and generally scowl in the direction of the TV whenever he's on, that they are not fans.

"That's the president," Daddy says. "I see you hiding those potatoes, girl."

"No, not him," I say quickly, removing the napkin from the top of the white pile of cold mess, which now has little bits of paper stuck to it. *Eww.* "That guy with the microphone."

From the kitchen, my mother squints at the TV as she scrapes the plates of everyone who has finished their dinner and has been allowed to get up from the table. "That's Sam Donaldson," she says as the man asks President Reagan a question. I can't make out what he's saying, but Reagan doesn't seem to be enjoying it.

"Isn't the president in charge of everything?" I ask.

My father sighs. "Unfortunately."

"So why is he afraid of that man?"

My father chuckles. "Because he's a journalist who's after the truth, and politicians don't always like that."

A journalist, huh?

"So his job is to, like, make people who are in charge of stuff nervous, just with his words?" I ask. This is interesting. Currently, my career aspirations are queen, veterinarian, and crossing guard, because crossing guards control the traffic with a whistle and a white glove. That impresses me.

"That's pretty much it," my mother says, stepping to the basement door. "Tonya! Don't fall asleep down there! I'm too tired to carry you up two flights of stairs."

"Yeah, Tonya!" I yell after her.

My mother rolls her eyes at me. "I wouldn't be too smug if I were you, my girl. At least Tonya's allowed to get up from the table because she's not messing around wasting my food."

I reluctantly force one more spoonful of hateful taters into my mouth, and as I make myself chew, I decide to find out more about this . . . what was it? Journalism? It was about writing, a thing I already like, and talking and being in charge, which I like even more.

"It's like being a crossing guard, but for the truth," I mumble.

"You're a very intense ten-year-old," Daddy says.

He has no idea. Tomorrow, all of Tonya's and my Barbies will be working in a fake newsroom for a paper called the *Morning Dawn*, and the editor, Superstar Christie, will be barking "Deadline!" and "Breaking news!" at all the other dolls and firing them at random, because Editor Superstar Christie is a tough, take-no-prisoners leader. (She'd survived having her plastic foot accidentally ironed.)

It does not matter that I have "technically" borrowed a portion of my staff from my sister's side of the room, where they'd been having a tea party and talking smack about how Superstar Christie's melted foot didn't quite fit into her hard pink plastic shoe.

"Always taking people's stuff!" I remember Tonya screaming. "This isn't fair!"

It would not be the last time that Superstar Christie's . . . er, my journalistic pursuits would be unfair to my sister. In my defense, her dolls were kind of mean.

Chapter 2

DEADLINES ARE A LOT

April 2023

"Fifteen minutes, Dawn!"

It's hard enough to concentrate on writing the perfect column under normal circumstances, and near impossible with someone literally breathing down your neck. It's especially insulting when you pay that someone's salary.

"Almost done!" I say, not trying to hide my annoyance. Pearl, my assistant editor, is hovering over my shoulder in the tiny newsroom of Glitter, the entertainment journalism start-up I created four years ago. *And* she's smirking. The disrespect!

"I'm just trying to help, Dawn," she says. "You have to get to this Vivienne St. Claire interview on time, and you have to finish this column before your flight tomorrow. I don't even have to ask if you're packed yet."

I am not. She knows me too well.

"You just don't have to be so smirky about it." I nod, scanning quickly for typos. I live by spell-check, because writing geniuses don't need to spell well. That's what Vernon, our ace copyeditor, is for.

"Chop, chop," Pearl says.

"Are you *trying* to get fired?" I ask, hitting "Save," and taking one more sip of cold coffee from the Baltimore Ravens mug next to the laptop. It's kind of gross, but I don't have time to refill it.

Vernon, sitting across from me, shakes his head. "I'd be careful, Pearl. It's rough out there. Every week, some old friend I haven't heard from in a decade suddenly texts me to ask if we're hiring. You can be replaced."

"See!" I say. "You need this job. How else are you going to pay for those expensive shoes you can't walk in?"

When I founded Glitter, which references both the glamour of the entertainment industry and the Mariah Carey movie you must never speak ill of, I had wondered if I'd ever be in a loud, hectic newsroom again. I used to be a staffer at the *Los Angeles Times*, but in case you've missed it, journalism is on life support and democracy is in the next bed in the ICU.

Pearl and I were both lucky enough to be offered substantial buyout checks from the *Times*, before they could lay us off for free, and she came with me to found Glitter, with business advice and support from my husband, Dale, a talent manager who worked with all the top artists. His faith in me paid off, and Glitter was an instant success. We've interviewed *everybody* you've heard of and even made a few stars with our features. Everybody, that is, *except* for monumental diva Vivienne St. Claire, or Miss Vivi, as she's known to those who love her, fear her, and secretly long for trending Google news of her death. She started as the lead singer of the 1960s girl group The Curtseys, and became a solo smash, fashion icon, and sufferer of absolutely no fools.

She's been dodging my interview requests for years. When I worked at the *Times*, her weaselly publicist Sebastian told me she was only doing exclusive outlets. I reminded him that I was from THEE *LA Times*, and he said "More exclusive than that" and hung up. That stung, because I'm a big deal, at least in this corner of the industry. But it makes a fun story on my Old Journalist Zoom Happy Hours.

But my luck seems to be changing. Last week, Sebastian reached out to say that I was supremely blessed that Miss Vivienne was granting me an interview from her suite at the Beverly Hilton. I better be there on time, and wear neutrals, as not to clash with her boa. He would be in touch with the specific color of the day.

"What's this, her third farewell tour? It takes this long to say goodbye?" Vernon asks, peering over my shoulder. "Dawn, that is NOT how you spell 'brouhaha.'"

"The *fourth*, and stop crowding me," I say, typing faster. "Creating magic here."

I get an email alert from someone or something called "B. L. James Investigates." I have no idea what that is, so I don't have time to deal with it now.

"You're going to hit traffic, and I hear she doesn't like being kept waiting," Pearl says, tapping her watch again. *Ugh*. The pressure is all part of the job, the incessant ringing of the phone, the last-minute tips, the madness of trying to pull it all together at the last possible second. I still get to do what I love, on my own terms, like Khadijah James on *Living Single*. I'm almost as fly as Queen Latifah!

"Done!" I say, jumping up out of my chair and grabbing my bag. "Pearl, I appreciate you taking the reins while I'm in Baltimore."

"No problem," Pearl says. "I wish you were going for a more pleasant reason."

"We both know that if it wasn't a thing like this, I probably wouldn't be going at all!" I say, to lighten the mood and because it's true.

Pearl smiles. "Good luck with Vivienne St. Claire. Don't get a wig thrown at you or anything."

"I'll try," I say. "But if she does throw something at me, the story might get more hits."

"You're always thinking," Pearl says. "Even though you can't spell."

"You're right. That's why I'm the boss," I say as the door closes behind me.

Chapter 3

I'm Just Trying to Avoid Getting a Wig Thrown at Me

"I know you from somewhere, don't I?"

I'm about an hour into my Miss Vivi interview, and it's been a while since she's acknowledged that there's another human being in the room.

As we all know—and she'd be insulted if you didn't—she went solo and rode her eagle-eyed ambition right to the top. This isn't me judging her. That's a quote from the *New York Times* review of her memoir, *Kiss the Ring*. I'm sure because she's mentioned it. Twice.

So far, I've heard about how she once arranged to have a romantic rival / backup singer "accidentally" left behind on the first ever—and last ever—tour of an Antarctic expedition station, in the frozen tundra wearing nothing but a sparkly jumpsuit and a pair of cheap sequined platform shoes.

"Didn't even let her keep her wig!" Miss Vivi divulges with something between a chortle and a cackle. "That wasn't cheap hair. So I had to repo that thing. A victim of wigflation! Wait, that's hilarious. Write that down."

I'm a journalist doing an interview, so *of course* I'm writing it down. I'm also recording it, which I'm glad of, because no one's going to believe this.

"What have you learned about yourself at this time in your life?"
I ask.

"I've had time to consider my legacy and those I've inspired, and honestly they need to give me more credit," she says. "Hold on, let me call somebody. These scones aren't scone-ing."

Now she's launched into a lengthy and possibly litigious litany of offenses by people whose names you'd recognize. We're talking about the dead, the living, and those she keeps referring to as "the late So-and-So" though they're very much alive. She's implied a scandalous affair with a fellow luminary whose name may or may not rhyme with Schmevie Schmonder.

"You know what *that* means!" she says, her elegant hand hovering over a fresh batch of scones that appear to be sufficiently scone-y because she hasn't lobbed them out the window. "At least one of the two albums in *Songs in the Key of Life* is about me."

This is all fascinating and over the top, and I feel like she's toying with me. I want her to be impressed with me, to not regret this interview and to feel bad that she'd blown someone with my credentials off for so long. Might as well ask my question and hope I don't get dropped through a secret hole in the floor.

"You said you recognized me. Was it from VH1's *Behind the Music*, maybe? Or my appearance on that Paula Abdul special? She choreographed one of your tours, right?"

Miss Vivi scoffs dismissively. I feel offended for Paula, and she's not even here.

"You think I watched *that*? After what she did to me?"

"What did she do to you?"

"Wouldn't you like to know, DeeDee?" she says.

Yes. Yes, I would.

"Again, ma'am, my name is Dawn."

"Dawwwwn! That's *right*! Like the Frankie Valli song!"

I nod. "That's what I'm named after, actually."

"Frankie was fiiine," she purrs. "He tried to get his writing partner—Bob, I think his name was—to do one called 'Vivi,' but you know how it was back then. I was Black, he was white. There was all that business with the USO tour. And that poor manatee . . ."

"I'm sorry?"

Miss Vivi takes a long look at me, and it feels like the heat of the sun and the hottest bonnet dryer at the salon on the back of your neck. Too intense.

"You're a big shot, then. How come you've never interviewed me before?"

Should I mention that she asked for me by whatever name she remembered to ask for me by?

"I've tried, ma'am! Never lucky enough. But I'm so honored that I am interviewing you now."

"Of course you are!"

Miss Vivi's publicist Sebastian steps back into the room as if secretly summoned, a sign that we are done. He refills her champagne as she gathers her caftan around her and rises dramatically from her chair.

"Thank you, Dawn," she says. She got my name right! This concerns me. Before I have time to consider what that means, Miss Vivi glides toward the door, blinding gold fringe trailing elegantly behind her. I'm so dazzled by the pageantry that I almost forget my last question.

"Miss Vivi?" I ask.

She turns slowly to face me.

"Yes, Damita Jo?"

"Do you ever talk to Veronica and Verlene? The other Curtseys?"

Miss Vivi pauses and gives what I'm almost sure is a friendly smile.

"We don't speak, but we're very close."

Interesting.

"And Daisy?"

I'm not even going to correct her.

"I don't know you from anything you've written," she says. "I wanted to see you because of the story you didn't write."

Huh?

Before I can get her to clarify, Vivienne St. Claire and her caftan have disappeared, and I wonder if any of this happened. No, wait, that's a marabou feather in my hair. It's real.

And weird.

"Something you didn't write? What does that mean?" Pearl asks when I fill her in during my drive home between bites of Burger King onion rings.

In all the years we've known each other, I've never told Pearl about the big story that got away from me when I was a fresh-faced reporter back east. Or about Eddie, the news photographer who really got me, before I messed it all up.

"What did she mean about the other Curtseys? How can you be close to someone but never speak to them?"

"It happens," I say. It's when you've been through the worst possible things together, but your history makes it hard to exist safely in the same zip code, let alone the same room. Still, when the chips are down or somebody's mama is sick, you'd show up. If that's the deal with Miss Vivi and The Curtseys, she and I have more in common than I would like to admit.

As for the story I *didn't* write?

I was working on what became the biggest story in ages when Joseph R. Perkins, currently of *National News Now* fame, got his big break. You remember. He wrote up that political scandal as a Pulitzer-winning story.

That he stole from me.

Maybe that's not what Miss Vivi is talking about—who even knows what she's ever talking about? She's so wacky and cryptic, she's probably forgotten about our whole conversation. But that story?

That's one I'm never going to forget.

Chapter 4

Your Cats Hate You

It's 3:46 a.m. My cats, George Michael and Andrew Wham!, are mad the alarm keeps waking them, and they are staring at me like "Lady who brings us the food! What's that noise?"

Groggy, I roll over, hoping I haven't woken Dale up. And then I remember.

I can't wake Dale up because Dale is dead.

"I know, I know. That man would have fed you by now," I tell them. "At least you don't have to take Daddy's ashes back to Baltimore for his brother to bury." They don't appear to be moved.

My phone buzzes. A text from my sister, Tonya. Hey girl. What's your flight number again?

I told her this already, so I'm tempted to ignore it. But since I'm up now, I give her a call.

"I just need your flight number—you didn't need to call," says my sister from a place where the sun is already up.

"Sure," I said. "My flight is United 1701."

Tonya pauses dramatically. It's too early for drama in either time zone.

"WHAT?" I yell.

"Nothing," she says hurriedly. "Just making sure. It's early."

"Even earlier here," I grouse, narrowly dodging George Michael's claw aimed at my neck. "What's your problem?"

She snorts. "It's not like you type well. Just clarifying so you can't blame me if I pick you up late. You're historically unreliable."

And there's the dig. My sister and I get along well, considering one party blames the other for fleeing town for a man. Also, maybe the fleeing party had something to do with the first party's boyfriend going to jail for fraud? Who knows?

It could have been anything, really.

I've had a good excuse for delaying this trip—excuses, plural. First, there was the pandemic: Dale died in 2021, and I didn't want to fly cross-country and get coughed on or punched out in a wild plane fight. It's not like I go home a lot anyway. Our initial move to the West Coast can be best described as . . . abrupt, and the next time I came back, both Dale and I were marrying someone our parents had never met, just like in a rom-com. But in the real-life version, no one pretends it's cute.

It was awkward for sure, and most everyone came to love each other over the years, with one notable exception. But the way I left town has always been a sore spot with my sister and me, and with work getting busy for us both, our planned twice-yearly visits after the wedding eventually became one, if that.

"Maybe if you had grandchildren for us to meet, you'd come more often," my daddy said once and then changed the subject because he knew that wasn't a thing he was supposed to say out loud. It burned. I loved him enough not to tell him and eat that acid burn in my chest silently.

We never had those grandkids, another thing for me to feel guilty about. And unfortunately, I can't delay this trip any longer for the worst reason. Dale's ashes—at least the half that's in the urn I'm taking with me and not the half that's in a Baltimore Orioles piggy bank on my bookcase in LA—are going to be interred in the family mausoleum along with his mother, Diane, who died not long after he did. I don't love his brother, Brent, but he asked me to bring Dale home, and I'm not petty enough to play games with ashes.

Here on the phone, it's quiet and uncomfortable, and I want to hang up, but someone has to speak, I guess.

"Maybe I'll fake a disease and not come at all."

"Oh, please. You can't mail ashes."

Tonya doesn't know that I have actually rehearsed wrapping this urn up in all the bubble wrap they have at the UPS Store and sending it on its way. I must hand deliver the ashes to Brent, who has never been my biggest fan. I wouldn't put it past him to run tests on the ashes to make sure they aren't really burned paint chips or Cheetos dust.

It's too early for this conversation, so I'm ending it.

"Now you know when my flight is," I say. "See you there. Don't be late. And thank you!"

She is confused by my politeness.

"Oh, OK," she says. "I'm going to be down there in Catonsville near the airport for work. Mrs. Mason—you know, Tammy's mother? She's refinancing, and she wants to talk about me being her broker."

"Oh her! Didn't she have Black lawn jockeys at some point?"

Tonya snorts. "Yeah, she did. But I can rise above. I'm a professional."

"A professional what, though?"

We both laugh, and just like that, we're cool again. Mostly.

"Listen, girl, let me get out of here," I say. "I have no idea how busy LAX is gonna be, or how weird the flight is going to be. People don't know how to act these days."

"Don't be nervous. I'm sure this won't be one of those situations where somebody trips a flight attendant, or where none of the pilots shows up and y'all get rerouted to Idaho. Don't worry about it. You'll be up in first class with all the ballers," Tonya says. "Even if something happens, you wouldn't notice with all the free champagne and extra blankets."

"You say that like it's a bad thing." I laugh. "I haven't flown in years. I deserve it."

Tonya scoffs.

"You always get what you deserve, I guess," she says, and hangs up.

Is it really early, or did that sound ominous? I start throwing stuff into my ridiculously nice suitcase, the one Dale bought me for our last anniversary. He was very sick and knew he wasn't going to be taking any more vacations, but it seemed important to him to give it to me.

"You're trying to encourage me to move on, but I don't want to move on anywhere you're not going," I'd said, wiping an angry tear from my cheek. I don't know if I was madder at cancer or at Dale for having it. Grief makes you illogical.

"You must," he said. Even pale and bald, he was still so beautiful. "You can't come with me, so you might as well go to Cabo. And now you won't have to throw all your stuff in a Target bag."

Cabo would be better than Baltimore—no funerals, no resentful and grieving relatives, no triggers of memories of almost burning down my career before there was anything to burn.

In about an hour, I'm getting out of the Uber at LAX, and I'm immediately reminded how much I hate flying. Apparently, in some long-ago time before I was born, air travel was glamorous, everybody all dressed up like they were headed to a Rat Pack show. Now it's hectic, rude, and even the little yappy dogs in the carriers look like they're one canceled flight away from biting you.

But there's something exciting about being in first class, and not just because there are better snacks. You get to board first, so you know there's going to be room for your carry-on. And as much as I believe in my connection with the common man, there's a perverse pleasure in seeing people walk past you to steerage, especially the ones who look at me like my Afro and I shouldn't be here. Enjoy bringing up the rear, Cletus! I feel like this is a posthumous victory for Rosa Parks.

There's no one sitting next to me, but across the aisle from me is a Mr. and Mrs. Howell–looking couple trying to shove an expensive leather satchel under their seat. A guy walks to the seat in front of me in a pair of aviators that cost more than his and the Howells' plane tickets. His whole vibe is "Idris Elba IS Gordon Gekko IN *Wall Street: The Musical*." He glances at me for a second, and the look on his face is a handsome sneer. Don't sneer, handsome man! You'll get wrinkles!

Wait . . . Is that . . . Yeah it is.

My grandmother used to warn me not to speak evil into existence, but I guess I never listen. I know that face. I've wanted to slap it for about thirty years.

"Well, hello, Dawn," mouths network news god Joseph "Joe" Perkins, my former mentor and friend and current demon, also known as the man who stole my Pulitzer Prize–winning story. That's the last thing he will say to me for the next five hours, but I will spend the whole flight thinking about him, as he becomes the star of an inner drama that will not be on the in-flight entertainment menu.

Chapter 5

WHAT I'M THINKING ABOUT FOR THE NEXT FIVE HOURS

1992

"Hey! Keep walking!"

A girl in line behind me on our tour of the *Baltimore Sentinel* newsroom is whispering at me in a less than cordial way. I'm so excited that I may have blacked out somewhere between the sports desk and the cafeteria.

I am officially an intern! I've waited for this moment ever since high school, where I followed in Editor Superstar Christie's melted plastic footsteps as a yell-y, tyrannical newsroom force of nature. At least no one ever tried to iron my foot. It would have been nice to have been loved. But I liked being right even more.

Now that I am at University of Maryland's journalism school, I've toned down the tyranny because I've accepted that journalism is a collaborative effort. Your staff is more inclined to collaborate with you if they don't hate you.

Our *Sentinel* summer intern class is composed of some of the most intense news dorks alive. But I'm not easily deterred. Ask that dining hall manager back at school who became the unwitting star of my campus paper exposé, "Mystery Meat: Do YOU Know What's in That Taco?" It was a big deal—I've already been recognized.

"Hey! I read your story!" a guy named Marco tells me when he reads my name tag. "You're why I'm vegan now!"

It has not escaped me that I am the only Black news dork among my cohorts. But I do know at least one other Black kid here, this guy Joe Perkins, who graduated Maryland a year ahead of me. He started interning here the summer after his freshman year, got a lot of bylines, and now, shortly after graduation, he's a real live reporter. Impressive. I hope he doesn't remember the one conversation we ever had back in the newsroom of the campus paper. He was an editor with a great reputation, and I was plugging away at exposing that smell in the Centreville Hall laundry room. (My money was on possums.)

My journalism power is more artistic than technical, so I'd hit a key and half my story disappeared.

"GREAT!" I screamed.

"Am I?" Joe said, because what else was there to say to some girl yelling out loud in your presence? I hadn't even noticed he was there.

"Are you what?"

"Great." Joe Perkins smiled, and it was a lovely smile.

"What?"

"I'm Joe," he said.

"I know," I answered and felt stupid for it. OH MY GOD. BE NORMAL, DAWN.

"Don't sweat it," Joe Perkins said, leaning over and hitting two buttons I probably should have written down so I'd remember them next time, and then "Return." My entire story popped back up on the screen.

"Well hey!" I said.

My editor, whose name was like Bryce or Trice or something, walked by.

"Hope you saved your story, Dawn," Bryce Trice said.

"Yeah, Dawn's got it, Bryce," Joe said brightly. "Don't act like it didn't take you months to remember how to even write your name on this thing."

Get him, I thought but did not say, as it was clearly not the time.

Bryce shut his mouth, and Joe had waved at me.

"Hey, Dawn," he said as he walked away. "Keep saving."

We hadn't talked since but I'd seen him everywhere, and he became my hero. And now The Joe Perkins strides sure-footed into the *Baltimore Sentinel* hallway. Instantly I turn back into that girl who can't use a computer. The real staffers are craning their necks to hear the police scanner so they don't miss, like, a bank robbery or something. Everything's busy, loud, and a little scary. I love it.

Joe's unruffled. He's been here since the summer after his freshman year and now is just one of the guys. He doesn't move like an intern but like he belongs here, grabbing lunch with the sports department and beers with the cops reporters after work.

"Hey, Joe," says a middle-aged man with the distinct air of someone in charge, offering a hearty handshake. "You left your shades at the house last night. You can come get them on the next poker night."

"Isn't that the managing editor, Bob Duncan?" the rude-ish girl behind me, whose name is Susan, whispers. "How did a guy who just got hired get invited to poker night?"

I shrug. "I guess he's that good."

"I guess," she says, and I clock Susan as very competitive. That's OK. Maybe it'll be like a movie, and we'll start off as rivals and then end up as best friends!

Joe walks toward us, his confidence ringing above the din of the scanner and the phones and the chatter. *How does he do that?* I think. It's like he's uncovered some secret to living, even at twenty-two. I haven't yet uncovered the secret to not losing my dorm mailbox key!

"Hey, it's Dawn!" he says, stopping right in front of me.

Aaack! My brain fumbles for something witty to say. I'm drawing a blank.

"You know each other, of course, since you both go to Maryland, or used to," says Jody, another new intern from Northwestern University, a school I didn't apply to but am pretty sure I could not have gotten into. The *And you're both Black!* goes unsaid. But it's super loud.

"Yes," Joe says brightly. "I saved her life once. She's very bad at computers."

I know he's being charming and not really calling me out as a technology-challenged loser. But I consider jumping out the window, catching the bus to the mall, and begging The Gap to take me back.

"What?" Jody says, confused.

"It's a joke," Joe says, shaking her hand. "I'm Joe. Dawn just had a weird technology moment, and I helped her out. We've all been there. I'm glad I helped her save her story. It was good."

The cool kid is vouching for me! There's no way that he remembers reading that story, but he's doing me a solid, even though I'm just a newbie. It's settled: I am always going to stick up for Joe, too, even if he doesn't need me to.

You know why? Even with his big-shot status and invitations to poker night, success in a mostly white newsroom in a mostly white profession is not a guarantee for Joe. He's earned his place in college and here at this newspaper because he's really good, and people don't just hand stuff to unqualified young Black men, no matter what your racist grandpa told you.

"You ever think about dating Joe?" Susan asks me once as we're drinking bad beer in the back parking lot sitting in the front of my not-good car. Susan and I aren't close, but you tend to hang out with the people your age. And whoever has beer.

I don't want to date Joe, or anyone. I'm working so hard to prove myself and not be exhausted all the time. But we are becoming close friends, and I rely on his advice. He asks me what I'm working on, has corrected some of my dumb spelling mistakes, and volunteered a source or two.

"You're pretty good at this journalism thing," he said last week, smiling. "You even know how to work the computer now!"

You ever been the teacher's pet? It can feel like the sun shining on you. I know it's a big-brother sun. But Susan is nosy, and I don't need her all in my business.

"You never even think about it?" she asks again.

"We're just friends," I say definitively, hoping Susan hears the door closing on this subject.

"Well, if you don't want him," she says, reaching into my bag o' beer for another can of Nature's Worst Beast.

Oh! I don't want him, but I also don't like her interest in Joe. I consider making up a girlfriend for Joe back at school or a wife he's been pledged to as a child in some ancient family pact. Fortunately, Susan just finishes her terrible beer and bounces. I notice she leaves the empties for me to clean up.

The rest of the internship goes well, although around the beginning of August, it's gotten sort of tense. Those of us about to be seniors are all wondering if we're going to be offered a real job for after graduation, like Joe had at the end of his internship.

I really want this. I'm keeping my head down, taking extra assignments to look ambitious, and not going out much unless it's for late-night coffee and hash browns. Still, networking is a thing, and I want to be a team player. So I reply yes when invited to see Jenn the copyeditor's boyfriend play bass in some band I've never heard of at a club in a neighborhood that does not historically welcome diversity. You know what I mean.

"You'll be fine," Jenn says when I hesitate, even though she has no basis for her confidence other than that she wants it to be true. She does not understand that this is not reassuring.

"I don't know," I hedge as Joe walks by.

"Perkins! You're coming to see Paul's band, right? Tell Dawn she should go," Jenn says. Joe gives me the "Girl, I got you" look. It's something you learn in Secret Black School.

"Sure, if Dawn goes," he says. Then he leans into my ear and whispers, "It'll be fine. Safety in numbers."

The bar is sketchy, as expected, and so is the band, Marshmallow Fluff. We all sit there trying not to make faces so Jenn doesn't know we think they suck while making "Oh my God, they SUCK" faces at each other when she is not looking.

"They're bad, right?" Susan whispers.

"They really are," Joe answers. "Jenn must really love him."

Susan looks over at me as I closely clutch my Jack and Diet Coke, which I've covered with a napkin because I've just written a story about girls getting roofied at bars, and I'm not going out like that. "Are you really that nervous about your drink?"

"Did you not read my story?" I ask.

"What story?"

Well, that answers that! Before I say something that will make the ride home super uncomfortable, the band starts playing "Blister in the Sun," one of those rock songs Black people of a certain age know even if they aren't into rock. And it's almost in tune! Joe and I are two of the three Black people in this place, including a girl at the bar who was introduced as the drummer's girlfriend. She's clapping way too hard. I feel people are looking at me weird, so I guess they're gonna do it anyway if I dance. I head to the floor and Joe follows.

"You look like you needed company," Joe yells over this blasphemous massacre of Violent Femmes.

"Thanks!" I yell back.

"What?"

"Thanks!"

I nod and do a little spin. Joe follows. We laugh. All my discomfort disappears.

"I'm glad you came!" I yell again. *"This is not my kind of place, you know?"*

Joe nods. *"Mine either! But I've got your back!"*

"You stepped on a tack?" I say, looking worriedly at my foot. If they're out here putting things in people's drinks, maybe they're putting tacks on the floor, too. I'm not getting got.

Joe laughs and shakes his head. *"Come here,"* he says, heading off the dance floor and beckoning for me to follow. I like this song, but this seems to be important. We head to a relatively quiet corner between the pay phone and a bathroom I can smell from here and am never, ever going into. I will pee in an alley first.

"Look," Joe says. "I see you working so hard, and I think you're really good. You might be a little in your head sometimes, but that's because you care so much."

"I do," I say. "This is everything to me."

"And that's why you're gonna be OK," Joe says. "Whether or not you work at the *Sentinel*—I'm always going to have your back. We have to stick together."

He extends his hand exaggeratedly, like we're about to shake on some sort of clubhouse oath.

"Absolutely," I say, returning his shake vigorously.

"I got you," he says. "No matter what."

Chapter 6

Et Tu, Tonya?

2023, still on this stupid plane

"Excuse me, ma'am," the flight attendant says. "We need your tray table up, please. We're about to land."

Had I been daydreaming about that dirtbag for five hours? He doesn't deserve one second of my time, let alone . . . however many seconds make up five hours. I'm not doing math for him!

I guess I slept through any opening to talk to Joe and ask him why he's going to Baltimore, or why he tried to ruin my life. At least I haven't kicked the back of his chair like I was tempted to. They'd probably dump me off in Topeka and I would never give Joe the satisfaction of seeing me dragged off a plane.

"I'm so sorry," I say to the flight attendant, hurriedly closing the tray. Joe's presence in Baltimore can't have anything to do with me, right? I'm gonna be here less than a week, and I'm certain that he's not going to be hanging out at Jewish cemeteries or anywhere near my mother, who hates him and has a licensed firearm.

I look in front of me through the space between seats, and I can see the expensive sleeve of Joe's coat on the armrest. I resist the urge to tug it and concentrate on not getting tackled by air marshals. When we land, I deliberately wait to get up until I see that sleeve disappear.

I half expect him to turn around and say something snide. But he just grabs his pricey-looking leather satchel and exits without a word.

"It's OK to deplane," the flight attendant tells me.

"But is it, though?"

She nods.

"You know who was sitting in front of you?" she asks.

"I have no earthly idea," I say, deadpan.

"Joe Perkins from the news! He signed my book!"

"You had a copy of his book on you?"

"He had an extra and gave me one," she says with the stupidest little look on her face. Poor kid. She has been Joe'd. Happens to the best of us.

"Well, at least he didn't charge you," I say, grabbing the rest of my stuff and hurrying off the plane. As I scurry, I think about that good friend and mentor who was willing to dance with me to a bad band at a dive bar, who swore to be my newspaper fairy godbrother and look out for me. Where did that guy go? And how has he been replaced with that over-moisturized picture of Dorian Black?

My suitcase should be off the baggage carousel by now so I can grab it and dash into the running car that my sister better be sitting in. Oh, good. There's Dale's guilt-gift suitcase, sitting on the belt. Where is Tonya? I told her we had to move quickly so I don't get in a fight here in this nice airport named after Thurgood Marshall, the first Black Supreme Court Justice. Justice Marshall was dedicated to his downtrodden brethren, but he probably wouldn't bother with "Black woman pops thieving former friend in the eye at the luggage area."

I reach into my pocket for my phone and realize it's in my bag. Maybe Tonya called and I didn't hear it? OK, here it is. Three missed calls. And some texts.

Grrrllle! the first text reads. *Grill?* Is that English?

Hrry up get yr bag we gotta goooo.

Huh?

I'ma leave my car running and you better be here!!

That one I understood. I look up to see my sister sprinting across several lanes of traffic, nearly colliding with the car rental shuttle bus. Has she ever moved that fast? Is she being chased?

"Tonya!" I say. "What are you doing? What's wrong? Did somebody die?"

She shakes her head furiously. "No, but I'm going to get a ticket. Can you run in those shoes?"

"Not with the urn! It's OK. You would never believe who was on my plane!"

Tonya's eyes get wide and she seems to be trying not to look at me. "Who?" she asks.

"Joe! I have no idea what he wants, or why he's here."

"No way!" Tonya says, and why does her voice sound like someone on *Murder, She Wrote* trying to pretend they're completely shocked about the dead body. "That's crazy!"

I pause, and take her hand carefully in mine.

"Is it crazy, Tonya?" I ask, pulling her around to face me.

"No, not really," a voice behind me says.

I don't want to turn around. But I do.

"Hello, Joe."

The well-preserved bane of my existence smiles at me from atop his very high horse. Pulling his gazillion-dollar shades down, he glances over to Tonya, who is trying to yank me toward the door.

"Hi, Tonya!" he says. "Nice to see you again."

"Yeah, yeah, yeah," she says, rushed and still yanking. "Bye."

"Looking forward to seeing you later," Joe says, which stops me in the middle of the automatic door. I stick my foot out to keep it open.

"See you later?" I hiss. "Why would she be seeing *you?*"

"DAWN!" my sister says. "Let's go!"

"Tonya, what is he talking about?"

Joe just stands there, glistening and amused. Tonya is almost outside, so close to freedom, but my bag that she's carrying is still setting off the sensors. Baltimore Washington International Airport is going to charge us for this door if she breaks it.

Tonya looks from me to Joe and back to me, like a caught rabbit who picked the wrong farmer to mess with. "I'll tell you in the car!"

"I'm not going anywhere until somebody explains!" I yell, attracting the attention of a young, uniformed army member trying to reunite with his family, who is forever going to have some unhinged lady screaming in their heartwarming video.

"Thank you for your service," I mumble.

Tonya is still trying to edge toward the car, but I tug on her arm. "Why does he think he's going to see you again?"

Joe's smirk is unsettling, which is what he's going for, I'm sure. "We're working together," he says. "I told her what flight I was on this morning, information I assume she wanted so she could make sure we weren't on the same one. Guess she's figured it out."

"Working together? How?" I demand. "Tonya, why didn't you tell me about this?"

My sister is silent, but Joe chuckles. I wish I'd kicked the back of his chair now.

"I imagine she didn't know how to tell you. I was just in LA finalizing a very special project, but now I'm here to announce it."

"Dating show?"

"No, thanks. Got that covered. It's a movie."

"Somebody was desperate enough to buy a script about that last exposé you did about the Amish crypto ring?"

"It's good to know that you keep track of my work, Dawn, but no. I've gone back to my roots."

"You're remaking *Roots?*" I spit. "It's been done, you hack."

"No, not *Roots. My* roots. My very first big story."

Oh wait.

"You know the one."

I do indeed.

"What does Tonya have to do with this?" I yell in the direction of my sister, who is attempting to fade into the well-trodden carpet in the vestibule.

"It's going to be great," Joe says. "Tonya can tell you all about it. She's a consultant on the film. She wants to make sure we get the story of *my* investigation exactly right."

I can barely see through the red flames of thirty years of betrayal. Wait, is that a camera flash? I must be hallucinating. All I can see is the man who stole my life float away on a cloud of smugness and expensive cologne. My sister flees out the door and back across the street to her car, narrowly avoiding getting clipped by the rental car shuttle van.

They missed. You can bet that when I figure out what in the world is going on, I won't.

Chapter 7

You Can't Always Get What You Want, Which Is to Push Your Sister into the Harbor

About thirty minutes later, I'm waiting for the girl at Avis to open the mechanical arm that stops you from stealing the rental car. That faithless Tonya lit out of the airport like a cat fleeing a bath, so I had to find my own transportation. I wish I could find the shuttle driver that almost hit her and tip him. I didn't really want her to get flattened by a bus full of blameless tourists who don't deserve to have their vacations ruined. I'm just confused and angry, and it's hard to drive with all these hot, livid tears stinging my eyes.

Does she not remember what Joe did to me? Sure, it didn't end up so well for her. I'm not heartless enough to forget that she and her ex paid dearly for the investigation I started into what was happening in city hall, when Titus "Junior" Blaylock, brother of then mayor Julius Blaylock Jr., went down for a nasty backroom deal. (I have never understood why the mayor, who was actually a junior, wasn't called "Junior," but nicknames have no rhyme or reason.) Regardless, Junior arranged to have several neighborhood schools condemned so a sleazy local amusement park owner could build a water park on the site and kick him back some cash.

Wait. Tonya's texting: How can you be mad at me when you know what happened to me? What that story did to me?

Look, I've felt bad about it for years. The story exposed a deep web of corruption that rocked city hall, the school system, at least one minor congressman, and a low-rent amusement park company, but my sister was caught under the rubble, so to speak. She got fired from her good city government job, and her boyfriend, Percy, who worked for the bad Junior, went to jail. He wasn't the ringleader, but he was guilty for sure. What's that they say about stupid games earning stupid prizes? My sister wasn't even in the game. She was just trying to do the right thing by asking me to look into it for the paper I worked for. I feel terrible about that.

I know how bad you feel about it! Tonya keeps texting. Let me explain.

Nah. It's not like I got to publish the story anyway. Joe, my alleged mentor, took advantage of my asking for advice and stole my story lock, stock, and essential witnesses for the *Sentinel*. It was stupid to even tell him, a reporter at a competing paper, about it. I *know*. Humiliated, I quit my job and ran off. I got none of the credit and had to start all over. Do I have things to feel guilty about? Yes.

But not right now. This movie? Not my fault. That Tonya! I wish they'd towed her stupid car.

Are you going to text me back?

Driving, I answer. See! I texted!

The drive up the Baltimore–Washington Parkway gives me time to reflect on recent events. I wish I hadn't fled without a witty rejoinder to Joe. He's still evil. Nothing left to say.

In moments like this, I try to channel all that therapy I've been paying for, reminded that even in my trauma, the world is in trauma, too. I just can't get over Joe's making a movie about that story—*my* story. I'm shocked it hasn't happened before now, because it's been three decades and he's not one to delay a coronation.

What I can't figure out is why Tonya is involved and why she didn't warn me. She was the whistleblower, and after what she went through, I should not begrudge her getting a bag. But I kind of do. This man stabbed me in the back, and yes, I got my own happy ending, at least until my Prince Charming died. I've done well, all things considered. But Joe stole from me, and she's going along with the lie he told my sources back then: that I had given up the story. And then he clean ran off with it.

I want to say this will not stand, but who am I kidding? It's probably going to stand, climb a chain-link fence, and do that crane kick Daniel-san whomped that dude with in *The Karate Kid*. At least I didn't have to pay full price for this Jeep. My one superpower is getting free upgrades from old Black dudes at car rental places, like I'm their granddaughter and they're slipping me an extra cookie when Big Mama's not looking. If these are reparations, I'll take them.

My phone beeps again, and I just know it's Tonya.

No, I text her. Let her suffer. I'm going to have to talk to her eventually because she's my sister, and I don't have the energy to edit her out of all my photos.

I also have to stop texting and driving.

I distract myself with an extra-long gaze at the Baltimore skyline rising before me. Maybe I don't see it enough. I should text my mother to tell her I've landed, although I'm pretty sure she knows because Tonya is loud and, like the guilty often do, she'll be looking for allies.

Never mind. I need to watch the road. I can't die today, with these ashes in the Jeep and this drama wafting out there. Not only would I be dead, but this would give Joe's movie a juicier, tragic ending, and I'm not helping this thing get on *CBS Mornings* with Joe fake-crying to Gayle.

Beep goes the phone. I shouldn't, but I take a glance at my phone again. Text from Brent. Great!

Just wanted to make sure you were clear on the time for the unveiling, he's typed. Dude. I'm not gonna get caught up in a *Real Housewives* reunion at the hotel, look up and go, "Oh no! I have forgotten to deliver this urn!" I'm tempted to turn around and head up to I-695, drop it off on Brent's doorstep, knock, and run away, like a sixth grader playing ding-dong ditch. But I think he half expects me to weasel out, and I don't ever like proving him right. So I keep driving on to the swanky Sagamore Pendry, my home for the next seventy-two hours overlooking the wharf at Fell's Point, this trendy little corner of downtown.

The building used to be the city's old recreational pier, then the set of *Homicide: Life on the Street*, and after that show was canceled, a decaying shell of what should have been. If you're new here, it's just fancy. Funny how a new coat of paint and not knowing history can change your opinions.

My room is, as expected, gorgeous. So many things in this part of town are. I had never been down here much before I went to that club where Joe and I first danced. I can't recall its name, but you or your cousin probably threw up there once. Baltimore, like most cities, had invisible lines—along with some actual real walls—determining who was welcome where, and this area was historically not so much Black girl friendly. I was young and broke, and they had cute boys and cheap Chinese food up my way, too. Didn't need to travel for that.

From that night we danced until the day he committed a journalistic felony, Joe and I were a team just like he promised, through graduation and separate jobs and bad relationships we used to make fun of each other for. We were pals, the potential Black Woodward and Bernstein, until we were not.

Geez! Why am I wandering down this particularly daft corner of memory lane?

"This is stupid!" I yell out loud, which makes me feel even stupider because why am I talking to myself? I should call Mommy, but she's just going to defend Tonya to me. So I text my mom Hey I'm here, in room 252. Call you later, and throw my phone behind the couch so I can't check every five seconds to see her response. At least she knows I'm not dead on the highway now.

Tonya and I were supposed to hang out here and then go back to my mother's house. Now I wonder if she's going to show up at all. I wouldn't if I were her, but she's not known for her good choices. I need to know more about this movie script. Am I in it? Does it make me look bad? It *has to be* bad enough that no one told me about it. Tonya's probably trying to explain her version of events in one of these seventeen voice messages and texts I'm not answering.

I remember something Dale used to tell the musicians, actors, and other entertainers he managed: "Never google yourself." It's easy to tumble down an inescapable rabbit hole of lies, hate, and clownery. If there was something his clients needed to know, they paid him enough to find out for them. Anyway, I'm not looking myself up. I'm investigating that demon, Joe Perkins.

I grab my phone from behind the couch and start searching. The first hits are images of Joe accepting his Pulitzer—Grrr—and his book covers. A still of him from the *National News Now* credits. Joe interviewing President Obama . . . Joe with President Carter building a house . . . Joe with Jennifer Hudson, who is serenading him with "Love You I Do" from *Dreamgirls* on his birthday on Jay-Z's yacht.

I'm not jealous at all!

Here's his Wikipedia with his origin story, which, of course, originates with a lie. Now, some photos from a 2019 *Rolling Stone* story about his series of speeches at African universities that had invited him to talk about fighting corruption. He looks too good. The power of shea butter compels you.

Enough stalling. I take a deep breath and type "new journalism movie." *Clickity-click click.* Here's a blind item on The Shade Room: *What celebrated journalist is headed to his hometown to start production on a film version of the book that started it all?* How the hell did I miss this? I run a whole entertainment site! I should fire myself!

I go back to the search page and type in that name I hate again, and here's an Instagram post of Joe and me AT THE AIRPORT. Wait, there were cameras? How did I miss cameras? What even is this account? "B. L. James Investigates"? Wait, that's whose email I ignored when I was running late to interview Miss Vivi.

They've got over two hundred thousand followers, which is nothing to sneeze at. But why would they care about a photo of me and Joe?

"Joseph Perkins of *National News Now* fame arrives in his hometown for the start of the movie based on his classic investigative nonfiction work, *Diving into Deception: Corruption Comes To School*, which toppled the government of a major city and changed the way we view power forever."

Well, that's a bit much.

"The movie, to be directed by acclaimed filmmaker Isaiah Greene, is set to start production this week. Among those involved are Tonya Roberts-Jenkins, the whistleblower who helped bring the conspiracy tying the brother of then mayor Julius Blaylock Jr. to a plot to raze several school buildings to build a water park worth millions of dollars. Also shown—Roberts-Jenkins's sister, Dawn, an entertainment journalist of some renown in Los Angeles."

Well, at least B. L. James, whoever they are, got that part right. Let me read that email they sent me.

Ms. Roberts. My name is Bria James, of the popular news site B. L. James Investigates. Confident, are we? I wanted to get a comment on a new movie about the 'Diving into Deception' story, in which you are mentioned. My deadline is tomorrow at 9 a.m. Thank you.

I guess that will teach me not to ignore my emails! Rookie move. And this Bria James? Bad journalism. She didn't even write "Dawn Roberts could not be reached for comment," or "Dawn Roberts did not respond to a request for comment." I hit "Reply" and start typing.

Miss James. I was on deadline and then traveling so I was unable to respond to your email. I don't appreciate the ambush. Why didn't you ask for a photo? What are you, BMZ?

I hit "Send." My Baltimore-related TMZ joke wasn't the freshest, but I think I made my point. I should call a lawyer about this. But I haven't seen a script, and they haven't started filming, so I would look preemptively petty. You know what? I don't want to think about this right now.

"Dale," I say out loud to my husband, who is not here, "what have I gotten myself into?"

My dead husband should be used to being a sounding board for my foolishness, at least in my head where I can hear him.

"Not sure yet," Dale says. *"But I'm sure it's going to be complicated, messy, and at least a little funny."*

I should probably go to my mother's right now, but if I do, she's going to want to talk about depressing things like why I'm mad at Tonya, or about Dale, or maybe about what happened thirty years ago that makes it so hard to come home. None of that seems like fun. So I'm not going to do it right now. I've been avoiding these conversations for decades.

I need a distraction. Work. I open my Miss Vivi notes and reach for my phone to get the recording of that crazy interview. Perhaps stories of sequins and drama will take my mind off it. I get to the part of my notes with Miss Vivi's weird comment about a story I didn't write. Could she have known something about this movie? How would she? I consider calling her publicist for a follow-up question, but with big stars, the time you get is the time you get. I'm sure she's just crazy and I'm paranoid.

I put on *Living Single* reruns in the background because *Flavor* and Khadijah are my inspiration. Look at them all young, Black, and wrinkleless, full of promise and confidence that everything was all gonna work out.

Chapter 8

YOUR FRIES ARE NOT SAFE WITH ME

"GIRL!"

Tonya is banging on the door. She's gonna get us both arrested, because the world hasn't changed so much that the cops wouldn't be called with a quickness on a loud Black woman banging on the door of an overpriced hotel room. And I might have to fight her. *Not* wanting to get arrested might be the only thing saving her life right now.

"Stop yelling! I'm coming!" I snarl. I'd gotten into a groove in the Miss Vivi story—somewhere around her Christmas special with Olivia Newton-John—and I'm irritated to have to stop.

When I open the door, Tonya's leaning in the doorway, wearing something completely different from what she had on at the airport. My life is falling apart, and she's had a costume change! The bangs of her pixie cut slide over her perfectly drawn smoky eye.

"It's happy hour downstairs!" Tonya says, stepping past me into the room. "Let's get martinis."

"Nope. NOPE. You don't get to act like we're cool. We are not."

Tonya walks past me to the hotel phone.

"What are you doing?"

She waves me off and speaks. "Hello? Yes, it's Roberts-Shaffer in"— she glances at the phone—"Room 252, right? We'd like to order two

Grey Goose martinis and some of those duck fat fries. We love those. Yes. Twenty minutes is fine. Sure. Thank you!"

I can't believe her. "Did you just order room service on my dime?"

"I sure did," she says. "Again, I feel like this is my last meal."

Unbelievable. And she didn't even ask if they honor happy hour prices at room service! Then again, if I were stabbing my widowed sister in the back, I'd be living my last few remaining moments to the fullest, too. Wordlessly, I point her to the couch.

"How could you let me fly in here and not tell me about this movie?"

Tonya plunks herself on the couch. "Ooh, this is nice!"

If I wasn't really mad right now, I'd admire her bravery. Because she's getting super close to getting snatched.

"Girl . . ."

"Fine. Remember when I asked you what flight you were on?"

"I certainly do. Is that when you *didn't* tell me that Joe was on the same flight, coming into town to make a movie about that book based on the story he stole from me, and that you are getting a check?"

Tonya drops her head like she's ashamed of herself. As she should be.

"I'm sorry," she says. "I mean it. I'm sorry! I wrote his flight number down wrong, and when I realized it, you were already on the plane, it was too late. It's just . . . this movie thing came up, and I was conflicted, but they said they were going to use a version of me and pay me. Everyone knows it's me, so I figured it was easier to just be involved and have some control, even a little bit. I honestly didn't know how to tell you."

Huh.

"How about, 'Sis, they're making a movie without you, about the story that changed your life, and here's the number of someone to call about it so you can control how you're presented'? Or even, 'Heads-up! Satan might be on your plane!'"

Tonya leans back into the fine leather couch.

"Don't get comfy," I snap. "You aren't staying long."

"But we ordered snacks!"

"Not *we*. *You*. And if I don't like what I hear, I'm gonna eat and drink it all."

Tonya rolls her eyes. "You're crazy enough to. Fine. Here's what happened. The production company—they're called Dockside Pictures—reached out to me a few months ago—"

"MONTHS? As in multiple weeks?"

"Yes. Can I finish?"

"I haven't decided yet."

Tonya presses her palms together, like she's weighing saying something rude, but she's hungry and doesn't wanna die. "Please let me explain, OK? I get why you'd be mad—"

"That's so big of you."

"DAWN! You wanna know what's going on or not?"

I do. "Fine. Talk."

Tonya glances at the door, as if willing the room service people to come now for backup. "They said there was going to be a movie and that there was a character that was supposed to be me, the whistleblower. And they found her to be, and I quote, 'lightly sketched.'"

"Did Joe write it?"

She nods.

"No wonder. Joe's become bad at things that aren't about him."

"It was a bad seventies sitcom nightmare," she says. "My character, Kitty, was a drunk dummy who popped gum and moved her neck and called everybody 'girlfriend.' They asked me to be a consultant to make sure it felt more authentic."

Hmm.

"So they were worried about getting sued, looking racist, and getting canceled, and they wanted you to sign off?"

"Something like that."

"Still, you didn't tell me about this for months," I remind her. "And now there are reporters asking me questions about a thing I know nothing about. And there are contracts. I'm sure you weren't supposed to say anything to anyone. But I'm not just anyone."

Tonya raises her finger in the air like a lawyer on *Matlock*. "I did wonder if they were gonna call you, because there's a character based on you in there—"

"Oh, is there?"

Tonya sighs, exasperated. "Can I talk?"

Might as well. I'm all out of words. Anything I'd have to say would come out like angry nonsensical *Sesame Street* lyrics.

"I read a little of it—they only gave me the parts about Kitty, so I don't know all of what they wrote about you—but in the parts they gave me, you're barely in it. It's not even really you. Her name is Fawn."

"Joe really got creative with that one, didn't he?"

"I know, right? But seriously, she's just a girl he works with who leaves the newspaper industry altogether because she's not very good, and she's never heard from again. I kept thinking that they had to talk to you. But then when they announced that they were going to start shooting this weekend and you didn't mention it, I realized they hadn't."

I frown. "He's been pretending I don't exist for thirty years. Why would he want to mention me at all in a movie? And as for you! When you learned the date, you had to know that we'd all be here in town at the same time, right? And that people talk . . . I mean, people who aren't you."

"Touché," she says.

"How were you planning to hide a whole movie from me? What if I'd emailed the reporter back, or if she were good enough to try to talk to me at the airport when she took our picture . . . You know she took our picture, right?"

I pull up the site, and she reads the item. "Oh, yeah, Bria!" she says. "I met her at one of the meetings." At the acknowledgment of meetings I didn't know about, I'm pissed all over again.

And Tonya knows it.

"Let me tell you . . . ," she begins.

"Nobody says 'Let me tell you' unless they're desperately trying to get their story straight," I say.

"Dawn . . . I was doing this for you."

Of all the Lifetime movie crap . . .

"You know you're lying!"

"I was hoping to get close enough to be able to make sure that whatever Joe wrote about you was more flattering," she says. "It's not like he's going to tell the truth about his stealing the story from you. That wasn't cool. Look, I wasn't cool about it, either. You know. You up and left. Percy went to jail. I felt alone. There were even rumors going around that I was in on it, and it was hard to find a job for a little while. That was hard to get over."

Points are being made.

"I was so mad at you," Tonya continues. "I was the one who brought the story to you in the first place, so I started it. I know that. But I could have used your support then, and you just left."

And even more points. I don't want to feel bad for her, but I do.

"OK," I say. I'm not ready to surrender the moral high ground just yet.

"Everyone's going to be there for the filming, including the former mayor."

"The mayor whose brother ruined his administration and who lost his next election because everyone thought he was part of the scandal?"

"You know how it is. He tried to play it off that Junior was just a bad apple. This makes him look magnanimous. He'll be at the press conference."

"When is that?"

Tonya suddenly looks super uncomfortable. "Tomorrow."

Hold up.

"Tomorrow is Dale's interment. How are you going to do all that on the same day?"

"It's before the cemetery."

"What if I needed you? This is for Dale . . . you loved Dale," I say, and the shaking in my voice is for real and not just me trying to make her feel guilty. I don't mind it if she does. Swim in that guilt. Get your silk press all wet.

"That's low," Tonya says softly. "I did love Dale. But I had to do what was best for me and my family."

"Fine," I say. "But you could have told me. Do you know how humiliating that was to run into Joe unprepared? And now I'm on some website looking like a troll."

"I'm sorry about that."

"That was a long flight! I had to sit there that whole time fantasizing about accidentally kicking him out of the air lock."

She nods. "Yeah, well, that particular thing wasn't fair to you. I admit that."

"Just that?"

"Just that."

I smirk and turn up my middle finger. She smirks back.

"I wish they had towed you, ticketed you, and then towed you again from wherever they towed you to."

"Well, they didn't," says my sister, who doesn't know when to stop talking. "But what would you have said if the movie people had called you, anyway? 'I lit a match and tossed it over my shoulder like Angela Bassett in *Waiting to Exhale* and let everything behind me burn—including my sister's life'?"

You ever say something that seemed like a clever thing to pop off with at the time, but it went different in your head? This is one of those times. Tonya sees my face and immediately knows she messed up. Before I can do anything to her, there's a knock on the door. Room service. She's lucky.

"Saved by the bell," I say. I don't want to be charged for these plates, so I'm probably not gonna throw them at Tonya, *Dynasty*-style.

Probably.

I sign the check and leave a very good tip in case I beat my sister up and need the room service guy to testify on my behalf. She reaches toward the plate of fries with one hand and a martini with the other.

"Mine," I say, grabbing the tray and settling it on my lap. "Get your own."

Tonya sighs. I wonder if she's going to attempt a half apology that lets her hold her self-appointed high ground while getting the fries back. Good luck with that.

"Can I have one?" she says, looking longingly at the plate. I pick up one fry and run my tongue across it slowly like I'm trying to get all the juice off a Jolly Rancher.

"That's nasty."

"It's gonna be a lot nastier when I lick them all," I say. "What was the plan once you knew we were on the same flight? Just to hope I didn't see him?"

Tonya nods. "It was not a good plan. I know that."

I hand her one. That's all she gets.

"You were going to just leave me hanging and looking stupid and not tell me?"

"Yes. I'm sorry. I am. But Dale's ceremony was already set, and it wasn't like I could tell you not to come since you were going to be busy and all . . ."

"You mean, I was going to be preoccupied with putting my husband's spirit at rest?"

"Yeah. That."

Then my sister does something sneaky and unexpected. She leans over and wraps her arms around me like an emotional ambush. Not fair! I'd forgotten how much I like her hugs . . . "Stop! I'm mad at you! *I am righteous in my anger!*"

"I'm so sorry," Tonya says, and I can tell she's not just talking about the fries. "I should have told you. And I just hoped, like I said, that you'd be busy and we wouldn't have to worry about it. I didn't want to be in the middle."

"I get it," I say, handing Tonya the fry plate back. "I know about avoidance. It's not like I didn't move cross-country to get away from this whole mess."

"Sometimes it felt like you were trying to get away from me."

Welp. Sometimes it feels like that to me, too. And I hate that.

"I'm sorry it felt that way," I say, and I mean it. "Here is what I don't get about this weekend, though: At no point did you think I was gonna call you and you were gonna have to play like you weren't in the middle of a movie set?"

"It's not like you're tracking my phone." Tonya laughs, running her finger around the crevices of the cup of sauce that came with the fries because she has no class. "You're *not* tracking my phone, are you? Anyway, like I said, the press conference is right before the interment, so I just wasn't going to answer any calls and be vague and hope you wouldn't ask where I was."

"How was that ever going to work? I'm a journalist who writes about movies, among other things. I'd have found out eventually."

Tonya smiles, leans over, and hugs me again. "I didn't say it was a good plan."

We both crack up, from sheer absurdity and emotion and just the joy of being in the same room, even if I'm super mad at her. And just like that, it's fine. At least fine enough for the moment. When you are sisters, you know when things are as settled as they have to be for now. You're never going to solve all the years of stuff between you in one sitting, and certainly not before the fries get cold. It'll have to do.

Tonya leaves after the martini and fries, and the plan is that we're going to meet up at my mom's later. "You've got gin and carbs in you now," she says as she hugs me. "It'll make it easier to deal with."

I guess. Now that we've gotten that conversation out of the way, I consider the larger mess I'm in. I know that wherever he is, my husband is making fun of me. When you're widowed, you think that what you're going to miss the most is the romance, the sex, and the "I love you" said with just his eyes from across a room. But I also miss my best friend, who was so much fun.

"We could have fun in a refrigerator box," Dale used to say to me. Once the horror of being trapped in said box had subsided, he would have made up some games, or sung silly songs, or asked, "You know what you smell like?" to make me laugh. Maybe the laughter would have busted us out of the box.

Dale is trapped in a box now, sort of, and I'm about to give him to his brother. Then he's going to be put in a wall. Oh, I'm being melodramatic. The other half of Dale's ashes is back in LA, and what's in either of those containers is not him. He's wherever the light in your eyes goes when it dims, when your hand stops gripping your wife's and you don't answer her when she calls your name. I wish I knew where that was. I don't want to die, but I'd sure like to be where Dale is. Someday. Not now. But someday.

I can't be mad at Brent for wanting to have his brother back in whatever form he can have him. He has the right to miss Dale and to insist on being able to mourn him in a way that gives him peace. Still doesn't mean I have to like him.

Then there's this stupid movie. After Joe stole my story, I fled my job at the *York Herald* in embarrassment. I was pretty sure my career was over before it began, because the editors I ran out on weren't itching to recommend me to future employers. But I hadn't been there for long, and it was in the days before you could just look someone up online. One of my journalism professors at Maryland put in a good word for me at a small paper near LA where a fellow alum worked. By the time I got to the *Times*, I had solid clips, and no one at the *Herald* seemed to care enough to ever contact me.

Somehow, I was able to board that part of my life up and leave it behind, but Joe's insisting on crowbarring it all open again.

Chapter 9

BACK DOWN THE RABBIT HOLE

1993

"You got this, kid," Joe says as we walk to the office of Barbara Smith, the assistant managing editor of the *Sentinel*, who is about to interview me for a general assignment position that I hope everyone in the office already agrees I'm qualified for. My previous summer internship was productive. I've gotten great feedback from editors and even some nice Letters to the Editor. There were also one or two not-nice ones, which I think means I'm on the Sam Donaldson path of annoying the right people.

My summer triumph was a sweet story I almost didn't get—I had left for my very regimented hour-long lunch break, but realized I left my wallet on my desk. As I was grabbing it, my phone rang with a random call about a dog that kept hanging around a bar in Fell's Point like it was sad and waiting for someone. As an intern, I'd gotten used to getting routed all the random weird stuff nobody knew what to do with, but this sounded potentially interesting, so I forgot about lunch and rushed down there.

Turns out the dog was named Stewie, and he used to go to that bar with his owner, Bill, for lunch every Wednesday for dollar wings before

Bill got too sick to go a few years ago. Since that time, the bar changed hands and staff, but nobody told Stewie, so when his owner died, the poor heartbroken dog escaped and went to look for him. Nobody at the bar seemed to recognize him, and he didn't have any tags, so I decided to ask people that usually get ignored, like the middle-aged parking attendant across the street and a nice homeless guy I'd seen down there before. They knew both Bill's and Stewie's names, so with their help we got the doggie back to his grateful family. And I got interviewed on Channel 13 for my heartwarming story—I'm on my way!

"Good catch," Joe had told me when the camera crew left. "What a lucky break that you forgot your wallet. Anybody could have picked up that phone."

"Sure," I had said. "But I did. And I hit it out of the park."

I kind of think he'd wished it was him, but who wouldn't? It's a competitive business, right? But Joe's a professional and that hasn't stopped him from becoming my journalistic sensei, talking me through everything from my résumé paper choices to what to expect in the interview. It'll be Barbara, our former internship supervisor, who just got a big promotion; James Patchett, the news editor; Thea Burke, the features editor; and Lisa Finch, the editor from one of the bureaus in a surrounding county. I'd work in an office on the moon if I could be under the big *Sentinel* umbrella.

"Hey! Good luck, lady," says Jenn, the copyeditor with the boyfriend in that bad band. We were not very close during my internship summer, but I called to check in and to use my reporting skills to subtly find out what had happened to Bad Band Boyfriend. (He'd left her for the drummer's girlfriend.) She's been super encouraging about my interview. It would be fun to have more work friends.

"Thanks, girl," I say as we get to the door of the office. Joe squeezes me on the shoulder.

"You got this," he says. "Just keep it simple, don't elaborate if unnecessary, and be confident."

And that's what I do. I go in, making sure my cute new Dressbarn sales-rack skirt suit isn't wrinkled and that there's no hummus in my teeth, and blow those folks away. I'm engaged and engaging, I ask good questions but not too many, and I make eye contact in a not-creepy way. I shake hands. I remember names. I don't have hummus teeth!

"I think I aced it," I tell Joe over celebratory tacos on two-for-one margarita night at Chi-Chi's.

Alas, the celebration was premature. Barbara's "Sorry, no job for you" call is short, polite, and manages to be encouraging about my future without implying that my future might be there at the *Sentinel*. Ever.

"Did she say anything to you?" I ask Joe, trying not to cry.

"No, and I can't really ask," he says. "It sucks. I was looking forward to working with you. It's OK. We'll have to conquer the world separately. But we're still in this together."

Joe is so good at talking me out of bad moments. He keeps encouraging me through a weeklong binge of pizza and tape-recorded *Simon & Simon* and *Magnum, P.I.* episodes in my mom's basement to apply to other places, like the *York Herald* in York, Pennsylvania. It's only an hour north of Baltimore, but I've only ever driven through it on the way to diving into a vat of chocolate at Hersheypark. It's very conservative and very . . . not urban. But the *Herald* is a good, scrappy paper. It's cheap to live there, and an hour isn't too far to do laundry for free at my folks'.

So I apply and get hired, which is swell because working at The Gap isn't paying off my The Gap card. On my first day, I pull up in a different Dressbarn discount-rack outfit, because what if the one I wore to my failed *Sentinel* interview had been a jinx? I'm standing in the lobby for a few minutes, noticing that the older lady at the desk is pretending not to see me. I didn't meet her during my interview. Maybe she was sick that day?

"Hello, ma'am," I say politely. "My name is Dawn Roberts! It's my first day as a reporter and I—"

This lady's look tells me I'm supposed to stop speaking, like I'm asking her to do something not in her job description. She hits a button on her phone. "Mike," she says. "Is there a new news clerk starting today?"

"No, ma'am," I say, thinking she must have misheard me but knowing she didn't. "I'm a reporter."

"Uh-huh," she says as the fuzzy, disembodied voice of managing editor Mike Finney comes over the phone. "It's a new reporter," the fuzzy voice says.

"Are you sure?" says this woman, who perhaps was not there the day of my interview because God was playing a cruel joke on me, lest I assume this was going to be easy. Her name is Evelyn, and I will continue to be nice to her, even though it's soon clear that she's a bitter person who goes out of her way to let me know she disapproves of my general presence. I don't have to ask to know that the news clerks, who do administrative work to assist the reporters, are mostly Black here, and that I am, in that moment, one of only two Black journalists in the newsroom. Well, I'm not technically in the newsroom yet because she won't let me up the steps.

"Hi," says someone behind me. It's a very good-looking brother with two cameras hanging around his neck. "You starting today?"

"I am!" I say, relieved to see both another Black person and someone who doesn't want me fired before I've gotten past the lobby. "I'm Dawn."

"Eddie," he says, shaking my hand. "Mike told me you're from Baltimore? I'm from Beltsville. Are you an O's fan?"

"You know it," I say.

Eddie glances past me to Evelyn, who still looks evil. "Hi, Evelyn!" he says chipperly. This appears to piss her off. Good. "I'll take Dawn up to the newsroom, thanks! Don't you worry about it!"

Relieved, I follow my new savior up the steps. "Is she always like that?" I ask. "She was so harsh, I was beginning to question whether I was mistaken that I really work here!"

Eddie laughs, holding the door open for me. He sits his cameras down. "Evelyn missed an opportunity to use her skills as a CIA investigator," he says. "Or to be the lady who checks Black people's bags at the door of Neiman Marcus."

Immediately, my nervousness is gone, and I have a new friend. I need one, because being a fresh little eager beaver reporter is a lot. I'm immediately thrown into the deep end of the reporting pool, faster than I would have been at the *Sentinel*, which has a bigger staff and more opportunities to ease in baby reporters like me. No easing here! I'm doing everything from checking the condition of car accident victims (hospitals would tell you before HIPAA laws) to traveling with Eddie to ruin my shoes tromping after fishermen on the first day of trout season. We all went out for beer and wings after that one, but I had to go home and change first because I smelled like creek water and fish.

I'm making other good friends, too, including Hattie, one of the news clerks; Stacy, the cops reporter; and Vince, who covers high school sports and has better cable than me, so we hang out sometimes at his place. But Eddie remains my favorite because he looks out for me, is fun to work with, and gives me the "Secret Black School" nod.

"Is that a Black thing?" Stacy asked me once as we passed Eddie in the stairwell.

Well, yeah, but we don't need to tell her all that. That's not the only reason I like Eddie, though. He's effortlessly nice, a great journalist, lets me pick the CDs on our drives, and doesn't laugh when I trip over my own feet, which is often. We all imagine ourselves young gazelles when we're baby elephants fumbling around in borrowed gazelle shoes. But I'm having a good time getting to know him, although there's still so much to discover. I know he was born in Chicago, raised in Maryland, and that he used to be a touring drummer when he was a kid. I haven't really been anywhere, so this is intriguing to me.

"Did you ever play for anyone I would know?" I ask once.

Eddie shrugs. "I'm not sure," he answers jokingly. "All you seem to listen to are obscure British eighties bands with weird names like Pestilence and Soup."

I giggle, because now I have a friend close enough to have a private joke of stupid made-up band names, and every time someone orders soup for lunch, we're gonna smile, knowing no one else gets it.

I know that our both being Black makes people want to pair us off like they did with Joe and me back at the *Sentinel*. I always knew that wasn't Joe's and my vibe. But here? I'm not so sure. Eddie's a little older than me and very self-assured. Plus, somebody tells me he's very friendly with Sabra Charles, who does weather over at the NBC station. She's shiny and skinny, and her hair looks like the hair on my Superstar Christie doll before I took her out of the box and tried to wash it with Head & Shoulders. I am disappointed in myself that I dislike Sabra instantly.

"Why don't you ask Eddie to the Christmas party and find out if they're serious?" Stacy asks over pancakes and hash browns at the diner. "You know he's cute."

"I'm not gonna set myself up like that," I say. "He's seeing Weather Barbie. And what if he says no? I still have to work with him, and everybody's gonna know he said no. I haven't lived down that time I almost threw up at the deer-processing plant."

"Yeah, that was funny," says Eddie, who I could have sworn was not here a few seconds ago. "But you held on to it till we got to the bathroom at the Turkey Hill convenience store. We can't ever go back to that store again, but it was impressive."

"You're the same color red as the ketchup," Stacy whispers as Eddie walks to the counter to grab his take-out order. "I didn't know Black people blushed."

"We do, and you're not supposed to say stuff like that," I bleat, now hiding behind my half-drank milkshake. "I'm gonna report you to . . . somebody." We laugh hysterically, but I still stay behind the milkshake until Eddie leaves.

I do not ask Eddie to the Christmas party, because I don't want to be turned down and look dumb. But I show up looking great in my new red velour dress, to approximate something Toni Braxton adjacent but with a Fashion Bug budget, and try not to look excited when he comes through the door. But it's hard not to care when he materializes behind me at the bar.

"Now that," he says approvingly, "is a dress."

"Is that what they're calling it these days?" I say, which sounded pithier in my head. I wait for Eddie to make gentle fun of me, like he does in the car when we ride together on assignments, but instead he leans back on the bar, looking at me like he's never seen me before.

"You know, Dawn," he says. "I've been meaning to talk to you . . ." and I can barely hear him. Is that butterflies? My heartbeat?

"Hey, Eddie, Sabra's here!" Judy, one of the education reporters, is saying.

The butterflies disappear and all I can hear now is a "womp-womp" sound in my ear. Eddie looks away as Sabra and her crown of princess hair float into the room, kissing him on the cheek.

"Sabra Charles," she says, holding her hand out to me like we've never met, like she does every time she sees me. I don't know if she's playing games or if she really doesn't remember me.

"Dawn Roberts," I say, not looking at Eddie as my face turns red. "I'm gonna go see if the DJ takes requests. See ya."

As I walk by, Eddie puts his hand lightly on my veloured shoulder.

"Dawn," he starts, but I smile tightly and just say "Have a great evening!" I hope nobody saw that, because I don't want to think about it. He's either a cheater and a player or he's clueless, and I have more important things to worry about, like continuing to prove myself at work. The next time I see him in the office, it's weird for a minute but nobody says anything about it, like it never happened.

I know I am on an unspoken short leash at the paper—I haven't been here long enough for anyone to miss me if I left or got fired—and

I'm still establishing myself as a professional to my bosses and to myself. I can't mess this up.

I'm not yet doing the serious investigative work I've dreamed of. It's all car accidents and the lady whose prize pumpkin got stolen. Sam Donaldson would have refused to do any of this, but it's gotten me on the map reporting-wise, and I just need to be patient.

"I wish I was down here with you," I tell Joe one afternoon at Faidley's Seafood in Baltimore for a crab cake on the way to my mom's to wash the meat smell out of my coat for free. "You're doing real stories about non-pumpkin crimes."

Joe is always busy, and we don't see each other as much as we used to. He's fitting in well—he's been at the paper so long, he's like part of the firmament. He also has a new girlfriend, Vanessa, a PR maven who pretends not to be suspicious of this girl who's hanging around but claims to just be his friend. In turn, I pretend to not think she sucks. It's OK, because Joe's too distracted with the job to be that serious about her.

"I just feel like there's more, you know?" he says, reaching for a napkin. "I really need a big story. An important one."

"You'll get there," I say. "Everyone knows you're destined for greatness."

"I hope they do. Here, let me get this," he says, wiping a glob of tartar sauce off my face. Later, when I'm watching *Oprah* as my jeans dry in the basement, I think about that moment and realize it bothers me. A humble person might have said, "Yes, we both are destined for greatness," but for the first time, I'm wondering if all the praise everyone, including me, has heaped on Joe all these years has gotten to his head.

Also, I think he did that tartar sauce thing just to mess with me.

Chapter 10

Who Says You Can't Go Home Even If You Don't Want To?

2023

Baltimore is one of those cities that people either know nothing about or think they know everything about because they've seen a couple of episodes of *The Wire* and both film versions of *Hairspray*. They believe it's a slightly cornier, grittier Philadelphia or a cornier, less sophisticated New York. Corny in general. That's sort of accurate. But shut up about it.

Northwood, where I'm from, is actually two neighborhoods, Original Northwood and New Northwood. Original Northwood has tree-lined streets with big, solitary homes made of stone or immaculate white clapboard and stately brick. It was mostly white when I was growing up. I lived in New Northwood, just across Loch Raven Boulevard from the OG. They only call something "New Whatever" to punctuate the difference between it and the first thing, like "we have to let people know that's not us."

No matter. We didn't need anyone else to love growing up here. Most of our neighbors owned their homes, and we all knew each other well enough that we would be lovingly in each other's business. Miss

Janey, who lived a few doors down, used to watch me and Joe closely when we visited my folks for free lunch as poor broke baby reporters.

"Hey, Roberts girl. That your boyfriend?"

"No, ma'am."

"Good. Watch out for him. He's too pretty," she'd say, closing her storm door and going back inside.

"She's sweet," Joe said, because he thought everyone should notice he was pretty.

"She's a silent assassin who probably has bodies buried under her azaleas," I answered.

A few years later, when I was leaving my parents' house in my wedding gown on the way to marry Dale, Miss Janey was sitting on her porch like always, and I suddenly felt bad because it occurred to me that we hadn't invited her.

"Roberts girl! You look good! You're not marrying that pretty one, are you?"

I remember smiling under my 1990s wedding top hat.

"No, ma'am."

Miss Janey nodded again, sagely. "Good. Never liked the looks of him."

I wish Miss Janey was still living so I could tell her she was right about Joe. She'd be pleased that whoever bought her house was keeping those azaleas beautiful and blooming. The neighborhood looks good, too. Gentrification hasn't hit yet. I don't want the original neighbors to have to move. I'd rather somebody invest in it so they can stay if they want to and have their property values rise. Just a coat of paint and some support.

As I pull up, my mother is on the porch watering one of the African violets my Aunt Marky literally left her in the will because she was sure all of our other relatives would kill them.

I start to be mad at her, about keeping this movie thing from me. But then she says, "Hey, Dawnie!" and suddenly all my anger at her evaporates. It's my mommy, right in front of me and not on a screen. I have not seen her in person since right after my husband died, and all of my widowed sadness, all of my sad and tired—plus the added recent subterfuge—starts leaking from my eyes. I had my reasons not to come home more, but right now none of them make sense. Before I know it, I've launched myself down the walk, up the stairs, and into her arms.

"Mommy," I sob. "I missed you so much."

"I missed you, too, girl," she says, smoothing my 'fro under her gloved hand. "I know you have things you want to say to me. But come inside. You know how nosy these people are."

I follow behind her, and she locks the dead bolt with an emphatic clank. I feel super safe. Some people boast about how where they live, they leave their door unlocked. That's why y'all get robbed.

My mother's sister, my Aunt Weedie, is in the dining room looking intently over a yellow pad. "Hey, Dawnie!" she says, not getting up.

I give her a side hug. "What are you writing?"

"Just checking off the list for the party and who's supposed to bring what. You're bringing the paper towels."

Paper towels for the *what*?

I look at my mother. "What party?"

Weedie smirks over her yellow pad. "Here we go!"

My mother rolls her eyes at her sister, then turns to me.

"Surprise!" she says, clapping her hands. "It's my seventieth birthday party!"

Now I know I don't come home a lot, but I can read a calendar. "Mommy, your birthday was two months ago. I distinctly remember serenading you over Zoom and sending you the most expensive Edible Arrangement available."

"Yes, you did, and it was delicious! We had so many of those pineapple flowers I made a ham just to find a use for them!" she says. "But you're never here, and I wanted a party, so I figured if you were going to be in town, we'd kill two birds with one stone."

Aunt Weedie raises her hand like a kid in school. "Nita! She's here to bury ashes! You can't be talking about killing anybody, birds or otherwise!"

My head is spinning—I came here to deal with Dale's family and be reminded of his death, and now I have not only a spectacle, because that's the only kind of party my mother throws, but this movie thing.

"This is a lot, Mommy," I tell her, because if we're at the stage where we're assigning tasks, it's impossible to stop.

"Yes, I am," my mother answers. "If you lived here I'd have put you on the list for food, but you don't have a kitchen at that hotel, and we didn't want you buying Twizzlers and frozen mozzarella sticks."

Rude.

"Tonya's making the potato salad," Weedie continues. "She's on her way."

Of course, I know my sister is coming, but just thinking about her being all casual with her starch-based salads and nobody mentioning her sketchiness with Joe pisses me off. Now I'm mad at everybody.

"Did you know that Joe is in town, and they're making a movie about that story you know was mine? And your other daughter is involved? Why didn't YOU tell me? Anything else you're hiding from me? HUH?"

"That's your mother," Weedie says, still scribbling. "Watch it."

My mother purses her lips. "I got this, Weedie. So, little girl, which disrespectful outburst am I supposed to address first?"

I may have earned that. "Sorry . . . but, Mommy, come on!"

"Yes. I knew. Tonya told me. It wasn't my news to share. And you get to be mad, but you're an adult, and you can pull yourself together like you've got some sense."

As old as I am—and make no mistake, I'm "holding up your boom box to the stereo to make a mixtape" old—I know I've come at her wrong. You just don't talk like that to your mother—your BLACK MOTHER—unless you enjoy getting snatched. And I do not.

"I'm sorry. It's just a lot. Joe was on my plane! Do you know how embarrassing that was? I didn't even have eyeliner on!"

"Didn't I always tell you to wear eyeliner? You never know who you are going to run into."

She's been saying that since I was going up for fried rice and chicken wings at the Chinese place with the bulletproof glass next to the library. And this time she's right!

"Mommy, it was so awful. I love you. But I'm still mad."

"I love you," she says. "Hug me and then yell at me later."

"Fine," I say, letting it go because I might have to fight folks later.

"Your mother tells me you interviewed Vivienne St. Claire!" Weedie says, changing the subject. "Which wig was she wearing?"

"An expensive one," I say.

"Was it the one she had on last week on *LIVE with Kelly and Mark*?" my mother asks. "It looked like a waterfall coming out of a wedding cake, like classic Diana Ross meets Marie Antoinette meets a Macy's Thanksgiving Day Parade float."

"You follow Vivienne St. Claire enough to tell her wigs apart?"

"You know I love her," my mother says. "I'm observant. I think that's where you get it from."

I hear the door opening, and here's my sister coming with a Giant Food bag that I'm assuming has potatoes in it.

"Hey, baby!" my mother says. "Marcus isn't with you?"

"No, he's working. Ricky's with the sitter. Help me with these bags, Dawn," Tonya says, all casual, like she's not a faithless hooker cheating on me with an entire movie. I know we were cool earlier, but I'm mad again. Emotions are mysterious.

"You can handle it," I say. "Gotta get your strength up for all that consulting."

Tonya glares and struggles to the kitchen, almost tripping over an errant onion that rolls out of the bag and between her feet. Karma!

"You are foul," she says. "That's why nobody tells you anything."

"Are you sure?" I reply. "It isn't because you're holding a thirty-year grudge and you're working with a man rocking a smoking jacket and a pipe on his latest book cover. Looking like a discount Hugh Hefner."

Tonya laughs. "Girl, get a mirror," she says, "because nobody holds a grudge longer than you."

Have I mentioned that I hate when she's right? I open my mouth to say something else, but my aunt raises her hand like she's forming a stop sign.

"No," Aunt Weedie says. "You don't need all that trouble, Dawnie. You have a fine life back in LA. What you want to be worried about Joe for? Let him make his movie. You have important work to do. You don't need to be involved."

"You can't turn down things dramatically if you weren't asked," Tonya said.

Well, that's just rude. My whole family is just rude!

"So, Dawn . . . speaking of being inviting . . . ," Aunt Weedie says, leaning over to duck the balled-up paper towel I've just chucked at her head. "Ha! Ya still slow!"

"I don't know what you're talking about, and I don't want to," I say.

"I'm talking about dating. It's been a while since Dale, God bless him, and I'm not trying to marry you off. I was just wondering if you'd . . . explored yet."

"I don't think I'm ready," I answer, either to date or to have this conversation. I haven't told anybody how I'd created and quickly deleted three separate Tinder profiles, because some of y'all get too familiar too quick on these chats. *Hi. I'm Frank. I've just "accidentally" sent you a picture of my junk.*

Weedie smirks. "Nobody's talking about dating. Isn't there an old friend you can accidentally run into? Nita! What was that cute man at her old paper's name?"

"Eddie! Yes, ma'am. He was a fine one," my mother says. "I met him a few times when I visited her newsroom. He made me a cup of coffee and let me sit in his nice swivel chair. He was such a gentleman. Why didn't anything ever happen there?"

"She was too busy ruining people's lives and sleeping with sources," Tonya says.

"I married that source, you cow," I say, rising up. "Say one more snide thing about my late husband."

Tonya's phone rings, and she glances down at it, shoves it back into her pocket, gets up, and goes to the kitchen.

"That's the second time in twenty-four hours a bell has saved your life!" I yell after her. "You're gonna run out of luck eventually."

"Dawn," Weedie says.

"NO. She should be apologizing for hiding stuff from me and taking shots at Dale. Tell her to calm down. I didn't fly three thousand miles to put up with this."

"Didn't you, though?" my mother says. "Welcome home."

Tonya comes back out of the kitchen, hurriedly.

"Who was that?" my mother asks.

"Marcus. He's getting off work late, and he needs me to come relieve the babysitter. I'll see y'all tomorrow at the grave?"

This seems weirdly abrupt, even for us.

"Is everything OK?"

"Yeah, yeah," she says distractedly. "You know how cheap Marcus is. He doesn't want to spend extra money on sitters when we're helping finance the queen's birthday."

My brother-in-law is certainly frugal, but something about the way she's saying this feels off, like she's covering something up. I wonder what it is. And it's more than just knowing about the secret party, another thing she didn't tell me about.

"Drive safe. See you tomorrow," I say, kissing her on the cheek. "You and I still have some talking to do."

Tonya smiles, relieved that I have kissed her cordially and not, say, ripped the hoop out of her ear with my teeth. "It'll keep," she says, scurrying out the door.

"Was that weird?" I ask my mom.

"You girls are both weird," she says. "It's hard to tell. Look, I know it has to hurt, this movie. You don't like that Joe; he don't like you—"

"Mother—"

"So you should be spending more time with people who really do like you, like me and Weedie. We love you. I know it had to hurt not getting the credit you should have gotten—"

"I got no credit."

She sighs. "Can I finish?"

"Can I stop you?"

"No. Maybe this all happening the same weekend is a sign."

"A sign that I'm paying for something I did in a past life?"

Mommy hugs me. "No, it's a sign that life goes on, and sometimes that's good, and sometimes it's bad until it's good again. Look at you and your website. It's going so well! I was mad that you left so suddenly, and I always hoped you'd come back. But maybe that was God's will— Stop rolling your eyes. You were happy for a long time. You can look at Joe, and that story, and all the stuff he got from it, but still see that you're complete. You don't need all that."

Aww.

"You have more faith in me than is warranted."

She kisses me on top of my head. I like that. "That's my job."

I decide to do something uncharacteristic and just let the moment end on this beautiful note.

"I'm hungry now. Wanna get fish sandwiches from Rudy's? They're still open?" I say.

My mother nods. "I'll order if you go pick it up for us," she says.

"They're not on Grubhub or something?"

"Rudy and them don't believe in sharing their cash with corporations," Aunt Weedie says. "Sometimes his son, Donnie, will bring it over for you, but only if he feels like it."

"I went to high school with Donnie! Isn't he an accountant? Why is he delivering fish sandwiches?"

Aunt Weedie shrugs. "Like I said. He usually doesn't feel like it. Nita, don't you have a coupon?"

"You know I do!"

They go to the kitchen while I remind myself to buy paper towels because I'm never going to remember that if I don't write it down. A phone rings near me—my mother's cordless landline. She is uppercase OLD.

"Can you get it?" she yells from the kitchen.

I pick it up and hit the "Talk" button. "Hello?"

"Hello," says the voice on the other end. "My name is Bria James from B. L. James Investigates," she says. To call my mother's house? Bria is a better investigative reporter than I gave her credit for. "I'm looking for Anita Roberts. I'm trying to reach her daughter, Dawn, who I'm writing about."

I start to panic, trying to conjure my best imitation of my mother, and then realize Bria James has never talked to her and has no idea what she sounds like.

"I'm sorry, they're on vacation!" I say, wrapping my palm around the receiver. "Last-minute cruise!"

Bria James pauses. "Are you sure? Dawn Roberts just landed in town today. I photographed her."

"It was VERY last minute," I say, still talking through my palm. Should I add an accent? That's too much. I can tell she's not buying a minute of this, but all reporters have been lied to by would-be subjects who claim to be out of town, or have moved, or to have died.

"All right, then," Bria James says. "If you hear from them tonight, please tell them I'm at Morgan State, at the Murphy Fine Arts Center, so I'm close by if they want to meet. There's a photo shoot for the movie. I believe Dawn's sister is in attendance."

"OK, bye," I say. So Tonya *was* being weird. I knew it! My mother is standing behind me, reaching for the phone. "Who was that?"

"Scam call," I say, and I'm not wrong.

My mother is no longer listening because she's already on the phone ordering the sandwiches. "Yes, yes . . . three fish . . . wait, do we need three? Should we just get two and share?"

"I want all of my sandwich," Weedie says. "You can afford it. Or Dawn can."

"OK," my mother says, rolling her eyes in her sister's direction. "THREE fish sandwiches, two with cheese and hots, one with no cheese and mushrooms."

I love that my mother still remembers my fish sandwich order. I do not love that my sister is most definitely a liar, and she's not even here to help me pay for these sandwiches.

I head out to the rental Jeep but just kinda sit there for a second and consider my next move. If my mother knew what I was thinking about, she'd have begged Rudy's son to bring the fish to us and not let me out of the house, because I'm seriously considering driving over to Morgan State University and crashing that photo shoot.

No, Dawn, Dale whispers to me. *It's bad enough that you're not invited. You wanna be uninvited* and *pathetic?*

No, I do not, Dale. And wow, that's mean.

I glance up at the porch and see my mother standing there quizzically. "Why you still here? They'll give away my sandwich!"

Because, I want to say, *I'm talking myself out of blowing everything up and shaming the family forever.*

"Checking work emails," I lie.

I turn on the radio to '80s on 8 on Sirius XM, where there's mostly music and no one will be talking to me, as I am sick of talking, particularly to myself.

"As promised," says former MTV VJ Martha Quinn, a voice of fun from my youth, "here's that punk block."

Great! I like punk! I feel like one!

"The Violent Femmes . . ."

Why is that familiar?

". . . it's one of my favorites . . ."

Oh, wait . . .

". . . one of those songs we sang as kids without really knowing what it was about . . ."

Hey, universe. What are you doing?

". . . it just makes you want to dance . . ."

Don't say it, Martha.

". . . I know you love it, too . . ."

Martha.

"Listeners, you know you love it . . ."

Don't play that song.

". . . It's 'Blister in the Sun.' You're listening to '80s on 8."

"I know that, Martha!" I screech. "But why?"

Maybe blowing stuff up is still on the schedule. I was JUST asked to accept God's will—that He knows best, and that even when things haven't worked out for you, you must believe there's a plan. I haven't heard this song on the radio in a thousand years, and if you were the kind of person who believes in signs, wouldn't it seem significant to hear the words that started your friendship with the world's worst person when right now he happens to be just minutes from delicious fried fish?

Of course it would. But I'm going to get the fish first.

Chapter 11

Sometimes Signs Are Just God Trying to Save You from Yourself

As I drive toward Rudy's, I try to reason out my plan here, and it's . . . hazy. Crashing this photo shoot might make things worse. I'm not blameless here. I was a sloppy young reporter, who let my story get stolen, and I did sleep with a source like Tonya said, even though I eventually married him. That could have gotten me fired at the *Herald* for sure because I hadn't been around long enough to be so important that anyone would overlook that. It's a journalistic no-no that would make anyone look flaky, especially as a young woman. I know plenty of men who did that kind of thing—newsroom hookups are common, and we all knew guys who were a little too friendly with the county clerks. But somehow no one ever called them a slut.

I know that before I left, I should have found a pay phone at LAX and called someone to explain—or to say goodbye. But I didn't, and I didn't apologize because in that moment, I was not sorry.

The *Law & Order* theme ringtone blares from under my purse. It's my mother. "Are you there yet? Get me some chips."

"I'm on the way," I answer, leaving out the "as I consider doing something really stupid" part. "Hey . . . you talk to Tonya? Did she get home OK?"

"She called and asked me to save her some fish. Why?"

"Oh, no reason," I lie. "See you soon."

"And, Dawn . . ."

Uh-oh. Can she smell the plotting through the phone? "What?"

"When you get back, I want to talk some more about what Weedie said. About dating. Sliding into somebody's DMs. Having a friend with benefits. All that stuff y'all say."

I'm so startled I almost run the light. "Thank GOD I'm in therapy," I say. "You spent my childhood telling me sex was going to send me to hell, and now you're encouraging it? And how do you know about 'sliding into DMs'?"

"I'm not dead, Dawn. And I'm aware you've had sex. You made the choices that you made, and now that you have new ones to make, maybe one of them should be a man," she says. "Now, just get me my fish sandwich, OK? And my chips. Barbecue."

"Fine," I say, and hang up. This conversation was more of a virtual slap in the face than a sign, but sometimes that's what you need. At the light, I flip down the mirror and look at myself. It's OK—Black don't crack and all that. But Joe looks like the very successful, wealthy star that he is, and I do not.

If I go near that man with cameras milling about, I am going to look stalky. *Craggy* and stalky! I also have to consider my reputation as a well-regarded journalist. I can't do this. Screw the signs. I need to just get through the next couple of days with my head down and my mouth shut. And then I'm getting back on a plane and back to my life.

Rudy's still looks like a hole-in-the-wall, a sketchy and reliable neighborhood joint. I get out, grab my food (almost forgetting my mother's coupon), and start back through the parking lot when I sense someone walking up on me. That's a very Baltimore survival skill.

"Excuse me? Dawn Roberts?"

I turn to see a kid . . . well, she's maybe thirtysomething, so she's a kid to me. She looks like the grown-up version of every Black funny friend from a Disney Channel sitcom. Quirky. Smarter than anyone gives her credit for. Annoying. Her voice sounds familiar.

"Yes?"

The kid sticks out her hand for me to shake, and I hesitate, because this could be a trap. "My name's Bria James."

Yes. It's a trap.

"B. L. James Investigates? You've been stalking me and my family." She shakes her head.

"You're a journalist. You know I'm just persistent," Bria James says, handing me her card.

"All I know is that you snapped and posted a photo of me without approaching me for a quote, and that you just called my mother's house. Nobody wants to talk to you."

Bria James's face lights up in a look I recognize instantly as polite gotcha.

"So that was you on the phone!" she says. "I thought that sounded like you."

"How would you know what I sound like?" I protest.

Her smile turns less confrontational. "I've done my research," Bria James answers. "I've watched several of your interviews, and you're very impressive. The way you got that *Survivor* winner to admit they'd smuggled beef jerky onto the island inside their boxers? Masterful."

Yes, it was. But this still seems like a setup.

"What do you want?" I ask, sounding harsher than I'd expected.

"Did you see my piece about Joseph Perkins and the new movie?"

"I saw an unflattering photo of myself, taken in a moment of grief holding my husband's ashes, just trying to mind my own business."

Bria James shrugs, and I have a wild urge to place my hands on her shoulders and push them down, like a stern ballet teacher in a movie.

"Journalism," she says. "You know how it is."

"Yes, I do know how journalism is. Do you?"

She laughs, and I don't like her laugh. I do like her coat, though.

"May I ask you a few questions?"

"No, you may not. I don't know anything about that movie, and it doesn't have anything to do with me."

"Are you sure?"

Don't hit her. They gonna arrest you.

"I don't know what you're talking about. I just want to get these sandwiches back to my mother," I say. Look, God, I said I wasn't going to that stupid photo shoot. Take it easy, please?

"Well," Bria James, who I have decided I hate, continues. I'm older than her and should be in my journalistic auntie bag giving her advice, but right now I just want to advise her to step off. But I don't, because she'll probably tell me she's confused by my outdated Gen X slang.

"Don't let me keep you," she says. "I just wanted to know if you had any comment on the new script."

"New script?"

I want to swing my purse at her and flee, but she's technically press, whatever that even means these days, and that's gonna make me look bad online. I run a start-up, not a shut-down. I have to be careful.

Bria James clears her throat. If I were a real celebrity, or a white woman, I might risk the jail time by punching her in it. "Well," she says conspiratorially, like we're buddies now, sharing a secret, "the previous version was pretty vague about the origins of the story."

"Vague how?"

Bria James smiles. I don't like her smile, either. "It said Joe had been given a tip from an old friend from college who worked at city hall."

Lies, I think silently. At least I hope it's silent. "And now?"

"Well," Bria James says, "now there's a reporter character, a real striver, that they've fleshed out."

"Fleshed out how?"

"She—her name is Fawn—overhears the story at a party, mentions it to the Joe character, is very jealous of his progress on it because he's a better reporter than her, freaks out, threatens to say it was all her idea, and then up and leaves town."

Stupid Fawn. "She does what now?"

"She's basically the villain now."

"She's the villain?"

"Yes."

"Like the villain, villain?"

"YES."

And all this is gonna come out when they announce the project on TV. While I'm interring my husband's ashes.

The chickens have come home to roost. I think I'm the chicken.

My head is spinning. I have no good comeback that doesn't involve violence or keying her car, so I just snap, "Whatever," and walk away.

This is bad. Really bad. I need a new plan.

Do you, Fawn? my conscience asks.

"Screw you, Conscience," I hiss. "And you know that's not my name."

Should I head over there and read them all for filth right now? That has a *Real Housewives of Atlanta* energy I don't want. I start backing out of Rudy's terrible parking lot carefully because I'm not going to risk my rental car deposit. I should call Bria James right now and ask what more she knows, but I think she's the sort to enjoy the begging, and I'm not a Boyz II Men ballad.

Oh, Dawn. Think of it this way. You have half your husband's ashes to inter and the surprise birthday party of the ages to attend and bring paper towels to. You don't have time to do damage.

I'm thankfully interrupted by the phone ringing. Oh, look. It's my own Diva Auntie Mame. "Hello, Miss Vivienne."

"Debbie Gibson!"

That's new.

"Where have you been? Are you working on my story?"

If anyone would understand the ego-driven revenge thing, it's her. I'm five seconds from telling her all about it and asking for advice, but she's an agent of chaos and feathered caftans and would probably weave this into her Instagram story.

"Actually, Miss Vivienne, I have, but I've been preparing to inter my husband's ashes tomorrow here in Baltimore. I'll let you know if I have any other questions."

It probably doesn't matter to her. I don't think she can process any words besides "Miss Vivienne," "You're the best," and "Here's your check." But there is silence. Her not talking is disconcerting.

"I'm sorry, Dawn. I didn't realize that. That's very sad. I was widowed a couple times myself. I was even sad about one of them."

"Which one?"

Miss Vivienne gives a long, throaty chuckle. "I'll tell you about it when we speak next. When we do, remind me to tell you about that time those girls tried to get back together without me."

"Who?"

"Those girls. In that group. They tried to do an anniversary tour and didn't tell me about it, because they knew I was never going to agree to it. I knew I was going to look like the bad guy. The nerve! Like anyone wants to see that. *Without me.*"

It's not a sign. *It's not a sign.*

And yet, Miss Vivienne keeps talking. She knows I'm listening very carefully. "What did I do when these people who owe me everything had the nerve to try to write me out?"

I lean into the phone.

"I shut it down."

Well then.

"I'll talk to you later, Doris," she says, and hangs up.

I'm still looking at my phone when it rings again. My mother must really want this fish, and if I don't take it to her, I will have failed to deliver the dinner of an old woman, and that is not how we take care of our ancestors.

"So you lied to me about who called the house before you left?" my mother says as we open the fish sandwiches over the coffee table, *Dateline* playing in the background on the big-screen TV.

"I just told you that my nemesis is rewriting history to make me the villain in the story he stole from me, and that's your takeaway?" I ask, biting into my sandwich and remembering how much I enjoy tartar sauce.

She shakes her head.

"Of course not. I just wanted to note it," my mother says. "It's good you came here to talk to us and didn't do something stupid like go over there and bust things up without a game plan."

"Don't say that, Anita," Aunt Weedie says. "Dawn's gonna think it's OK to bust things up if she has a game plan." My aunt knows me too well.

"I don't like that look on your face," my mother says. "You should leave it alone."

"Are you kidding?" I say, and get the "Girl, you're too loud" look. "Sorry. But you think I should just let this stand, knowing that it's not going to take too long for people to figure out he's talking about me? I have a business and a reputation—"

"And also, you don't like that man!" Aunt Weedie agrees, slapping her hand on the coffee table.

"You're gonna leave a mark on my good furniture, and I have people coming over!" my mother admonishes her. "Look, I know you have to respond, especially now that this reporter is onto it, and knows how to find you. But why don't you sleep on it? Do some research. Use all that journalistic experience you're so proud of. Popping off to the wrong person is what got your story taken in the first place. Slow down and craft a response."

I hate when she's right. "So I can't politely trip him?" I ask.

My mother chuckles.

"I wish you could," she says, "because I don't like him, either. But if I were you, I'd work on a statement, call that reporter back, and then move on. Nothing good comes from confronting him. Just leave Joe alone."

This is good advice. But she's been away from me too long if she thinks I'm actually going to do that.

Chapter 12

Well, If It Isn't the Consequences of My Own Decisions

1994

"What is up with you?"

Tonya is fidgeting on the Ferris wheel high above the York State Fair, the biggest event in town. The big-city girl in me used to make fun of that, but then I walked onto the midway for the first time and was introduced to apple dumplings. A little bit of cinnamon, flaky dough, and hot fresh fruit will change your life.

My sister's visiting me as I interview 4-H kids about the pigs they've raised since birth and are about to sell off to Hormel for chili purposes. I've been impressed by their professional ability to not get all *Charlotte's Web* about it. Circle of life, you know. Enjoy being chili, Babe!

Tonya says she drove all the way up here for the food, but really, she needs a break. She's been working in the mayor's office in Baltimore since graduating from Morgan a semester early because she's an overachiever and wants everyone to know it. She's on a respectable professional path, but her personal choices are more suspect, particularly this dude she's been dating named Percy, the assistant to the mayor's brother.

"What does the mayor's brother need assistance with?" I asked her once.

She shrugged. "Something that makes money, and Percy makes sure he knows when and where to do it," she'd said cavalierly. But she doesn't seem so cavalier right now, floating above the concourse.

"Look," she says, and sighs. "I think Percy's up to something."

"I know he is," I say, trying to calculate how many calories an apple dumpling is and how much food I really need to eat the rest of this week. "Did he ever pay you back that five thousand dollars he borrowed from you? I know he said he was helping his mother buy shrubs for her yard, but I went to her house for that cookout, and those things are scraggly. I bet that money's in a strip club in Atlantic City. And not even a good strip club."

"You sound like a judgmental shrew," Tonya says. "How long is this stupid ride?"

"As long as the ride is, I guess," I reply. "So . . . what did he do?"

She clears her throat and starts talking, and what she says is so startling, I want to whip my reporter's pad out and start to take notes. From her nervousness, I suspect she'd slap it out of my hand if I did, though. Last week, she was at Percy's place looking for something to write down the number for Little Caesars on and accidentally picked up a receipt for a lunch Junior Blaylock had with Guy Nederlander, shady middle son of the Nederlander amusement park family. You know—Dream Village, Tomorrow Planet, and Balloon Kingdom? The places your parents take you when they can't afford Disney?

"I thought, 'Why did he go to lunch with that guy? His parks suck.' The costumed characters are clearly rip-offs," Tonya explains later as we're eating our zillion-calorie treats in my car. "Hoagie Bear? Ricky Mouse? Who are we kidding?"

Percy didn't want to talk about it, but when she wouldn't let it go, he admitted that his boss had met Guy at a ribbon-cutting for a mini golf place because he's in the nepotism job that his brother gave him, and that's the kind of inconsequential garbage the taxpayers pay him to do. They'd struck up a conversation about how the Nederlanders could work with the city and bring something really big there to benefit the citizens. Wouldn't that look great for his brother's administration? How about a water park? And we know just the spot! Of course, there are schools on that spot, right next to some shopping centers that had seen better days.

How good were those schools, anyway?

"Scandalous!" I say, so offended that I stop eating, and you know that's significant.

"I know!" Tonya says. "Percy hasn't told me everything, and I don't know if he's involved at all, but as a Baltimore City Public Schools graduate, I take this stuff personally. Maybe if someone could get to the bottom of this, Percy might realize it's shady and walk away."

"Huh," I said, because if there's something shady happening, I'm pretty sure that guy's involved. More importantly . . . this is a potential story. I don't want to freak her out and, say "Oh, my God, you have to let me write about this." But she really does have to let me write about this.

Here's the thing I've been waiting for! It's not happening in York, but the Nederlanders live up here, and Balloon Kingdom is right on the state line. The implications are huge: a major city's first family involved in a pay-for-play scandal that would disenfranchise mostly Black kids in a mostly Black city. It's a microcosm of the greed-fueled nastiness that happens around the country, leaving minorities holding the bag and, in this case, unable to read.

And it could be *my* scoop.

By the time we wake up the next morning, still hungover on fried food and cinnamon, she's agreed to let me tell my editor, Zach. He's kind of skeptical.

"Do you have time to do this?" he says. "You're pretty busy, and this could be a heavy lift." I am now the unofficial festival and car accident reporter. How will I have time to write about the Skunks As Pets club (which voluntarily calls itself SAP) and the new flavor down at Maple Donuts if I'm busy with a side project that isn't even really about Pennsylvania?

"I can do this," I say confidently. "My sister is willing to talk to me, on the record, and she thinks she can get me some other people, too. Let me just see if it goes anywhere, OK? Please?"

Zach says yes because he sort of believes in me, and because I agree to work the next couple of shifts that need coverage when someone is sick or has the funeral of a close relative who totally exists and who is not a Dave Matthews Band show. He needs me. No one else wants to cover the skunks.

I start slow with my investigation, having coffee with Tonya and this lady, Sheila from Permits, who introduces me to Bobby, Junior's driver. I'm cobbling together a narrative. Veering between caution and candor, everyone agrees that something shady is going on. Nobody likes what they think is happening, but everybody likes being employed and paying their bills. I've got some well-founded suspicions, a receipt or two, and a promise from Sheila to check on relevant permits if she can do it without Junior or anyone else finding out.

When I sit down with all my notes, jotted in reporter's pads with the words "Water Park Story" written on the cover so I can tell them from my notes on skunks and oyster festivals, it's overwhelming. The story is growing branches and leaves and squirrelly choking vines. I need someone to bounce stuff off. But who? I don't want to bother anyone at the *Herald* lest they complain to Zach about it and he pulls the plug because I'm too distracted to cover Pug Fest.

"What's on your mind, kid?" Eddie asks me on the back steps of the newsroom, where other people are smoking and I'm just taking a minute to make some sense of my interviews. "Pug Fest's got you that stressed?"

"No," I say quickly, shoving my pad into my bag. "Just trying to keep all the names straight. There's a Peg, a Bug, and a Rug. All too cutesy."

He laughs. "Well, let me know if you ever want to talk about it," Eddie says. "Coffee later?"

That's an interesting offer. Between assignments, we sometimes drink coffee, or we have donuts, or we eat fried rice in the car with our hands like fiends with no home training. Does he mean a non-car coffee? Is this a thing? Oh, Dawn, too much in your head. So much work to do. Be silly later.

"Maybe next week," I say.

"Sure thing," he says, and I can't tell if he's disappointed. Do I care if he is? I saw Sabra Charles and her beautiful weave sniffing around him at that bank robbery the other day, and I'm sweaty and covered in adorable pug licks. I can't compete with all that, and I don't have the time to dissect it.

I do need an ear, though. What if I went to another reporter at a different paper who was good at this sort of thing? Normally, the idea of telling anybody about a potentially huge story like I know this one could be would be considered handing a scoop over to the competition. But this is Joe! My good friend! I can trust him. I just won't tell Zach. He wouldn't like me talking to someone from another paper in case it turns out to be something. He wouldn't get that Joe would never stab me in the back.

Because he wouldn't!

"Is there something here?" I ask him later that night as we split a slice from Marcello's on my plastic coffee table. I would like my own slice, but then again, I'd like to be able to afford that and a coffee table not made of plastic. These are goals.

"Maybe. Let me read what you've got," he says, reaching for my reporter's pad.

I giggle and hold it over my head. "Hey," I say playfully. "You aren't gonna steal my story, are you?"

Joe smiles again and jovially hits me on the shoulder. "Of course not," he says. "I promise."

Sam Donaldson would have slapped me across the face with his microphone for so rookie a move. Because I do not see that his fingers are crossed under that paper plate.

Chapter 13

I See My Invitation Got Lost in the Mail

The next morning, after an abnormally fitful night of rest, I drive onto Morgan State's campus. I attribute this to my clear conscience about what I have to do this morning. That does not mean that I'm not planning to start chaos. Just that I feel OK with it.

Here is my plan: I'm going to use my press credentials to get in the door and then try to figure out how to get a copy of the script so I can confirm what Bria James told me. I've already texted her a simple "Expect me," which is intentionally ominous. I'm going to need receipts for what Joe's planning and, eventually, that he stole my story. As my mother would say, I'll fall off that bridge when I get to it.

Who I don't text is my sister, because I can't stop thinking about her helping power the bus about to drive over my head. I wish I didn't know that Tonya was a faithless betrayer. She also gives great hugs and I could use one right now. But they are warm, tight, faithless betrayer hugs. She'll see me when she sees me.

Turning the corner, I recognize the telltale signs of a press event—TV trucks, emphatic traffic cones, and tape around sections of the parking lot, with on-air reporters pretending to be shocked when they're recognized and producers sitting in cars trying to look important. That tape is the velvet rope of journalistic events. It seems performative, but we have to park and get in and out if there's a deadline or something even more important about to happen.

I'm not gonna lie—it feels great, being allowed on the other side of those cones. A VIP bouncer in South Beach once told me that he'd prepared for his job by reading psychology books. "If there is a closed door, people want to know what's on the other side of it," he explained. "And they're willing to pay extra and wait in line to get in there and find out, even if all there is, is another door. Then they'll pay double to get into that one, too."

That brother was very smart. I hope he quit bouncing and went to grad school, or at least has some sort of highly lucrative online coaching classes.

"Ma'am, you can't park here," I hear someone say. It's a college kid in a Kappa Alpha Psi hat and a "Security" jacket. He could be doing anything with his time, and he's spending it in my business.

"I'm sorry?"

"Ma'am," he says again, peering closer because it's his job to figure out who is on his campus. He's good at it. Too good. "This is for media only."

Media, you say? This is always my favorite part, flashing my credentials at gatekeepers who don't believe I belong within the gate. I've worked too hard to be denied my rightful place in this industry I've given and lost so much to. It takes great restraint not to yell, "Take that!" But I am not a twelve-year-old boy.

"Dawn Roberts, Glitter," I say, handing him my card. "We're an award-winning entertainment site in Los Angeles."

"LA?" he says, eyebrows cocked behind his shades, taking maybe too long of a look at my card. It's not in Sanskrit, my dude. It's not like I'm using my professional credentials to further a personal plot against my former mentor and blow his life to high heaven!

It's not like that *at all*.

For all my planning, I haven't done everything right. In all the excitement, I never called Pearl, who I left in charge at Glitter, to tell her any of this, and if I do what I'm thinking about doing, she's gonna find out. I'm the boss, but I'm only as good as my staff, who have helped me build this site. Nobody wants to work for an unpredictable liar. I mean, I have—plenty of times. But that doesn't suggest job security.

Kappa Security Guy hands me the card back and nods, pulling the cones aside and gesturing toward a space next to the Channel 13 van. I grab the reporter's notebook with my Miss Vivi interview notes in it, hoping there's enough blank pages. Am I prepared to write about myself, warts and all—in my own publication? That's like Drew Barrymore in *Never Been Kissed* begging a man to come kiss her from the pages of a major Chicago daily. Hideous. Then again, if I do, at least I'll make my own deadline.

I get out, nodding at a woman with a mike sitting in the news van, hoping it's not anyone I went to school with. They should know who I am—I'm no slouch, plus the Smalltimore of it all demands that at least some old acquaintance is gonna pop up, and I don't want anyone tipping Joe off. That snob Susan McNally is now one of the *Sentinel's* columnists. She's a good writer. Probably still a meh person.

I bet the *York Herald* sent someone. The water park's location makes it local for them. Does anyone there even remember that it was originally my story? Time and the official mythology have probably obscured all that.

I follow the signs to the press conference. What am I even going to say when I get there? Should I grab the mike and say, "See here, suckers!!"—risking being forcibly removed, staining my career, and embarrassing my poor mother?

"Dawn?" Busted. It's Bria James, because of course it is. "What are you doing here?"

"What do you think I'm doing here?" I hiss. "I told you to expect me."

"You did," she says evenly. "And it sounded like a threat."

"Not a threat. Just some information," I say, pulling her by the arm into the alcove of a locked classroom.

"Hey!"

"Don't 'Hey' me," I hiss. This may be an all-hiss conversation. "You knew you were starting trouble last night by telling me about that script, and I'm not proud to admit that I fell for it, so here I am. I don't know how you even got a copy, but I want to see it."

Bria James now looks 15 percent less smug. Good.

"I don't know if I can do that. I gave it back to the person who showed it to me."

"Then get it back! I do the same thing you do, kind of, so I know how you work. You ask leading questions and goad people into acting a fool so you can get them on the record. I know you told me about the script so I would do something stupid so your site gets more clicks and maybe an exclusive. You're obviously buddy-buddy with the production."

Bria James shakes her head. "I am not 'buddy-buddy,' and wow, how old are you?" she says. "I know how to get access."

"Fine," I say. "Just trust that I'm prepared to tell everyone you leaked me information and let's see how exclusive you are then."

Yeah, she's shook. I am quite enjoying it.

"OK," Bria James says calmly. "What's your play here?"

That's a good question. Self, what *is* your play?

Girl, I don't know. Here is where a better plan would have come in handy.

"Dawn!"

Someone else is calling my name, but it's coming from behind me.

"Dawn! What are you doing here?"

My sister is standing behind me, with even better bangs that she usually has. She's going to be on camera, after all.

"I could ask you the same thing," I tell Tonya, pulling her into the doorway, trying the handle on what I thought was a locked classroom. It gives, creaking more loudly than I expected. I pull them both inside and shut the door, turning to my sister, who looks satisfyingly guilty.

"So what's up with that secret photo shoot you didn't tell anyone about last night?" I say quietly, because I don't want anyone in the hallway to hear a confrontation.

Tonya's eyes widen. "How did you find out about that?"

"This one," I say, gesturing toward Bria James. "She called the landline at Mommy's, stalking me—"

"Reporting," Bria James objects.

"In a stalky way," I answer.

Tonya gives a deep sigh. "Would bringing it up have helped anything? You already knew about this press conference. You know I didn't tell you about the movie in the first place. I'm the bad guy no matter what."

I laugh. "If that's a ploy for sympathy, it's not working."

Bria James clears her throat, and I consider that maybe kidnapping a person with a significant media presence is unwise. Also, I've always been proud of being a Black woman who supports other Black women, no matter what. Jesus is testing me.

"You're not a captive," I snap, hoping that she doesn't figure out that being pulled into a room against one's will is the textbook definition of captivity. "We gotta go before anyone misses Tonya at this godforsaken press conference."

"I have to go, too!" Bria says, her voice rising to a low panic. "That last story did really well, and the movie's producers have noticed! I'm risking my access."

I step back enough so that when the cops are called, she can't say I was in her face. "Bria. Ma'am. MA'AM. If you just listen to me, I think I can get you a better story."

She scoffs, straightening up to look me in the eye. If I didn't hate her so much, I might be impressed.

"What could you possibly have to share that's bigger than one of the bestselling nonfiction books of all time, written by a major news star, becoming a probably Oscar-winning movie?"

Tonya raises her hand slowly. "I know this one."

"OK," Bria says. "Shoot." She pauses and looks squarely at me. "Not literally, of course."

"I'm going to ignore that," I say. "Tonya?"

"What if we have proof that Joe stole that whole story that the movie is based on from Dawn, and that this new script is a final attempt to muddy the waters so that no one ever believes her?"

Tonya looks at me. "Dawn, is that what you were trying to say?"

I nod. "Almost exactly."

We both turn to Bria James, whose mind appears to be blown. "Is this true?"

"Of course it's true," Tonya says. "We literally just told you so."

"Why didn't you ever say anything before?"

"It's a very long story, but it could be *your* story if you play ball and get me a copy of that script so we have some leverage and I know exactly what to refute," I say hurriedly.

Bria James is quiet for a moment, hedging her bets and running the numbers. What's better—the original plan or the wild promises of bizarre ladies who barricade her in classrooms?

"I know you won't give me a complete exclusive because you'll want that yourself. And the press conference starts in, like, three minutes," she says. "How am I supposed to get a copy of the script by then?"

"How did you see it the first time?" I ask.

She smiles. "I have a source."

"I bet you it's that cute little assistant girl. She had a script in her hands at the photo thing last night," Tonya whispers. "She looks dumb enough to be charmed by this one's flirting."

"Maria's not dumb," Bria James says. "And that's not very feminist of you."

"Go tell your cute, little, not-dumb source you want to take some notes," I say. "The two of you get out there. I'll figure it out."

Tonya straightens her bangs, because whatever happens, she knows she's about to be on Instagram. A lot. "What are you going to do?" she asks me.

"I'm not sure yet. I'll figure it out."

Tonya laughs. "That's the scariest thing you could say."

"My friend," I say, hugging her and shoving her toward the door, "you are not wrong."

Chapter 14

This Is Me Figuring It Out

As I walk into the press conference, I wonder what I'm actually here to do. I've changed my mind on this about twelve times since the parking lot at Rudy's. If I confront Joe publicly, I'm going to be called a hater, or a grieving madwoman who has one less Pulitzer than him. Whatever narrative wins, it's all bad. But if I don't say anything, everyone is still going to think that I'm a jealous hag when that movie comes out.

What's that saying—print the legend? Joe printed the legend, and now he's projecting it onto a screen. It's going to blow up my life, and I'm either going to lose my business and reputation or wind up with a facelift as the hanger-on friend of a Bravo show star, holding her handbag. Nobody wants that.

As a journalist, I know I need more proof than just Tonya and vibes. And I'm afraid she's signed something legal that could cost her money if she helps me.

You don't have to do this, says a voice in my head that I fear is either Dale or my conscience again. Dale is the better part of my conscience, but it's not fair to blame him. I am, however, not above blaming the loss of him and the trauma of grief should I get sued.

I do have to, Voice, I say in my head. *I already told Tonya and Bria James something was going down.*

Both of them would be happy to let this go, assures the Voice. *You're the captain of this ship. And think about what happens at your mother's surprise birthday party if you do this. There are deaconesses from the church coming! You can't embarrass her in front of the deaconesses and the Lord!*

Wait. Is the Voice my mother?

Before my current nervous breakdown can continue, I'm ushered into the press area, where I am careful to try to blend into the back, away from the lights or anyone local who might recognize me. This better start soon, before I lose my nerve.

Something's starting to happen up on the stage. Lights come on, and some official college-looking people start walking in. There's Morgan State University President George Eaton. I see my sister up there, holding her hand over her eyes to shield them from the lights. Her gaze meets mine.

"Girl, this better be good," she mouths.

I'm gonna try.

Taking the stage behind her is . . . Michael Ealy's stunt double? Terrence Howard's little cousin? No, it's Joe, as if he materialized directly from hair and makeup. Hair glistening. Fake glasses shining. Fangs hidden.

President Eaton taps the microphone.

"Thank you all for coming. Several years ago, this young man— well, he was a young man then . . . ," President Eaton says to laughter. Joe's perfect brow furrows just a teeny bit because someone has noticed him aging. This pleases me. "This young man single-handedly brought a city to its knees, spoke truth to power, and eventually wrote his second book, *Speaking Truth to Power,* here in our library. He also holds an honorary doctorate from this great institution."

Single-handedly? Bull. But please continue, sir.

"This brave journalist worked tirelessly to stop an injustice, and though it was not Baltimore's finest hour, we have been grateful ever since for this steward of the truth"—OH COME ON—"risking it all to get to the bottom of it. We are proud of his hard work and that his

Pulitzer Prize–winning series has made some real change. City hall was cleaned up, the nefarious business that threatened the education of so many of our precious children was shut down in disgrace, and cities all over our country, including ours, have tightened the reins on the relationship between private industry and the public good."

I have to stop rolling my eyes so publicly, but come on, dude. This is Baltimore. It's not like no elected official has gotten arrested for anything since 1994. They just never again tried to demolish elementary schools and risked sending thousands of kiddies to take to the streets selling pencils in tin cups.

President Eaton is still droning on about how special Joe is. Snooze.

"Mr. Perkins went on to the big time, to *National News Now* and more books. Now, we're delighted to announce that *Diving into Deception* is, after so many years, coming to the big screen, filming in and around the area, including some scenes here on campus!"

Applause, applause. Fine. Get to the weasel.

"And we're honored to have with us some of the principal cast, the director, and some people who played such a big role in bringing the culprits to justice. All of them are notable, but none of this would have happened without our own Pulitzer Prize–winning journalist, Joseph R. Perkins."

"R" is for Ronald, but it might as well stand for "Rat." Or "Rat fink." Something squarely in the rodent family.

Joe sidles up to the mike and looks out into the crowd. I instinctively duck.

"Thank you all for being here," he says. "It wasn't an easy journey. I've lost friends and made enemies doing this job, but as I stand here, I am truly humbled that this important story is finally going to be documented on film in all its truths."

One of the criticisms of modern journalism is that no one does any actual journalism anymore. We just ask publicist-approved questions and avoid anything our subjects might not like. We're too worried about losing access, about not getting through that VIP door. I've done it, too. And I'm not proud of it.

Joe is getting applause. He appears to like it. Stop doing stuff Joe likes!

"First, I'd like to introduce our director, Isaiah Greene, and our stars, Keith Daniels, Martin Epperson, Regina Mattson, Helen Richardson, and Crystal Dirkins."

I've actually met Keith Daniels, the latest in a line of young-ish Black actors dubbed The Next Denzel because no one can imagine that two Black actors could exist in power and popularity at the same time. I'd love to say casting a man this fine to play Joe is a reach, but it's not. That stupid perfect face.

The minute I see Miss Crystal Dirkins, who you may recognize as every trifling ex-girlfriend ever to appear in a Lifetime movie with Black people, I know who she's playing. If I were vainer, I'd be excited that she's hot. Evil hot. I haven't seen her movie wig yet. It's probably made from used macramé cord.

"Dawn?" someone whispers. How can I conduct a secret undercover plot if people won't stop saying my name out loud? I don't turn around, but I recognize the voice. It's still snooty.

"Dawn?" Susan McNally, columnist and fellow annoying fellow intern, tries again. "Who are you here with?"

Busted.

"Glitter. My own Los Angeles–based entertainment site."

"Oh, that's you? I didn't know that! Huh."

Yep. Still hate her.

"I'll shoot you the link," I say. "Our next story is gonna be a blockbuster."

Susan smiles and goes back to reading her phone and looking for someone more interesting to talk to. Boy, is she gonna look stupid. This is one more reason to bust this all up.

One busybody reporter diverted, at least for now. I look back to the stage, where Joe is still on his pedestal. He's just introduced former mayor Julius Blaylock Jr., who's had some tasteful work done and seems to be enjoying the attention. I almost felt bad for that guy at the time, although I was never convinced that he was completely in the dark about the scandal. Bet he's a "consultant," too.

"Now I'd like you to meet some brave souls whose efforts and bravery made my reporting, and the discovery of this terrible injustice, possible. Here are Holly Jarvis, George Middleton, Sherri Simpson, and Tonya Roberts-Jenkins, whistleblowers who placed doing the right thing over their careers and personal relationships."

Huh. No Sheila from Permits? I know Joe's talking about me with that last dig. He's not gonna be so smug when I do . . . whatever it is I'm about to do. Tonya gives the crowd a nervous half-wave. She really does look good today. You're never going to catch my sister slipping, face and hair-wise, whether it's a press conference or a run to the corner store for slushies.

Her eyes meet mine again. "Well?" she mouths at me.

I shrug. She gives me the "Girl, get it together" eye roll.

There is applause as Joe pauses to let the crowd acknowledge other people who are not him and then nods. "I thank these brave people again. This is an exciting project, and I can't wait to start filming tomorrow. I think we have time for a few questions."

Here we go. Maybe I'll wait to see where it's going before I say anything. The minute I raise my hand, it's on.

"Hey," I hear Bria James whisper behind me, shoving something into my hand.

I glance down at a bound stack of papers. "Diving into Deception," it says. It's the script! Susan glances from me to Bria, trying to figure out what's up. Eyes on your own paper, kid.

"Where's the part about me? Do you know what page I'm on?" I whisper.

"You're on a lot of pages," Bria James whispers back.

I flip it open wide enough to read but not so wide that prying eyes might be able to read it, too. It takes three flips to see the name

"Fawn." Of course, he wants me to know it's about me. The allusion to scandalous Fawn Hall, famous for helping her boss, Oliver North, shred state secrets while having big, gorgeous hair, makes his point.

FAWN

Where are you going?

JOE

I'm going to meet the woman from the mayor's brother's office. There's something there, I just know it.

FAWN

I don't trust her. I think she's full of it. And she's hitting on you.

JOE

What about the truth?

FAWN

The truth is that this skank is making things up.

I'm trying to listen to what's being asked in the press conference as I read quickly, and wow, did Joe become a hack!

"Mr. Perkins? Tyler Murphy, *Baltimore Weekly News*. Why has it taken so long for this story to come to the big screen?"

"Tyler . . . and thank you for being here, man . . . I've had so many other stories to tell on TV and in print that it took a while to be able to focus on sitting down and writing this the way it deserves to be. Drawing attention to myself and my own efforts seemed self-indulgent. That's not what I'm about."

Lord Jesus, please spare me when the lightning bolt from on high strikes this loser. I flip through the script. It's like a Rolodex of evil. Here's Fake Dumb Skanky Me again.

FAWN

Look, I know he's up to something. I didn't think there was anything to that story he's doing! I do want to get a look at that notebook, though.

CHIP

That sounds like a good idea. Maybe there's something you can get in on.

Who in the world is Chip?

FAWN

I've been looking for a scoop. Maybe this could be my ticket out of this little town. They never took me seriously at the big paper. If I can just get that notebook, they'll have to now!

CHIP

Maybe. Wanna have a drink later? Unless you're still on deadline.

FAWN

Oh, that's not important. Just my review of the Shoo Fly Pie Parade. Screw that.

CHIP [*laughing*]

Speaking of screwing . . .

FAWN

Come here, you. Help me with this bra, and then we can go see that band you manage. They don't suck as much as I thought they would. If you make me happy, I can see about getting them on the front page of the Features section.

This is libelous and horrible. Can you retroactively snatch back a Pulitzer?

CHIP

Wow, I have to be good in bed on top of the money I paid you?

WAIT A COTTON-PICKING MINUTE. Fawn is Dawn, obviously. And Chip . . .

No, he didn't.

Chip is Dale. *My* Dale. That unimaginative prick couldn't just drag me into his self-serving crap, he had to drag my dead husband in there, too? And he's doing this now as I bring his ashes home? Joe's actually implying that I took money and orgasms in exchange for better story placement? Lay for pay, as it were?

If he's willing to go this low, I know it has to go lower.

"It gets worse, right?" I whisper to Bria James as Joe takes a question from a local radio guy about the movie's soundtrack and how much Babyface is in it.

"Where are you?" she whispers back.

"Where I'm offering to screw 'Chip' in exchange for writing about his band."

She nods. "Oh, it gets worse."

"Really bad?"

"Bad. Chip's a liar and a sleaze, who, it's suggested, is stealing from his family's accounting business—"

Oh no.

"And he convinces Fawn to try to get the Joe character in trouble by claiming the story is hers. Also the script implies that Fawn is open to this sort of . . . exchange with other sources, which, as you know, makes her look like the worst, sluttiest, most unethical journalist in the world. No one would ever trust her, or you, again."

I feel like I've been punched in the face by a ream of paper. Bria James sees the "Oof" wash over me.

"Maybe he did steal your story," she says. "Because this is scorched-earth territory."

Is it ever. I have spent my life and career trying not to be the angry Black woman stereotype people assume I am. But Joe's messing with me and my legacy. And my man.

I look up from the script, and Tonya's staring at me from the stage like she's worried. "What are you gonna do?" she mouths.

"This," I mouth back, raising my hand.

"And so it begins," she says. She does not mouth this.

Joe turns to Tonya, then sees my face, and for half a second, his smugness slips. He's so used to controlling the narrative, and at this, his big moment, he has no clue what's coming. He can't ignore my hand like he could if no one else in the room knew who I was, and he can't be initially nasty to me because he's in Clark Kent mode. He can't go full General Zod just yet.

"Yes?" Joe says. He hates this. Good.

"Dawn Roberts-Shaffer, *Glitter*," I say. I have never professionally gone by my married name, but I suddenly feel like I'm a knight avenging my fallen family. You've got to use the whole name.

"Is that a real publication?" he says. "Sounds like a nineties movie about a past-her-prime prima donna."

"Mariah Carey was triumphant!" I say. "And you *know* it's a real publication."

"Fine. You have a question?"

"Many," I shoot back. I can feel the temperature in the room change a little, because this is reading a wee hostile.

"You get one," Joe says. "Shoot."

"Do we know her?" someone behind me asks.

"I do," Susan answers, leaning closer.

"I wanted to ask about the script. I understand you're the writer?"

"Sure am," Joe says. "Very proud of it."

"I'm sure you are. Having covered Hollywood for decades, I understand that there are usually liberties taken. I'm curious about any details you've changed."

"Well," Joe says, "I changed some names and rearranged some of the events to streamline them, but for the most part, it's exactly what happened."

"Is it now?"

"Yes," Joe says definitively, looking for someone else to call on. "Thank you for your question, Ms. Roberts."

"*Roberts-Shaffer*. One more thing," I say, Columbo-like, holding up the script dramatically. "I've perused this script, and while I see that yes, you've certainly changed some names—like mine—I know that you've changed the most important detail of all."

Ever wonder what a Scooby-Doo villain looks like right before Fred and Shaggy pull his ghost mask off? I imagine that it's something like Joe's face right now.

"And what is that?"

"That you've made me look bad in this script on purpose. Because you stole the story from *me*."

All the cameras in the room turn in my direction. Wow, these lights are bright.

"DAWN!" Susan says, recorder in my face. "What are you saying?"

"I said what I said," I answer. "Mr. Perkins?"

Joe pauses, then leans forward. He's pivoting. Bring it.

"That's a very serious accusation, Ms. Roberts, and it's very curious that you'd wait almost thirty years to make it. It's absurd, of course. And that you'd do this publicly is very sad. I understand you've had some personal challenges lately and that this is an emotional time. I am sorry for the solemn occasion that brings you back to our city. But that doesn't excuse these blatant lies."

"Are these lies, Dawn?" Susan says. I'ma slap that mike out of her hand.

"No, Susan, they're not. That's enough questions right now. I'll let you know when I have more to say."

"Are you done?" Joe says, snarl no longer hidden.

"Oh, sweetie," I say, matching his snarl with a smirk, "not anywhere close."

I turn to leave and stride out triumphantly, but there are too many reporters in my way.

"I gotta go, y'all," I yell as the cameras and flashes edge closer. Bria James appears behind me. She may have been there all along. I was having too much fun roasting Joe to notice.

"You're gonna talk to me later, right?" she asks.

"Of course," I say as Susan and some others push toward me. "I promised. But I really do have to go. Y'all, back up!"

"Dawn, you can't expect to just drop a bombshell like that and walk away," Susan says before pursing her lips.

"Yes, she can!" says Tonya, now flanking me. "She has a funeral thing to get to."

"A funeral thing?" Susan says, confused. "Who died?"

"Everyone, girl."

Tonya grabs me by the arm and starts clearing the way in front of her with her other arm. "MOVE!" she bellows. Bria James follows behind quickly in the hastily made clearing. We push forward, and the crowd parts. They're afraid of Tonya now. Wise.

"How do you know Joseph Perkins?" someone yells.

"Do you have any proof of these serious accusations?"

"Did you really name your publication after a Mariah Carey movie?"

"Who are you wearing?"

I must answer that one. "Old Talbots and a no-name skirt I stress-bought on Amazon in the middle of the night in 2020."

"Where'd you park?" Tonya asks, pulling me through the door.

"In the media lot, where all the vultures are gonna be."

"You better run fast then," she says, and we start booking it toward my rental Jeep. Some students look at us weird—it's odd enough to see lots of old people on your campus, but then some of them are running in dress clothes. A kid in a Tupac hoodie looks behind him as if there might be something he should be running from, too. He was raised right.

I quickly hit the unlock button on the rental Jeep key fob, and the three of us jump in—me in the driver's seat, Tonya and Bria in the back—as a bunch of reporters follow us.

"I know y'all aren't surrounding my car," I say.

"Dawn, if you just give us a statement," Susan says, tapping on the window.

I was never a "tapping on the car window" reporter, but I'm not shocked that Susan is.

"Tonya," I say. "Get me the urn."

"It's right next to you," my sister whispers. "What are you doing?"

Honestly, I'm not sure. Maybe that's better. If it gets crunchy, I can say it wasn't premeditated. I reach carefully for the urn holding half of Dale's ashes, strapped into the passenger side.

I lift it to the window.

"This is my late husband, Dale," I say.

"Well, half of him," Tonya says under her breath.

"Is that real?" Susan says.

"No, it's an urn I always carry in my car to confuse nosy reporters. Girl, bye," I say, quickly restrapping the urn back to the seat as we jet out of there.

Bria James, who I had forgotten was in the car for a minute, lets out a long sigh. "That press conference was intense!" she said. "Dawn, I can't believe you confronted Joe Perkins and then just left like that."

"I can," Tonya says. "That's how Dawn works. She's good at dropping bombshells and fleeing. And the only choice you have is to hop on board or get run over."

"Shut up. And thank you."

"Of course," Tonya says. "I got you."

And I believe her. "Are they following me?" I ask.

"I can't tell," Bria James says. "How am I gonna get back to my car?"

I snort. "Ma'am, I don't have time to be caught in the mob I just escaped. And I really do have to get to the cemetery. Your choices are Ubering back to your car or walking. You're young."

She considers this. "What if I come with and you let me interview you while you drive? I have so many questions! Was this your plan all along? What do you want from Joe Perkins? Are you trying to stop the movie, or do you just want to rewrite the script? Maybe you're after a cut of the film's earnings, or maybe you just want to mess with the guy who messed with you?"

The answers to those questions have changed constantly over the last several hours. What I mostly want is to stop this clownery and not have Dale's and my lasting legacy be as Baltimore's bungling Boris and Natasha, without the moose or squirrel.

"I'm not really in the headspace for that," I say. "I'm wired and sad, and I'm bound to say something stupid that I'll want to sue you for if published."

"She's a weasel website newsperson," Tonya says. "That's the exact headspace she wants you in."

"That's not really fair," Bria James says.

From the front seat I hear furious clicking on her phone. *Uh-oh.*

"Bria James! Are you writing a story right now?"

Tonya snatches the phone out of her hand.

"Hey!"

"Girl, nobody cares."

"What did she write?"

"'I've been kidnapped on the way to a funeral!'" Bria James yells.

"You did not!" I yell back, hoping she didn't, because I'm not trying to get arrested.

"Fine!" Bria James says, snatching her phone back. "I just sent a post on X saying that explosive things had happened at the press conference and that *National News Now* star Joe Perkins's former friend, noted journalist Dawn Roberts, accused him of stealing the Pulitzer Prize–winning story from her."

Tonya whistles. "Accurate. You type fast."

"Part of the job."

"At least I get to be 'noted,'" I say. "Fine. But you have to be discreet. I can't have this scene at the cemetery becoming a circus on my account. I can't be the black sheep bringing this drama to them."

"And the BLACK black sheep, to boot," Tonya notes.

"If anyone asks, you're a young journalist I've been mentoring," I decide.

Bria James's face is doing something weird.

"What?"

"Nothing."

Deep breaths, Dawn, I think, trying to find a bit of uncharacteristic Zen from somewhere deep in my soul. "Look, kid. I know you think I'm a journalistic dinosaur and you're the new era. You're probably right. But you need something from me, so I'm gonna insist that you keep your snark to a minimum, or you and your Temu pumps are hitting the street. Got it?"

She nods reluctantly.

"Great. And no more posting unless you clear it with me. I have my own site, and trusting the competition is what got me into this mess in the first place. But I'm happy to share some details on my terms."

Bria James rolls her eyes. "You're a journalist. You know you can't control my story."

I turn the wheel sharply into a check-cashing store parking lot and unlock her door. "I *am* the story. Do you want it or not?"

Bria James looks at Tonya. "Is she serious?"

"I think you know she is."

She pauses, then puts her phone on her lap.

"Good choice. Thank you, Bria James."

"You can just call me Bria."

"I'll promise to not call you what I was calling you in my head."

I take a moment to listen to my voicemails, because I keep feeling the beep of my phone blowing up. My mother has called three times, because I bet the usher board was watching. I've also ignored a call from Pearl as well as a cryptic text from Miss Vivi that simply says, "Ask me about Teena Marie in New Mexico!" I really want to hear that story, but I have my own crazy to navigate, so hers is gonna have to wait.

"Why is your phone still out?" Tonya asks Bria James. "I'm close enough to throw it out the window."

As I pause at a red light, I glance back at Bria James. She smiles. Settles forward in the seat. Goes to Voice Memos on her phone and hovers her finger over the red "Record" button. "How long does it take to get to the cemetery?"

"I don't know, a half hour?"

"Good," she says. "You promised me a story. You probably have time to tell most of it."

Chapter 15

The Story I Almost Have Time to Tell Bria James

1994

"What are all those notebooks for?"

I'm hunched over in the passenger seat of Eddie's truck, tossing everything that just fell on the floor from out of my big, overstuffed duffel back into the bag, making sure I scoop up the crumbs from the crumpled-up bag of Combos I had for breakfast. I know I shouldn't consider my rancid nutrition a badge of honor, but . . . deadlines!

"It's a thing I'm working on," I say hurriedly.

Eddie reaches down and picks up a notebook that's fallen behind my fake Doc Martens boot. "'Water Park,'" he reads. "What's that?"

"It's a long story," I say. "What time was that band contest starting again? We're gonna be late."

Eddie laughs. "When was being late ever a problem for you?"

"Whatever," I say. He's not wrong, but I'm not in the mood. I've been doing all my regular cops and cupcake-baking stories while heading to Baltimore as much as possible for this water park project. And it's hard. I'm making definite but slow progress. Tonya and I have been having secret lunches and coffee with some of the witnesses to this scandal, and I need to prove that there is, indeed, a scandal. Sheila from Permits has been especially helpful because she's seen paperwork to demolish one of the schools where the water park is supposed to go, and she knows it's bull. She went to high school with the principal of that school, and when she asked him casually where he was going to be next year, he said, "Who can say?" and then added something about buying a new stereo.

Also, one of the Ricky Mouses is willing to talk in exchange for a better whiskey than he can afford. This is neither ethical nor in my budget, so we move on. Meanwhile, Tonya has been very vague with Percy about what we're doing—so vague that she hasn't really told him. He's not going to hear it from me because we don't deal with each other.

The last thing I need is to be teased by Eddie, who I want to respect me as a journalist and not see me as the happy-go-lucky newsroom version of Tootie from *The Facts of Life*. He also is looking very cute today—as always. I still wonder sometimes if there's a thing between us, but I'm bad at guessing about this stuff and also too much in my head.

As I am right now.

"You're writing a story about a water park?" Eddie says, turning into the West Manchester Mall parking lot and pulling up as close as he can to the door because those cameras are heavy. Not that his arms aren't strong enough to carry them . . . and probably me.

OH MY GOD, DAWN. STOP.

"It's a thing I'm doing on enterprise, on my own," I answer, hoping it's not obvious that I was inner-monologuing about his arms.

"That's cool," Eddie says, now out of the truck and getting his equipment from the back. "What's it about?"

"It's a whole thing," I say quickly. "I don't want to jinx it, and I want to do more work on it before I talk about it. Zach said it was OK. I want him to know that I can do more than this."

"Are you telling me that you didn't dream of covering drunk guys with mullets singing Van Halen covers in a mall?"

I laugh, holding the door open for Eddie. "No, I did not. Maybe if they suck, you can jump in on drums."

He laughs. "I'm very rusty. They'd have to be really bad for me to be an improvement."

"Why do I think you're downplaying your talent? Am I gonna find out you were a secret child drum prodigy who flamed out on *The Gong Show* in front of Gene Gene the Dancing Machine and never recovered?"

Eddie laughs again.

"Nothing that dramatic," he said. "The singer I was playing with and I parted ways in the middle of her tour."

This sounds like a good story.

"What did you do? Was it a big scandal? Is it anyone I've heard of?" I ask.

Eddie looks like he's weighing whether to get into it, and then shrugs.

"It was someone from the sixties, on a comeback tour of sorts. Don't know if you've ever heard of her. She wound up coming back without me, but it was hard to keep Vivienne down."

I sit up.

"Vivienne St. Claire? Didn't she challenge an Ice Capades skater to a duel live on TV or something?"

Eddie shakes his head, like he's got so much to share, but isn't going to. "Just go do your story, girl," he says. "If anyone can make something worthwhile out of this, it's you."

I may not be excited about Corn Pudding RockFest '94 or whatever this is, but I'm the only one. The crowds are packed around the stage in the middle of the mall, and the line at the pretzel store is massive. If you're moving that many pretzels in central Pennsylvania, it's probably a big to-do.

Eddie starts setting up while I wander around to interview people. It's the usual "I'm here to see my boyfriend / grandson / watercooler delivery guy's band and they RAWK!" I have a rule of three: I need to interview at least three people not related to the event and hope at least one of them has more to say than "They RAWK!" What I've learned is that it's easier to get good quotes at a place people are happy to be at than at, like, a ten-car pileup.

So far I've talked to a nice Mennonite lady who seems proud of her guitarist nephew but also slightly confused that he's playing rock music in a mall and not milking a cow like a nice boy, plus a girl named Kayla who keeps trying to tell me what a good bassist her boyfriend is but keeps bursting into tears. I probably can't use her quotes because they're sort of nonsense. I need more.

"Excuse me? Are you with the newspaper?"

I'm literally holding a pen and a reporter pad and wearing a press pass, and after a year in this business, I'm beginning to understand that some people don't expect a Black girl. I'm mad now.

"Yeah," I say sharply, turning toward the voice and hoping the person it belongs to understands they're pissing me off. And that person is . . .

Whoa.

"Hello . . . Dawn!" says the person—who looks like Ethan Hawke's character in *Reality Bites* if he'd bathed and had a job—as he peers at my press pass. "I'm Dale Shaffer. I manage a band called Wingling, and they're playing third. Can't wait for you to hear them."

I normally hate hustle like this, because what if the band sucks and it becomes awkward? But this Dale is charming. Nice. Probably not a hustler? Wait, he's a manager of a band playing a battle of the bands at a mall in York, Pennsylvania. He has to be a little bit of a hustler.

I don't hate it.

"Are they good?" I ask, a stupid question considering he's their manager and he's not going to admit they aren't.

"Honestly, Dawn," Dale says, and hearing my name from that voice tingles something in my fingers, which is bad because I'm trying to use them to write. "They're better than they were, but not as good as they're going to be, which is epic."

That's a great quote. I write it down and keep talking. "What does Wingling mean?" I ask, copying down the names of the musicians from the flyer he's handed me.

"It's a play on words, like Yuengling, the beer," Dale says, pointing at the logo that's a knockoff of the logo of the local-ish brew, but with extra wings.

"Isn't that copyright infringement?" asks Eddie, who has suddenly appeared behind me like he does.

"I keep telling them that," Dale says, laughing and sticking out his hand. "Dale Shaffer. Manager of Wingling."

Eddie shakes his hand and nods. "Man, I hope they're good enough to win so they can pay off those lawsuits," he says. "I know someone in the business, and she'd have been on the phone with her lawyer already."

"I hope they're that good, too!" Dale says, turning toward the stage. "Be right back. Let me know if you need anything else, Dawn."

"What's that about?" Eddie asks.

"What's *what* about?" I answer, trying not to be flustered. "Hey, they're starting!"

Wingling is taking the stage early because the Yeastie Boys, a bread-based white-boy rap cover group who all work at the same bakery, has dropped out. I will be forever curious about what that might sound like, but I guess we'll never know because I don't care enough to look them up. Wingling is pretty good, though. They do mostly covers—Aerosmith, Bon Jovi—but throw in an original that I don't hate.

"I'm not sure that's wise," Eddie whispers. "Remember on *Star Search* when the singers would say, 'I'm singing a song I wrote?' Nobody likes that."

"Shh," I shush, because I like the song and for some reason it has become very, very important that this Dale Shaffer knows I am taking his little band very seriously. Eddie looks amused, as if he knows something I don't.

"What?"

"Don't mind me," he says, lifting his camera and walking toward the stage stairs to get ready for the next act, a cute eleven-year-old named Ellen Strausbaugh who, like many young singers before her, completely misunderstands the key "I am a dirty mistress" theme of the lyrics to "Saving All My Love for You."

As the singers and bands and alleged rap groups come and go, I learn a little about Dale. He's from Baltimore County, like most of the members of Wingling, but the bass player's mom has a barn nearby where they practice. He has a brand-new business degree from Towson University, not far from where I grew up, but turned down a job with his family's accounting firm to pursue a career in music management, which isn't the most direct route to making a living in the northern Maryland / southern Pennsylvania shopping mall market.

"But I think I'm onto something," Dale says as Wingling is announced the winner and an automatic entrant in a statewide contest at State College. "I know a good thing when I see it."

And then he winks at me. Oh my. Did someone turn on a Bunsen burner under my face?

Later in the car, that warmth still in my cheeks and Dale's business card in my pocket, I start marking up my notes so I can run into the newsroom and write this story quickly. I need to get done and get down to Baltimore so I can try to persuade some of the other city hall people to talk to me. I also need to have dinner with Joe. I think he can help me out of some of these corners I've reported myself into.

"Where you headed, kid?" Eddie says as I start packing up.

"Baltimore. See my sister. Work on some stuff."

Eddie pauses in a way that seems significant and perhaps like I've done something wrong.

"What?"

He shakes his head. "Nothing . . . I don't want to be in your business," Eddie says in a way that plants him squarely in that business. Oh, for Pete's sake.

"Say what you're saying, dude!" I blurt, and I think this is the first time I've ever raised my voice in the slightest with Eddie. I wonder if he notices.

He gets the weirdest look on his face, something like soft affection and sharper concern. "Well, have fun. Just take a beat."

"What does that mean?" I am always on alert for signs of being insulted or not taken seriously, and my meter is going off.

"I just mean . . . There was some flirting back there with that guy. Remember church and state. Ethics . . . Business and pleasure and all that," Eddie says. "Drive safe."

Is he jealous? Being a hater? I don't know. Is he wrong about flirting with a source, if that was indeed what was happening? I don't want to look unprofessional, and Dale's not cute enough to throw my career away over, is he? Of course not.

But am I thinking about any of that as I drive off to meet Joe, making note of all the things I want to tell him about the water park story?

I am not.

Chapter 16

THE MORE YOU KNOW

2023

"Telling Joe anything about your story doesn't seem very wise, does it?" Bria James says from the back seat of my rental Jeep as we drive toward the cemetery. "I mean, like, in retrospect."

"You think?" Tonya says. "Like it's not the thing she's been regretting for decades."

"No offense," Bria James mutters, looking down. "You've been doing this so long, and not flirting with a source or sharing notes seems like Journalism 101."

"I was literally twenty-three years old and thought I could trust this man who said he had my back. It was dumb, but what did I know?"

"And you flirted with that PA girl on the movie to get the script, even before we asked you to," Tonya notes. "So don't be so smug."

Get her!

"Anyway, what do you know about Journalism 101?" I say sharply.

Bria James's face tells me she's weighing her next words carefully, as she doesn't want to be kicked out of the car. "I think I know a lot about it, since I got an A in it at Morgan."

"You went to J-school? You're a blogger."

She snorts the righteous snort of a savvy younger woman about to educate an elder. I've been that woman and trust me, she's highly annoying.

"Yes, ma'am," she says, the "ma'am" dripping with condescension. "There are not as many opportunities in legacy media as there were in your day, so we have to be creative in the digital space."

That's a lot of fancy words to say, *Handle the business that is yours, you old cow.*

"Sorry," I say. "That was presumptuous of me, but like I said, I was a little baby reporter. I made a mistake and paid for it."

Bria James shrugs. "I'm just trying to understand. It seems like a red flag."

Tonya laughs. "It was!"

"Percy was a red flag all on his own," I say.

Tonya bops me on the arm. "He had his moments."

"Those moments when he was lying to you and borrowing money, and those moments when he was selling church-lady chicken dinners out of your kitchen to fund his beeper side-hustle business?"

"He was a businessman."

"It was your chicken! From your freezer! On your power bill!"

Bria James dramatically clears her throat. I glance back, and she's raising her hand like she's a tenth grader with a question.

"Yes, Bria James?"

"Beepers?"

Tonya smacks her on the arm. "You know good and well what a beeper is. You're not that young."

Bria James starts to laugh. It's the first time we've had a human moment, and it's nice. "Sorry about that," she says. "Joking. So did you start seeing Dale then?"

"Define 'seeing,'" I say, and Tonya smacks me on the arm. "Can you stop smacking people?"

"You know what she means," my sister says. "I will refrain."

"I don't believe you," I answer. "Is this my exit?"

Tonya laughs. "Like I ever come out here . . . Hey, Bria James. We're not in class. Speak up."

"What was going on with you guys then? And what about Eddie?"

Tonya chuckles. "Yes, what about you and Eddie?"

"There wasn't a me and Eddie."

Tonya raises an eyebrow. "Well, maybe not for you, but I think he was sweet on you to go through all that effort."

I'm so confused I almost miss the exit. "What effort?"

"He sent Mommy some of the stuff off your desk after you left. I think it was like a Terps mug and an old photo of you interviewing Billy Ray Cyrus at the York State Fair. And Bria, if you ask if that's Miley's cousin, I'm stripping your phone back to factory settings."

I turn to Tonya as much as possible without taking my eyes off the road and killing us all. "How come nobody ever told me Eddie sent my stuff back to me?"

She shrugs. "I wasn't speaking to you, and that was actually Mommy's mug you stole, so nobody bothered."

Wait . . .

"Just a mug and Billy Ray? No notepads?"

Tonya shakes her head. "That would be great, given recent events, but no, sadly. Hey! Have you ever Facebooked him?"

"I've been afraid to. I don't love revisiting that time of my life," I said.

"I got it," Tonya answers.

I hear her typing. I'm tempted to turn around and look, but I'm trying not to kill us all, so I let Tonya tell me what she's found. He doesn't work at the *Herald* anymore. He's shooting weddings and headshots, and of course he's good at them.

"Look," she says, flashing her phone at me from the back seat. He's still handsome.

"Marital status?" I ask.

"Single. Why?"

"Just wondering," I say, relieved that no one can see the goofy look on my face.

"He's attractive," Bria James says. "But can we go back to the story? How did you end up losing the story and leaving town? Is there enough time for that part?"

"Not really," I say, and sigh. "But I guess there has to be."

Chapter 17

REALITY SMITES

1994

"Joe's not here," says Vanessa, Joe's irritating girlfriend. I can hear her rolling her eyes through the phone.

"OK, but I just wanted to make sure he knows I'm coming down for his mom's party," I answer.

"I'll tell him," Vanessa says, eyes still probably rolling. "It's a long way to drive. You sure you want to come?"

I take a deliberate pause that I know Vanessa can hear before not saying what I want, which would ruin my friendship with Joe once and for all. So I just say, "It's no trouble at all! Tell him I'll meet him at his place."

"Can't wait," says Vanessa, who doesn't seem to mean that at all.

I'm calling from a quiet part of the downstairs newsroom, speaking softly because I'm supposed to be upstairs finishing the third installment in what has become a series about Wingling. Who could have guessed there was anything more to say about those copyright-infringing idiots? They won the statewide Battle of the Bands that their mall win qualified them for, and they've been on the rise ever since while dodging a cease-and-desist lawsuit from the Yuengling beer people, just as Eddie predicted. Whatever it was he needed to tell me at the Christmas party has still not been mentioned. Maybe it was the wine.

"I told you," he said. "This kind of thing used to happen to Vivienne St. Claire all the time."

"She got sued all the time?" I ask.

"She sued, they sued, lots of suing," Eddie answered. "Those kids don't want any part of that."

I kind of think they do, because Wingling has become a "local boys who do good and might do better" story, and it's oddly compelling because everyone's meemaw subscribes and it sells papers. I think it's good. I know, I'm biased. I'm writing it.

Meanwhile, their manager, Dale, has been happy to keep me informed of every detail, and I don't mind it. He's funny and ambitious like me, and he's cute. I shouldn't be noticing that part—professionalism!—but it makes the band practices more fun. I even got Eddie to come to one to take photos for my story.

"I feel kind of bad for them," he said while the band took one of their smoke breaks. It's almost like the rehearsal was the break from their smoking. "I know this is a 'Stars on the Rise' story, but I'm afraid these photos are going to be used in an account of how their mothers lost their homes after the beer company takes it all."

"I'm pulling for them," I said. "I believe in them. There's something there."

"There is, is there?" Eddie said as Dale suddenly emerged holding two beers from the garage, which was, indeed, in somebody's mother's house.

"Hey, guys!" he said. "Thought you might want one of these."

"No thanks, we're on the clock," Eddie said even as I took the beer from Dale's hand. The frost on the bottle was cold, but the warmth of his palm gave me a spark. Caught out being unprofessional.

"I'm sorry," Dale said, his face reddening. "I didn't mean to put you in a bad position, Dawn."

"It's fine," I said, glaring at Eddie, who was suddenly very intensely wiping off one of his lenses. It'd been weird with us since I started working on the Wingling stories. The first time Dale stopped by the newsroom to drop off a flyer for the band's next performance, Eddie and I had been coming back from a fire on a horse farm. All the animals made it out, but we both smelled like embers and hay, which isn't sexy.

Even so, Dale smiled and told me he was glad he could give the flyer to me in person, and Eddie looked . . . disappointed? Disapproving? Hungry? Something unhappy. He'd had that look since then, and I don't know if he's jealous or if he thinks I'm an unprofessional ninny getting too chummy with a source. I tried to get another photographer to come with me, but wouldn't you know that no one else was available. Whatever. If he wants to be weird about it, that's on him. He's the one with a Sabra.

Since then, I've been trying to keep my Wingling stories close to the vest, because Eddie is my friend and I can't stand to have him think badly of me, and because I know this . . . whatever it is with Dale is probably stupid. There have been some deep-ish conversations at rehearsals, and maybe some chats on the phone between rehearsals, and a beer or two to go over notes or whatever. He even drove me back to my terrible apartment once when that beer or two became three. I started to ask him in but didn't want him to get the wrong idea. Sometimes I'm not sure what the right idea is.

I know his mother's name is Diane, and she's the life of everything in Green Spring Valley, a fancy place that's Baltimore adjacent but with absolutely no Chinese corner joints with bulletproof glass. His dad is very driven with their family accounting business, and his brother, Brent, studied accounting but went to law school because, as Dale says, "He does too much and doesn't know how not to."

I've enjoyed getting to know Dale and hearing all about his world. OK, I admit it: I like him. Shut up. I've not been all that successful in relationships, mostly because I'm always too focused on work to know if anyone is flirting with me.

"That guy is flirting with you," Tonya said once when I called Dale from her place while we rehashed the covert meeting we'd just had with Sheila from Permits behind a 7-Eleven.

"No, he's not," I said, my cheeks beginning to heat.

"You're blushing, and I'm Black, too, so I can tell," my sister answered.

What is wrong with me? I'm making all kinds of stupid choices. My job is to write about this band and not overanalyze hugs from their manager, a source I should not be hugging. And it could jack up my career, making me look flighty and silly. As a woman—as a Black woman—I can't afford anything that would bring my ethics and professionalism into question. Sam Donaldson is scowling at me from behind the collar of his raincoat. I am ashamed.

I'm also trying to be quiet around here about the water park story, which has hit a weird slowdown as of late. I was bumping along, pacing myself with my interviews for that story and my beat, but the last week or so it's been harder to get people on the phone. And I think I'm missing a notepad. I've never been the most organized person, but this is important. Must be around somewhere.

It seems like when I'm not working on my various stories, I'm leaving messages for Vanessa, which both of us are sick of. I try Joe directly at his desk, and he picks up on the first ring.

"Yes, Dawn?" he says a little brusquely.

"Oh, sorry. Don't mean to interrupt you," I answer, caught a little off guard. "Just wanted to make sure Vanessa gave you my message about coming to your mom's party."

"Sure," he says absently. "Got it. Anything else?"

I want to ask him why he sounds so weird, but that's going to irritate him further, and I don't want to do that.

"Sure, sure. You must be busy. Your big story is on its way," I say encouragingly. "I believe in you."

"You've always been so corny, Dawn," Joe says back. "It's very cute." Then he hangs up.

I've been trying to see Joe whenever I come down, but he's been very busy at the *Sentinel*, and sometimes I get the feeling that he's stuck. My friend, Jenn the copyeditor, tells me he's been stressed chasing some stories that fell through, and she thinks he feels pressure to live up to that super intern he was. Maybe that's it. Lately he's a little short with me, like just now? And he never calls me back right away anymore.

I have been chalking the weirdness up to stress and Vanessa's influence, because we don't like each other. I know, I know . . . it's easier to pretend that your friend is acting off because of who they're dating and not because something is off between you.

"What are you doing? Your deadline is in, like, ten minutes!" says Eddie, who has got to stop walking up on people. That used to be cute, and now it's just irritating.

"I know," I snap, even though I tried not to.

"Just trying to help, Dawn," he says. "Carmen the night editor was wondering where you were, and I didn't want to bust you."

"Bust me, how?"

Eddie sighs, and those pretty lips turn up into a grimace. "By telling her that you're either down here making plans for a story other than the one you were assigned, which is due in ten minutes, or that you're all chummy with the guy you're quoting in the story that's due in ten minutes."

I have been avoiding this conversation with Eddie for a month now, but the shadiness and the scowls and the feeling I'm supposed to be sorry for something I can't define is too much. "What is your deal?" I ask, draining the remnants of the bottle of Diet Coke I've been nursing since I've been here. "Why are you being such a jerk?"

"I'm not being a jerk, Dawn," Eddie says. I'm not sure I like the way he's saying my name. "I said I'm trying to help you. You've been so distracted, and I'm not the only one who's noticed."

That's not great. "What have you heard?"

"You made a phone call before you came down here that didn't sound like work, and as you got up to come down here, Carmen yelled,

'I don't hear clicking!' because you know she clocks when you're typing. You *should* be typing. And—"

"And what?" I do not want to have this fight. I've got, what, eight minutes left till my deadline? I'm trying to keep all this emotion and stress from spilling from my mouth, bubbling in my ears like I'm on a plane in a mess of turbulence. But I'm mad now, and tired. I'm feeling something for Dale that's becoming less of a crush and more of a thing. And I know he's feeling it, too. Why is Eddie so mad about this? It can't just be journalistic integrity.

Isn't that enough? Sam Donaldson says from behind an old-timey CBS News microphone. Not now, Sam! It's about to get wild!

"Hey," Eddie says, beginning to realize that maybe he's opened a can of worms. "Slow down."

"NO!" I say. "I'm sick of it. You've been weird to me for weeks now, and I didn't want to think this because it's ridiculous, but I think you're jealous of Dale."

"Why would I be? There shouldn't be anything happening with Dale to be jealous of," Eddie says.

"That's not the point," I spit at him, and now I have seven minutes. "You're so high and mighty about how bad a reporter I am, but you're acting like you're my boyfriend, and I'm pretty sure you are not my boyfriend because I'm pretty sure you have a girlfriend. And you've never asked me out."

Are you sure about that? Sam Donaldson asks in my head. I see all the times Eddie kind of suggested getting a drink. And he was the last one to leave the Halloween party I threw at my terrible apartment when I dressed as Clair Huxtable and he came as Sho'nuff from *The Last Dragon*, before things got odd at Christmas. I thought he stayed around to help to be nice, but was it more than that? I can recall smiles, and looks, and the word "Kid" said with what I probably used to hope was affection beyond that of a more experienced staff member and the spunky new reporter.

Oh.

"*Oh,*" Eddie says, and there's a terrible hurt in his eyes and a finality in his voice. "Guess that's true."

The silence isn't just deafening. It's banging the drum solo of "In the Air Tonight" between my shoulder blades.

"Eddie," I say, my voice shaky, but he puts his hand up as if there's nothing more to discuss. Oh no. I've broken it. And I don't even know what "it" is.

"Dawn!"

Carmen the night editor is standing in the doorway. That's bad. She had to come downstairs to find me, and she hates to move.

"You've got five minutes! What's going on? Am I interrupting something?" she says, glancing at Eddie, still silent, leaning against the wall of the sports department.

"There's nothing to interrupt," he says, pulling himself off the wall and toward the door. The cool in the air could chill a thousand illicitly procured Yuenglings.

"Well, good," Carmen says. "Dale, the guy from the band, called to follow up, but I told him you were on deadline and you'd call him later."

Carmen talks too much! At the sound of Dale's name, Eddie flings the door open and walks out into the darkened parking lot. I want to go after him, to make this right. I want to yell, "Why didn't you just tell me you liked me? I thought you had a girlfriend who is on TV and is prettier than me! I am very confused, and I cannot take your being mad at me!"

But I don't.

Carmen clears her throat.

"I would ask what that was about, but you don't have time to tell me," she says. She's right, and I'm probably wrong, about a lot of things. I run upstairs and put the finishing touches on the story, but I get a little guilty gurgle in my stomach when I read the phrase "said manager Dale Shaffer." I don't call him back because suddenly I'm afraid that talking to him in the newsroom—even about the band, which is my job—seems unprofessional. I have been denying every flitter and flutter, between Eddie and me and now with Dale, and I'm being both a terrible reporter and a terrible human. I have failed to juggle journalism and dating, proving again that I am not Khadijah James.

After I send the story to Carmen, I put the water park story notebooks in my desk drawer because that will force me to look at them the next shift I work, and then I leave another message for Sheila from Permits and one with Percy, who is never going to call me back. Finally, I read the message from Dale, who said he was making sure I didn't have any more questions. I have so. Many. Questions.

But I also have a birthday party in Baltimore to get to, and I'm hoping that the hour-long drive will clear my head and that Joe and I can talk through whatever weirdness has been going on there.

I hate this. All I want to do is save public schools, bury some weasels, and see my star rise into the stratosphere and beyond whatever's beyond the stratosphere—and don't ask me what that is. I am not the science reporter.

The newsroom phone rings, and Carmen answers. "Dawn!" she yells, though I am sitting three feet away. "Call."

I pick up at my desk.

"Dawn!" Joe says. "Glad I caught you. Listen, don't bother coming down. My mom got that thing that's going around."

"What thing?"

"You know, the stomach thing," he says hurriedly. "We've canceled the party."

"Oh no! Does your mom need anything?"

He chuckles. "Just some rest and a little Pepto. We've got it all handled here. Don't worry about us."

"I'm so sorry that she's going to miss her party," I say. "And I wanted to talk to you. I feel like there's been so much going on, we haven't had a chance to catch up. Is everything OK?"

There's something in the background, some sort of buzzing behind Joe. Sounds like people.

"Are you with your mom?" I ask. "Are you sure I can't bring down her apple butter and help pass the Pepto?"

"No," Joe says a little more forcefully. "Don't come. It's fine." Then he pauses, like he meant that to come out differently. "Sorry. Didn't mean to snap at you," he says, and that force is gone from his voice. All smiles again! "Just worried about her, and we have to call everyone to cancel."

"I understand," I say. I get the feeling there is more to understand, but I don't want to make him explain with his mother projectile-vomiting over her cake. "Don't sweat it. I'll check in tomorrow."

"Oh, OK," Joe says, the slightest weirdness back again. "Talk soon."

The hang up is kind of abrupt. Maybe it's the connection? Carmen gives me the thumbs-up across the room. My story is done. I'm not sure what to do with myself if I don't have to drive to Baltimore now. Maybe I could go try to find Dale? No, don't do that.

As I head to my car, I trip over my feet on the last step, dropping my keys. "Oh, for God's sake!" I say, leaning over to grab them by the faded Orioles key chain. But Dale has already picked them up.

Guess I don't have to find him after all.

"Hi," he says softly.

"Hi back," I say, too softly. What should I do? Lie. "I'm on my way to Baltimore for my friend's mom's birthday," I say, wondering if my pants are on fire.

"Oh yeah, you said that. Joe, right?" Dale says, walking behind me as I scuttle to my car.

"Yeah, Joe," I answer. Too much in my head. I look around for Eddie's car, hoping he's left, because this is already messy. "What's up, Dale?"

Dale's smile, always so steady, falters a little because I have never been less than European-Michael-Jackson-fan-in-the-Thriller-World-Tour-videos-level excited to see him.

"Something wrong?" he asks.

"No," I lie. "I'm just late. Why are you here?"

He takes a deep breath. The smile is back stronger, if a little urgent, and all the things I have been imagining might happen, which should not happen, seem to be happening. My timing blows.

"I was hoping I could tempt you to have a beer, but you're leaving. You wanna call me when you come back?"

Yes, I do.

"I don't think I can, Dale," I say.

"'Cause you're busy?"

"Because I'm covering your band. And it's a rookie move. If something happens with us, and people find out, it makes me look bad. It could get me fired, or at least make things harder for me at work. So whatever is going on with us can't happen."

Dale's smile softens, like he's gotten the answer to a mystery he's been trying to solve. "So there is something," he says, brushing my cheek with his finger. That didn't feel bad.

"Hey," I say just above a whisper.

"Eyelash," Dale says.

"You're a liar," I say, now legitimately whispering. "Haven't you heard anything I'm saying? Showing up here like this, coming up on my job? I have a lot of eyes on me as the only Black reporter—the only other Black journalist besides Eddie, who hates me now. No one expects a lot of me, and this could kill it. This is really bad."

Dale smiles again, the sweetest smile of . . . what? Regret? Resolve? "I don't want to ruin your job," he says, matching my whisper. "But I don't want to stop . . . whatever this is."

"You're gonna be the end of me," I say as his forefinger lightly meets my chin and lifts it to meet his face, leading me forward.

"God, I hope not."

The kiss is both gentle and insistent, like when you're telling yourself you're going to save some of this cookie for later, but you want it too bad not to eat it all right now. As Dale's arm, now around the waist of my faded The Gap jeans, begins to pull me closer, my makeup bag full of Clinique samples and whatever they had on sale at the Rite

Aid crashes onto the ground. And the spell is, if not broken, at least shaken violently into focus. I'm also reminded that I don't know if I have eyeliner on and am caught lacking, just like my mother always warned me.

"No," I say, grabbing the bag and scurrying past him into my driver's seat. "I can't do this."

"Dawn, wait," Dale says. I've never seen him less than sure of himself, and it's both scary and intoxicating, because the thing shaking that confidence is little old me.

"NO!" I say, pulling the door closed. "Don't come back here. I wrote the last story I have to write about Wingling. I can send you the name of the court reporter, and you can tell him what happens with the lawsuit."

My brain is screaming at me that if I stop writing about Wingling, I can date Dale. But it's going to look suspicious if I suddenly dump this series I've been working so hard on and show up shagging my source the next day. It makes me look like a lightweight. I've screwed this up so bad. It's terrible either way.

The car door has closed, and so has my Dale window. I don't want to close it. I want to be on the other side of that door kissing that man, or on this side of it in my back seat like a teenage loon. Then again, teenagers who make out in parking lots get killed in slasher movies.

Especially the Black teenagers.

"Please," I hear Dale say through the window. Is he crying? "Won't you call me when you get back, at least?"

I can't answer that because I know what my answer would be, and it should not be that. I'm not fit for human connection, even the connection my lips can still taste.

I peel off like an unsteady stuntman, and in a few frenzied moments, I am parking at my terrible apartment. It's a bad parking job. I can't care about it. I run up to my place, unlock the door, and slam it behind me. It's so quiet here. Solitary. I don't have to be solitary if I don't want to. But I'd better. Oh my God, have I ruined things with every single man in my life? This is not something that would have happened to Mary Tyler Moore. Maybe I should call Eddie and try to make things right. What would I even say? I am a journalistic ho. I see the jar of apple butter on the counter that I bought for Joe's mother. I wish I was driving down to Baltimore, sharing this delicious apple butter with the Perkins family. I'd even deal with Vanessa to not be up here plotting foolishness.

What if I go down, crash with Tonya, and work on the water park story? She's expecting me anyway, and with her good government job she can afford better booze. I'll just give Joe a call to let him know I'll be in tomorrow. I don't have his mom's number, so I'll leave a message with my favorite person.

"Hello?" Vanessa says.

"Hey, it's Dawn," I say.

There's a brief pause, as if she had been assured she wouldn't have to deal with me tonight and now finds the promise was a cruel farce. Not my fault she didn't check her caller ID before she picked up. "Joe's not here."

"I know," I say. "He's at his mother's, taking care of her."

Silence.

"Hello?"

"Why would he be taking care of her? She's at her birthday party. I came back to grab more wine. I guess that means you won't be there?"

What?

"I thought she was sick."

The silence is punctuated with impatience and slight scoffing. "I don't know where you heard that, but she's fine. He's just not there."

What?

"Then where is he?" I ask. There has to be some simple explanation.

"He had to run out and do a last-minute interview for his big story that's running tomorrow."

"Which story?" I say, feeling stupid. I hate that Vanessa knows something I don't. Why wouldn't he tell me about something so big?

"You know," Vanessa says in a way that tells me there's about fifteen more seconds left of my dance around her last nerve. "The one about the water park."

Umm.

"The what?" I say, but she hangs up. Something erupts in my chest. In my limbs. I'm hot and cold all at once, a sensation of unbearable fire and unsettling chill, like my body is trying desperately to figure out whether to explode or melt. I want to call Vanessa back and make her repeat that last part to me, but she's either not going to answer, or she's going to say those words again, and this desperate feeling is going to drown me.

She doesn't know what this means, but I do. Joe took my notebook. Joe took my sources. Joe took my story.

Joe took everything.

Oh my God. I think I black out for a moment and come to as my butt is headed toward the floor. I have only a split second to twist myself before my left side hits the milk crate coffee table. The cordless phone crashes to the ground as the batteries clank violently out of the back.

Joe, my mentor and trusted friend, has betrayed me. And I gave him the road map.

"Oh my God, you're so stupid!" I scream out loud, hot tears searing my face as I fall to the ground. Now I'm glad I forgot that eyeliner because it would have been a mess. This is *bad*. I haven't shared anything with Zach about the progress of the story, and maybe he just assumed I dropped it because he didn't need it anyway. But when it comes out in tomorrow's *Sentinel*, it's going to ring a bell, and he's going to have questions, the answer to all of which is "I messed up. I trusted the wrong person and handed a potentially huge story to my friend because he danced with me to the Violent Femmes at a dive bar."

I don't know if I'm sprawled here on the floor for a minute or a half hour, but I'm slapped out of my daze by a loud knock on the door. I take a sharp breath because I don't even know if I can talk when all the air has left my body.

"Hold on!" I yell, crab-crawling toward the knock and struggling to hoist myself onto the doorknob. I lean back against the wall and pull the door open. And there he is.

"You didn't go to Baltimore," Dale says.

"I did not. Why are you here if you thought I did?"

He pauses. "Can I come in?"

My career is probably over so I don't know what it's going to hurt at this point. I wince as I gingerly tilt to the side so he can come in. Instinctively he grabs my arm for support. I like it too much.

Dale helps me to my giant papasan.

"You OK? I was going to leave you a message, but now I can tell you in person."

"Tell me what? Is this about before? I'm sorry . . . ," I start to say, but he stops me, touching my cheek gently.

"I'm not," he says, and I want to return the kiss he hasn't given me yet but knows he wants to. This is so cheesy. I kind of hate everything right now. And yet I don't hate this as much.

"What are you talking about?"

"I'm leaving."

I lean forward, the hard wicker frame of the papasan burrowing into my thighs. "Why? You just got here!"

Dale laughs. I love his laugh because it's deep and warm and not directed at me. "No, I mean I'm leaving town. I just got a call that a band in a big festival in Los Angeles suddenly dropped out, and the producers are desperate to replace them. I guess they started asking around for anyone that won anything, which might mean they are not terrible, and they found Wingling."

I giggle. "Are we sure they're not terrible?"

"No," Dale says, returning my giggle and lifting the mood. "But it doesn't matter. They're in. But we have to be on the West Coast by tomorrow afternoon, so we leave now."

"For how long?" I ask.

"A long time, I think," Dale answers, and something in my chest shifts, like the air is escaping again. "I have no idea how they're going to do, but this seems like a sign that I should try to make a go of it out there in LA. It's where I want to be, where I think my future is, with Wingling and with other artists soon. I know it sounds crazy, and my family is never going to get it. But I have to try. And I can't go without you."

I'm confused. "You mean you can't go without telling me?" Even as I say it, I know that's not what he means. This fool.

"That's not what I mean," he says, and the kiss comes right on time, like the money note in a Whitney Houston key change—powerful and sweet, a catharsis of all the heaviness and need you've been holding on to, the thing you've been waiting for. We fall deeper into the papasan, not frantically or quickly but kissing and breathing just enough to fuel more kissing. I can see clearly now, like the song says. I'm liking what I see.

"I know it's crazy," he says.

"No talking. Just kiss," I whisper, pulling myself up to his face again, but he stops me. "Whiplash, dude! What are you doing?"

Dale takes both of my wrists in his hands and pulls me to face him. "WHAT?"

"I have no right to ask what I'm asking, but I don't know if or when I'm coming back. And the only thing I could think of during that phone call that could change my life was that I didn't want it without you. I want you to come with me. I know that's stupid, and you have a lease and a job that means so much to you, and we just kissed for the first time like an hour ago. We aren't officially anything to each other . . ."

I take my hand out of his and squeeze his shoulder. "I think we kind of are, though," I say, and Dale lets go a sigh of relief I can read all over that beautiful, employed Ethan Hawke–character face.

"Me too," he says. "So . . . would you do this crazy thing and get on that plane with me? I bought my ticket, but I called and there's one more seat left in our section. Do you have any vacation time to take? A great-aunt who no one has ever heard of on her deathbed you must visit for a week or two?"

As stupid as this idea would have been even an hour ago, in light of very recent events I find myself considering it. Usually, you ask for vacation before you're on the plane, but I need to get out of here. I can't tell what's going to happen when the paper hits the doorsteps in Baltimore tomorrow. I could fight this, but I can't prove it. If Joe has interviewed people, that's his work. Of course, he sourced that work from my stolen notes—I'm positive of that. But what do I do? Do I call the *Herald*, or run back there and grab my notebooks and call the *Sentinel* and yell, "Stop the presses!" I always wanted to yell that.

Wait, hold on. That would make me look worse, being close enough to a reporter at another paper for him to get ahold of my notes. For a story I told him about. The only thing that would make me look worse? To flee town with a major source in the other story I'm working on.

"I don't mean to rush you," Dale says, rushing me. "But we should be down to BWI in a few hours if we're gonna make the flight. Would you think about it?"

I'm so sick of thinking. I want to do something wild and stupid when I don't have much else to lose. My family will be OK—if the story is coming out, Tonya will be vindicated. The schools will be saved. I don't know if I have a job to save. They're probably gonna fire me. *I* would fire me. It would be so weird there with . . . oh, crap—Eddie.

Yeah. I guess I'm proving him right with the Dale thing, because either I'm delusional and desperate to run away, or I really am falling for him after all. I can't think about what could have been with Eddie because it's all in flames.

I look at this beautiful man in front of me, and I know there are no more thoughts to think.

"Kiss me," I say, falling back against the papasan. "I pack light, and if we leave in an hour, I think we have a little time."

Dale smiles a relieved smile that is not completely honorable. "Time for what?"

"Time," I say, leaning up and pulling him down with me, "to not think."

Chapter 18

On the Road Again

2023

"Well?"

The car is very quiet. Tonya and Bria James both look like they've been watching a *Dateline* murder mystery only to find out the whole case was an elaborate sting, and the victim is still alive and talking to Josh Mankiewicz. Shocking cliff-hanger magic.

"You tell that so good," Tonya says approvingly.

Bria James is speechless. This is a first. "It's a really good story," she says. "Why haven't you told it all before?"

"How old are you, Bria James?" I ask.

"Thirty-two. Why?"

"Because if you live to be my age—"

"God, what are you, eighty?" Tonya says.

I clear my throat. "*If you live to be my age*," I repeat, "you'll know that you can spend a literal lifetime relitigating a decision made in a split second. Everything was bad; I was heartbroken, embarrassed, and in love, so I dried my face and kept moving."

"OK," she says. "I understand why you went with Dale, but why did you wait until now to tell anyone?"

"It was done," I say, raising my voice louder than I probably mean to. "I had done so much work on that story that my editors in York didn't know about, and I couldn't prove it. I ran out of the house without my notes, most of which were at the paper, some of which were missing, and I had just realized why. I looked like an idiot."

"Couldn't you have stopped by the paper and gotten the notepads so you guys could have written your own story that day to refute what Joe had written? To hang on to your scoop?"

"Maybe," I say. "But all that would prove was that I was working on it at some point. I guess Joe would have had to explain why I hadn't given him all the notebooks. But at that point, his story would be in print. He would have lied about it, and it would take lawyers and investigations and I was already . . . entangled with Dale at that point."

"So what?" Bria says.

"Between losing the story and sleeping with the subject of a series, everything pointed to my looking untrustworthy. Does that make sense?"

Tonya clears her throat. "Can I suggest something?"

"When did you ever ask before suggesting something?"

She laughs. "It's just . . . this is a sensitive thing . . . but do you think that maybe you were so embarrassed and overwhelmed at that moment, and also really digging on Dale, that you just fled and didn't think that you could have pleaded your case and seen this through?"

I do not recognize the sound that rises from my throat, because it's kind of a whimper mixed with that sound Chewbacca makes when stupid Kylo Ren murders poor Han Solo. Tonya, concerned, grabs my shoulder and gives it a squeeze. "Dawn! Are you OK?"

I am not.

Bria James sounds absolutely shook, like maybe they broke me. "What's happening? Should she be driving? Is she gonna kill us?"

Wordlessly I pull the car over to the shoulder and hope no one stops to ask if we need help, because I can't deal with that right now.

"Dawn," Tonya says gently. "You are freaking me and the blogger girl out, and you have to tell us if you're breaking down so we can take you to the ER or back to your hotel and not to this very important family funeral thing."

I nod slowly. This moment needs an explanation that I'm not sure my brain and mouth can muster. But here goes.

"It's just that . . . Oh man . . . I have spent three decades telling myself that I had no choice, that I was backed into a corner," I say softly. "Does that make sense? I convinced myself that the crazy move I made was the right one. I ripped up my life and left you and everyone else, but I was sure that I was right. Leaving with Dale and starting over seemed like a clean slate, because it made me happy and solved everything. I was so positive that it had . . . at least for me. But maybe I'm really like a bride in a rom-com who leaves a dude at the altar and runs off with someone else, but their friends and family shelled out for gifts and plane tickets. And now they're sitting there looking stupid, like, 'We've been conned!'"

"That is a popular Gen-X trope," Bria James says as if she's discussing ancient Egyptian architecture.

"Are you having a nervous breakdown?" Tonya asks. "I've had a few, so I know what they look like."

I start laughing in a rapid sputter, which, I realize, does not make me look like I am *not* having a nervous breakdown. "No," I say. "I'm just having a realization that I have been talking nonsense for thirty years. I don't regret Dale, or leaving, or staying in LA. But I couldn't even allow for having done it differently because once it was done, I didn't want to hear about it. I felt I had to put up this wall around me and my decisions because if I had to justify them too much, it might turn out they were stupid. And I'm sorry."

Tonya looks truly gobsmacked and just squeezes my shoulder again because she probably doesn't want Ashton Kutcher to jump out of the trunk and tell her she's being punked. "OK," she says. "Thank you."

I exhale and start driving again. It's peaceful for the moment, so of course I'm gonna say something to mess it up. "Tonya, I better not find out you had those notebooks and tossed them."

She snorts. "I did not. But if I did, you'd never know."

"But did you?"

"I told you, you would never know."

My phone rings, and Tonya takes a glance. "It's Pearl."

Oops. I've been avoiding Pearl's calls, and she and the Glitter crew must be pissed we're being scooped temporarily on their founder's own drama. I have some calls to make and myriad apology Edible Arrangements to buy. I'm not ready to deal with her yet, so I grab the phone from Tonya, hit "Decline," and then text, "Driving. Kill me later." I'm sure she will.

Bria James's phone beeps an alert. "What's that alert for?" I ask.

"I set one for your name," she answers. This seems complimentary and creepy at the same time.

"What does it say?"

"Was Susan that unpleasant woman banging on the window?" Bria James asks.

"That was her," I say. "Did she write something?"

Bria James clears her throat and reads: "An unexpected guest showed up to the announcement of the movie version of the Baltimore-bred *Diving into Deception* at Morgan State University this morning. Dawn Roberts-Shaffer, an entertainment journalist, Baltimore City native, and an intern at this very paper back in the 1990s, dropped a bombshell: she alleges that *National News Now* star Joseph Perkins, who, like me, was an intern, stole the idea from her. We don't have any details on this yet. Roberts-Shaffer bolted almost immediately, wielding an urn and claiming that she had to go bury her late husband's ashes somewhere locally. We'll update you as soon as we can, although Mr. Perkins says these accusations are 'the egregiously false and probably actionable ravings of a grieving, stunted widow.'"

"Wielding an urn? What if Dale's family sees that? They're gonna think I was threatening to throw him at people!"

"I seriously doubt they're reading this right now, and by the time they do, they'll have the ashes back and know you didn't toss their loved one's remains at the press," Tonya says. "Speaking of which, that's it, the funeral home."

Oh no. So soon? I'm not ready for this, not that it ever matters to the universe. But after so much pain and avoidance, here we are.

And so is my mother.

Chapter 19

YEAH, THIS SUCKS

"What are you going to say to her?" Tonya whispers.

"I have no idea," I whisper back as our mother, perfectly coiffed and fueled by righteous anger, slams the door of her CR-V and propels herself across the lot to our window. I assume several members of Dale's family already think we're a Tyler Perry play, and we're just waiting to start shouting and dancing in the name of Jesus, so I can't cause a scene.

My mother taps on the window, holding a bag of cheddar cheese Combos with the pretzel topping against it. "I got you something," she says.

"What's this for?" I ask, rolling down the window and taking the snacks because they're my favorite.

"Well, you broke up a press conference and caused a scene. I thought you may have worked up an appetite."

Busted.

"You saw that?"

"Yes, I did. I watched it to see Tonya, but there you are showing out at this press conference. You told everybody Joe stole your thing from you! What happened to you just talking to the reporter and leaving him alone?"

I raise my hand. "I never actually agreed to that part. I did talk to the reporter, who is in the back seat. This seemed more efficient. Can I eat my Combos now?"

My mother smiles, and I tear the little bag open savagely, like a bear ripping the head off a live salmon. Vengeance makes you hungry. My mother shakes her head, smiling, and turns her gaze to Bria James.

"Hello, cute little girl! What's your name?"

Bria James perks up. "I'm Bria James from B. L. Investigates."

My mother raises her eyebrows. "Dawn, Dale's family can't stand you, and you're bringing an extra reporter with you?"

"It's a long story, but yes. We sort of kidnapped her, but she's promised not to call attention to herself in any way, or else."

"Hey!" Bria James whispers. "I didn't agree to any 'Or else.'"

"It was implied," Tonya says.

"Well, if something goes bad, I'm not going to claim prior knowledge," my mother says, "so let's do this."

"Do we have to?" I ask.

"Sadly, we do," my mother says. "They're going to ask questions about the urn if you don't."

I toss the rest of the Combos into my mouth and think about the last time Dale and I were in town together on the way to my cousin's graduation from Baltimore School for the Arts. Dale was sick, but not as sick as he was going to be. We were downtown at the Admiral Fell Inn, just across from where I'm staying now. Dale invited Brent and his family to come down for lunch on a Saturday before we left. As much as they loved each other, Dale knew it was easier to get him to commit if we could say, "Hey, we're only in town a few hours more, so come see us now or you'll miss us."

You shouldn't have to play those kinds of games to get the people who love you to spend time with you. We knew Brent didn't want to come downtown for reasons of traffic and parking and I think probably Black people, because race has so much to do with why people don't want to come into Baltimore City. Fell's Point is not as white as it used to be, and I think that was a factor. He asked to meet somewhere that was, as he put it, "more neutral," like Towson, which isn't a long drive. But I didn't want to give in.

"I'm not sure that's going to work, man," I remember Dale saying on the phone, and he held his hand up to me in a "Stop" gesture because he didn't want me to make it worse. "We want to be able to get on the road soon to BWI and take this rental car back early. There's a hot dog place right across from the hotel. The kids will love it. Doesn't have to be long. I'd really love to see you."

"He can't come see his brother who's dying of kidney cancer?" I mouthed. I wanted Brent to feel bad, and I had no idea that I wasn't just exaggerating for effect because at that time, Dale's prognosis was OK—not sparkling, but not dire. Dire was yet to come.

But no, Brent couldn't come see Dale, because traffic and, oh, Emily has a soccer game this afternoon, and it would help us so much if you came out here, and I'm sorry it's not going to work this time. Next time.

Brent's next time with Dale is ashes in a box, and their mother is dead now, too. There's a lot of sorry behavior you can't take back. I feel sorry for Brent because none of us wanted this. And I feel sorry for myself, because in the end, here I am still driving out to the county for this, which in a weird way means that Brent won.

Having a competition over ashes is very petty, I can hear Dale saying.

"Stop judging me. You know who you married," I whisper back, low enough that no one hears me.

I talk to Dale in the car by myself all the time. And because of Bluetooth, the people in the next car probably think I'm buying stock or something.

After Dale's death, I sometimes fantasized about pulling a Tracy Chapman, driving a car really fast to flee the grief and the anguish and the day-to-day drudgery. That would have been nice, the forgetting part. Didn't happen.

Turns out that pain is already deep in your veins, polluting your heart as it spreads through to the rest of your body. It's what you breathe into your lungs now. It's everywhere. Grief is basically the plague. And there's no vaccine. Even now, with all these people in my car, my brain is screaming, *Flee. This car could be fast. Tracy Chapman would want you to.*

Nah, Brain. It's like my mother said when I was almost late to our wedding, "It's not like they can start without you."

There are many nice but not-too-nice cars: normal, well-off, but not LA / Palm Beach "Lookit My Trust Fund" cars. Mercedes. BMW. There's a newish but not-too-new Volvo station wagon that I'll bet is Brent and Sarah's, because it's station wagon enough to be practical but expensive enough that everyone knows what they paid for it.

I know I'm being cruel about people who are hurting worse than I am today. Brent was not only worried for his brother, who was dying of cancer during a pandemic, but watching his mom die, too. I should give him some grace.

It's just hitting that for me, this is Diane's funeral in a way, since I didn't get to go to the real one. Skipping town and starting a life with Dale three thousand miles away from our families was abrupt not just for us but for them, because it was all like "Who is that girl?" His dad was not welcoming—I wasn't Jewish, and even though moving to LA was Dale's mad idea in the first place, it was obviously my fault. Brent, who was in school at the time, took his dad's lead.

But Diane? From the very first time Dale put me on the phone with her, she'd decided to try to make it work.

"Mom, this is Dawn," Dale had said into the receiver as we crowded onto a bed at a cheap-ass hotel outside LA, the kind I'd never think of staying at now. "I think I love her."

I could hear her taking a deep breath on the other end. "Well, my baby boy, I don't understand any of this," Diane had answered. "But I guess I'm going to have to love her, too." And that was that. For the next three decades, this woman went out of her way to be my friend—to be my mother-in-law. To be my family. I'm running out of family.

"HEY!"

My mother is staring at me and I have no snappy comeback—I'm all out of snap. I take the urn carefully from the passenger seat, where it's been riding with the seatbelt secured around it. As it retracts, I realize that, in a way, Dale has been riding shotgun with me one more time. I'm about to hand him over, and when I get back in the car, that urn will be gone.

But that's *not* my husband. My husband is dead. This—plus the half that's on the bookcase in our house in LA—is what's left of a body that got too sick to hold all of him in. I got used to having all of Dale. Now that I say that in my head, it sounds like I was playing keep-away with a grieving family. . . . Wait. Am I awful?

Let's revisit that later.

"Tonya," I say as I close the car door, "can I ask you something?"

"I was hoping you would. Yes, that dress is a little high on your butt, but you can borrow my jacket if you want. Honestly, I don't think anyone's going to be looking. How dare they at a moment like this?"

"No, not that, but thank you," I say. "Hey, Bria James, can you give us a minute? Can I trust you to not immediately broadcast our GPS coordinates on Instagram?"

She smiles. "If I did, it would be on my own site," she says, reluctantly shuffling ahead, scrunching her face. I know that look. That's a "I really wish I had a tape recorder to plant on one of those ladies for journalistic purposes" look.

"She's like a millennial version of you," Tonya says. "Annoying, but in cuter shoes."

"I'd admire her more if she wasn't a little know-it-all," I concede. "And we owe her for the script. She still sucks."

"Like you!" Tonya says, laughing.

"Touché. I just wanted to say I love you, and that I didn't mean to drag you into this further, especially since you've probably voided whatever check they wrote you."

"Don't think I haven't thought about THAT," Tonya says. "I love you, too. Plus, I imagine this is gonna be a bigger story, and you're going to come into your own checks. You'll pay me back. I'll figure out the interest."

We're at the funeral home entrance, and my mother, waiting outside for us, opens the door for me and the urn. A man in a nice suit materializes in the lobby. "Mrs. Shaffer?"

"Yes." I nod. I'm technically not Mrs. Shaffer because I hyphenate in my personal life, but not for work. Yet here, in this moment, I'm going to be.

"It's so good of you to come," says the man, who is Frank Ehrlich, the funeral director. "It's good of you to come" is not what you say to the widow interring the ashes of her husband, unless someone told you she may not show up.

"Wouldn't have missed it," I say. I'm lying.

I shuffle in the direction of the door with my mother, Bria James, and Tonya behind me.

"Hello, Dawn," Brent says. Not sure he means that welcome.

"Hello, Brent," I say. "You remember my mother and my sister, Tonya?"

He nods and looks expectantly at Bria James.

"Oh yes, hi. I'm Bria. I'm . . . their cousin! I came for moral support."

"Right. Hello," Brent says.

Sarah is standing next to him looking protective. Does she think I'm gonna start swinging? I get it. She's Brent's wife. It's her job to protect her man from his heifer-in-law. I concede the point. Not that this is a competition. Well, it shouldn't be.

But she doesn't say anything, and neither does Brent, but he is staring at me. His eyes are wide, and I realize he's not actually looking at me. All he can see is the urn. His mouth turns down and then up into a squiggle, like he can't decide how to feel. I have had that squiggle mouth, so I know that his already shattered heart is rebreaking into pieces impossible to glue back together. In this moment, he's not my snotty brother-in-law but this sad, grieving man having the worst day of his life. And this woman he blames for keeping his brother away is holding his remains. His family of origin is all gone, and his least favorite person is guest-starring as the Grim Reaper.

I would hate me, too.

"I want to tell you, again, that I am truly sorry for your loss . . . your losses," I say, and I mean it.

Brent looks surprised, and his eyes turn instantly glassy. "Thank you, Dawn. Truly," he says softly.

Sarah's hand on her husband's shoulder loosens a little. Maybe she doesn't have to start swinging on people just yet. I extend the urn toward Brent, and he takes it, clutching it to his chest with a sigh of relief. His little brother is finally home. I start to break. Why didn't I think about how sad this was going to be for him? Have I never thought of him as a human person with emotions? Is this what my therapist has been talking about?

My mother puts her hand on my shoulder. "You're doing great, girl," she whispers, and I want to sink into her. Sarah smiles at me for maybe the first time ever.

"You have no idea what this means to our family," she says, and I stop myself from reminding her that I'm part of that family. *My family, too!* But it's not the time. Also, I have a lot of pity-charged texts to my sister explaining how *not* part of this family I feel. But that's not for today. Sometimes you just shut up.

"You're welcome, Sarah," I say. All this genuine niceness and gratitude floating through the room, and then it's completely silent. I'm so overwhelmed, I don't know what else to say, so I don't say anything at all.

"How was your flight?" Brent says, snapping me back into the moment. *Is he making small talk?* This is new.

"Uneventful, thank goodness."

I'm afraid I've misread this rare moment of comfortable familiarity with these people I've been related to for decades. Maybe we're just grateful the space between us and the dead people is filled with something other than sobbing.

"How is your website going?" Sarah says.

"Really well, thank you," I answer, stunned she's showing personal interest in me. It almost seems too good to be true.

"Good for you. Making the best of a dying industry, I bet."

WHOA. We have established that journalism is my boyfriend, and I can talk about it and its weaknesses, but outside people better shut their mouths.

"We're doing what we can to save it," I say as the pleasant air seems sucked into the urn like a malevolent genie. "Let's not talk about dying things in front of my husband's ashes, OK?"

Sarah shrinks back as if I'm threatening her. I might be. But I'm the widow, and she's pushing it.

"Let it go," Tonya whispers in my ear. "She's grieving, too."

"She's lucky I'm not trying to get arrested today."

Brent squeezes Sarah's hand in that "slow your roll" motion married people do. "Sorry, sorry. She didn't mean anything by it. We're all on edge today."

Sarah nods. I don't know if she is sorry, but I'm a little jealous that she still has a living husband to defend her. I used to have one of those. Now we just stand there waiting for something else to happen outside of our silence. I wonder if Brent has been practicing this moment in the car mirror and bracing for the uncomfortableness, just like I have. We all lost Dale and Diane, and though not in the same way, I know how empty this moment feels, how much more the world sucks with their absence.

I don't have to like him to feel bad for him. Look! Growth!

Mr. Ehrlich clears his throat. Was he here this whole time? "Let's go over the order of the service," he says, and I wonder if he likes his job. Necessary but morbid. I unconsciously pat my side like I've forgotten something. My keys? No, they're in my pocket. My purse is on my shoulder. There's an uncomfortable flutter under my bra. I know what I've forgotten now.

Dale.

Oh God. I don't like this. Dale's really gone.

"It's OK," my sister whispers.

It's not OK. But I can pretend for as long as I need to. I recognize Diane's sister, Aunt Judy, never my biggest fan, and their neighbor, Mrs. Weitz, who once called the cops on me when I was feeding Diane's cat when she was in New York on an old lady bus trip.

"Isn't that . . . what's his name . . . Herman?" Tonya says, pointing in an all-too-obvious way to a slight man in a professorial tweed jacket standing off to the side.

"That's Diane's boyfriend?" my mother asks. "He's adorable. But never tell him that. Old people don't like being described in the same way you'd talk about babies and puppies."

My family and Bria James do some awkward mingling while I make my way around the room, starting with people I know and don't think I'll be too weird with. "Aunt Judy," I say softly, tapping her on the shoulder. "I'm so sorry, again, about your loss . . . losses."

"Thank you, Dawn," she says, squeezing my hand. "I got your flowers. It would have been nice to see you at the funeral, but we understood."

Aunt Judy's shade game is impressive. I nod goodbye and make my way over to Herman, who has now crossed into silver fox territory. Maybe not a fox. Foxes are sleek and look like they're hiding something. Maybe Herman is something more trustworthy and cuddlier . . . Silver bear? Silver walrus?

"Hello, Dawn," Herman says, and there's a catch in his voice. He's widow-adjacent, and this man being honored is the child of his beloved. Now I feel I must protect him, officially embracing our membership in this morose club of people who have loved and lost Shaffers.

"I'm so sorry, Herman," I say, hugging him. "I wish I'd been here for the funeral."

"No one could blame you. There was a pandemic, and you, losing Dale so soon," he says. "Dale was such a good boy."

Herman and his late wife, Elaine, were in the Shaffers' social circle. There had been some . . . rumblings that there had been a historic flirtation, or at least a mildly significant and wistful look or two at somebody's Hanukkah party. I don't care. Who wouldn't have fallen in love with Diane? I was a little in love with her myself.

"He really was a good boy," I say, finding that catch in the throat contagious. The catch is catching. "I wish I had . . . that we had . . . you know, been more a part of things with all of you here."

"No, you don't," he says, and we both laugh. Maybe I've lost a Diane and gained a Herman? I give him one more good squeeze and turn toward Mr. Ehrlich, who is clearing his throat.

"We will be driving over to the mausoleum now," he announces, and we all shuffle back to our cars.

"Hey, can I sit shotgun now that we don't have the urn anymore?" Tonya says. "I want to make sure I'm next to you."

"That's very sweet," I say, sincerely moved.

"Also, everyone knows you can't drive. I can't have you running over people in your grief."

I laugh. "You had to mess that up, didn't you?"

Like an inquisitive bad penny, Bria James turns up next to the car.

"You gotta stop popping up like that! Where were you?"

Bria James slides into the back seat like a little kid riding behind her parents. "Don't worry, I didn't talk to anyone. Just observed. I told your brother-in-law I was sorry for his loss."

"OK," I say. "Can you just chill, please?"

Bria James nods, not saying what she's thinking. She's not good at that. Me neither. Maybe we have more in common than I thought.

When we get to the mausoleum, we get the lay of the land. Dale and Brent's father is buried with his own mother nearby, so this part of Dale is going to be buried in Diane's mausoleum. I am probably not going to be buried anywhere since I don't have kids, but whatever commemorative Obama presidential bank my ashes wind up in will probably be with my own family. Half of Dale's remains will be with his people. Half of them with me.

And when I go, we'll be wherever that light is. And that's all that matters. I can't wait for him to tell me what I've missed.

The small service we had for Dale in LA was in the park where we used to sit after chemo, just to rest and not be at chemo. Our friend Alan asked if I wanted him to do some prayers in Hebrew. Dale's Judaism was cultural in some ways—he had married the Christian Black goy lady—and he didn't keep kosher or anything. But he prayed, and we did the high holidays. They say you get closer to God when you think you might be meeting Him soon.

So yes, we told Alan we wanted the prayers. I wanted to hear whatever language I thought would honor Dale and his time with the rabbi—whatever would honor his mother who was struggling with her own illness on the East Coast. I wanted to do whatever might make his transition easier, what might bend the ear of Whoever was listening on the other side in the hope that the Whoever would find it familiar and lovely and grant him rest.

"We gather here today with the family of Dale Shaffer at his final resting place," begins a rabbi I don't know. Am I crying?

"I know that guy!" Tonya whispers. "Rabbi Maslin. He married this girl in my office and her boyfriend we never liked. They got divorced a year later. I hope he's not a jinx."

"How do you jinx a funeral? The bad thing already happened," I whisper.

"Dale is being laid to rest with his mother, Diane, who went to meet Hashem not long after," Rabbi Maslin continues.

I don't want to think about that, so I think about what might be happening beyond this cemetery, with Joe and the story and whoever else is involved in this movie who may be gunning for me. Also, the ghosts of Mike Wallace and Joseph Pulitzer are sitting with Sam Donaldson and, boy, does he have some disappointing events to catch them up on. I really want to google myself right now, but this seems . . . not the venue.

The rabbi calls up a few people I don't recognize to do readings from Psalms. They read the same ones when we buried Daddy, when he was literally being made to lie down in a green pasture on the other side of Baltimore. Nobody wanted him to have to lie down, anywhere. We wanted him here with us. When we sang "It Is Well with My Soul," I whispered to my mother, "I am about to straight up lie to Jesus, because this is not well with my soul or any other part of me."

Dale and I were not particularly religious, but it's helpful in this quietly painful moment to remember that both of us hoped to be greeted by God when we left this plane of existence.

"We now call on a few of Dale's loved ones, who miss him so much," the rabbi says. At Daddy's funeral, Reverend McComb made the point that we were on a schedule and that remarks would be three minutes or less, *strictly enforced*. Mrs. Wilkins, the organist, raised her hands over the keys as if to say, "I will play you off like the Oscars." It would have been funnier if not for all the sobbing.

We have agreed that Brent is going to speak first. Brent squeezes Sarah's hand as he steps to the front. He looks smaller today. Slightly bent, reduced. Weirdly, I want to hug him. I'm probably not going to.

"Today, we dedicate this memorial for my mother and for my brother, Dale, who died not long before my mother did, and who, as the rabbi said, will be laid to rest here with her so they are always together."

Tears will mess up your carefully drawn eyeliner.

"I'd like to ask Dale's wife, Dawn, to say a few words."

"Was this planned?" Tonya whispers.

I make my way to the front awkwardly. "Hello," I say. "Thank you for having me."

They had to have you. You brought half the dead guy, Dale whispers.

This is not a 1990s comedy about a wacky ghost and his living wife who looks crazy when she responds, so I will not be answering him out loud. "I'm Dawn . . . Dale's wife . . . you probably know that. I just wanted to say how happy I am that a part of him will always be with Diane." I hear myself say the word "part" and think about how I'm sneaking half a dude past these nice people.

"They're together now, and it's so hard not to have them both here with us. If anything could make us feel better, this does. Thank you, Brent and Sarah, and Rabbi . . ." Oh crap, what's his name? "Rabbi . . . Thank you, Rabbi."

Tonya mouths "Oof" at me and starts giving me the sweeping motion, like she's Sandman Sims on *Showtime at the Apollo* and I'm dodging boos and tomatoes. Am I bombing at a cemetery?

"But, you know, it's wonderful that at least we could be together like this. I mean, the occasion isn't wonderful, but . . . you know what I mean. Never mind. OK. Thanks. Bye."

"You did good," my mother says as I come slinking back to where they're standing.

"Don't lie to the girl," Tonya says, squeezing my shoulder. "Somebody pays you to write words?"

I fight the urge to run back to my car in shame, but I stay for the rest of the remarks, which unsurprisingly go better than mine. Rabbi Maslin and Brent go over to the memorial. On one side is a plaque that reads DIANE REBECCA SHALIT-SHAFFER. SEPTEMBER 18, 1944–APRIL 9, 2022. BELOVED WIFE, MOTHER, GRANDMOTHER, AND FRIEND. HER JOY WAS CONTAGIOUS. MAY HER MEMORY BE A BLESSING.

There's another plaque next to it that reads DALE SHERMAN SHAFFER. JULY 19, 1971–FEBRUARY 28, 2021. BELOVED HUSBAND, SON, BROTHER, AND FRIEND. A JOY TO ALL WHO KNEW HIM.

Dale being dead is not a surprise, obviously. But the reminder is always a gut punch.

"We are now going to recite the Mourner's Kaddish, first in Hebrew, then in English," Rabbi Maslin says, and someone passes out pieces of white paper among the crowd. They start with us, maybe because they think we need prayer more than anyone else. The words wash over me, comfort me. I think a lot about God's will, about our will, about what we have control over and what we don't. It's mostly don't.

I think about the things that I would change about my life—funerals and such make one reflective—and what got me here. If I had not left town and married Dale, I would not be with these people, saying these words. I got him just to lose him like this. Would I rather not have had him? No. Does it make the tiny pointy shards of hurt any less real, even now? Absolutely not.

I guess we're done with the reading. I wasn't paying attention again. I hope I read the right thing. People start dispersing, and now I have to make my goodbye rounds. Tonya hugs me.

"This was beautiful. I think it's just the break you need before things stir up, you know?"

Oh yes, girl. I know.

Bria James does that point you do without wanting people to know that you're pointing. "Isn't that Susan? That lady I believe you don't like?"

Indeed, over on the other side of the parking lot is Susan. She waves.

"Want me to go say something?" Tonya says. "You know I will."

"Remember what I said about not throwing hands today?"

"Well, you're no fun."

My mother comes over to us. "That was beautiful," she says, kissing me on the cheek. "Y'all headed over to the house now?"

"Eventually," I say. "I need to say some goodbyes."

She looks across the parking lot. "Isn't that Susan McNally from the *Sentinel*? She has some opinions about Baltimore City that are . . . well. You know. Did she follow you here? That's terrible. Want me to say something?"

Ladies and gentlemen, my family. Surprised none of us are in jail. Yet.

"Nah," I say. "I got this."

My mother waves and walks to her car. Susan seems to calculate that this means one less person to beat her up and decides to finally make her move. "Dawn, I'm so sorry," she says.

"You are not," I toss back, "or you wouldn't be here. I bet you didn't even believe me. You probably thought the urn was fake, too."

Susan just purses her lips. Yeah, she totally thought it was fake. "Dawn, again, I am so sorry that I had to do this on a day like this—"

"No, you're not," I say, louder than I need to. "You don't come up to me today, in this place, and make demands. I know you want a story. Screw your story. You are not gonna come up in here with my family and demand anything from me. I know that your editors and readers wouldn't like that you accosted a widow after she just interred her husband's ashes. You wanna back off me now?"

Susan's lips are still pursed. This is not where she saw this going. "That's fine," she says. It is not fine. "Is there somewhere to talk later?" Susan asks, trying to gain some semblance of control over the situation. That's not going to happen.

"Seriously!" I say, because the nerve of her! "I have to go join my family now. Write what you want, but leave me alone. And tell your editors that you just blew any interviews you might have gotten on account of our having worked together once. That's on you. Have fun."

With that, I march back toward the other mourners. I wish I had one of Miss Vivi's capes to flourish behind me.

Herman comes over and takes my hand in his. "Diane and Dale would have liked what you said," he assures me.

"Even when I couldn't remember the rabbi's name?"

"Especially that. A laugh's a laugh. How long are you in town?"

"Just two more days. Tomorrow is my mother's birthday party, and I'm out early the next morning."

This nice widowed-ish man doesn't need to know I might stay longer to continue to destroy a major pop cultural event. Herman smiles. "Too bad. It would have been nice to have coffee. She loved you, you know," he says.

I know, but it's always nice to hear it. I just nod, because I don't want to cry. How terrible to be running out of people who love me.

"Dawn?" Brent is standing beside me.

"Hey," I say. "Again, so sorry," I say. I mean about his loss, but maybe for other stuff?

"Me too. Say . . . we are having people over to the house, just a few people, if you want to stop by."

Maybe I should to keep this fragile peace. But there's so much going on with the Joe stuff, and I can't make their grieving be about this. I start to tell him just that, but it seems like too much, so I just say, "I appreciate that, Brent. But I'm gonna head back to my mother's. We're planning her big birthday for tomorrow, which I actually just found out about, and I'm pretty tired with the jet lag and all . . ."

Brent is already nodding, as if he already expected to be turned down. Maybe it was just a polite invite, and he didn't want me to come in the first place. He probably thinks I'm making up this surprise birthday party. "I get it. I get it," he says, a hint of an edge forming around the last "it."

Oh no. I've ruined it. Good job, Dawn.

"I just wanted you to know you are welcome to come. I've got to go talk to more people." He shakes my hand, just a little more formally than before. "Thanks again."

"I really do appreciate the invitation, Brent. Maybe I'll have more time next time." He nods again, smiling slightly, and walks away.

I don't even know what the next time would be. Dale was the only thing connecting us. We didn't have kids, and I don't know the kids well enough to show up at birthday parties unannounced. We'd kept our connection threadbare, and now maybe that thread is cut for good. I wish I had known it would matter.

"That looked sad," Tonya says when I join them.

"It was," I confirm. "He asked me to come back to the house, and I said no. Now I feel bad."

Bria James looks sad, too. "At least they asked you, right?"

Right. Am I starting to like her?

"What now?" I say. "Back to Mommy's?"

"Not yet," Tonya says. "We should regroup somewhere more private to make a plan. You never know who's going to be over there at Mommy's house, and we need a united front."

"What do you suggest?" I ask.

"Let's go back to your hotel. It's secluded. They have security that aren't going to let just anyone up to your room," Tonya says.

"You want to hit that bar again."

She shrugs. "They do make a fine martini."

Bria James raises her hand.

"Yes, Bria James."

"I like martinis."

"Good," I say. "You're buying."

Chapter 20

Coo Coo Ca-Choo, Mrs. Roberts-Shaffer

The drive back to the city feels anticlimactic. Tonya, Bria James, and I were all high on causing a commotion with Susan and such, but reality has smacked us in the face. Now we have to deal with all the fallout, starting with finally answering the texts and phone calls we've been avoiding.

"Do we have to?" Tonya asks, gingerly turning her phone back on in the passenger seat. "I should probably check in on my kid."

"He's still at day care, right?" I say. "He's fine, unlike the rest of us. Look, people are gonna be mad, probably, but we're communicators, right, Bria James? How are the numbers on your site today? Better than they were yesterday?"

"Sure. Let's just keep it this way," Bria James says. "That means I need to write more. I know you've gotta feed your site first, but I have to hustle in a way you don't. You have a foot in the door. Your whole generation pats themselves on the back about being mentors and trying to help the rest of us up the ladder as this industry crumbles, but somehow that ladder keeps getting pulled up."

Did I miss the sign for the Young Journalist with Grievances convention? I don't remember registering and ordering the chicken luncheon option.

"Bria, you are very impressive, and I see how hard you work, but I don't have time for this debate. We can chat later when my reputation is saved and people stop coming at me. Cool?"

From the corner of my eye, I see her throw her hands up, and I have a feeling that if we weren't in the car, we might have more words. But she thinks better of it. "Holding you to that, ma'am," she says, and the "ma'am" is a fiery arrow aimed at my head. I catch it mentally.

OK! Whatever that was is quashed for a moment. Now let's check those voicemails. No one leaves them anymore, and there are eight so you know it's serious.

Number 1: Pearl, wanting to make sure I got her text messages. Yes, I did.

Number 2: "Dawn, Dawn, this is Susan." How did she get my number? "Please call me at your earliest convenience." Girl, that's never going to be convenient.

Numbers 3 and 4: Someone calling about my car's extended warranty. Delete, delete.

Number 5: My mother, telling me that her pastor wants to know if I'll be at service this Sunday, because I need Jesus.

Number 6: "Dawn! This is Luke Willis from the *Baltimore Sentinel*. I'd love a comment on today's events." Good luck with that.

Number 7: "Girl, this is Natalie. I can't get anyone on the phone, but your mom knows I'm bringing my boyfriend to the party, right? And maybe his cousin? He's in town, and we can't leave him home. That's rude." My cousin has been, and stays, trifling. God, I love her.

Number 8: "Daisy Fuentes! It's Vivienne St. Claire! I see you were paying attention during our last conversation. Call me!"

Is it wrong that with all these other critical messages, I almost return the call from my crazed fairy revenge godmother first? But I don't, because I have some money to make off my own misfortune. So I call Pearl instead.

"Hey, Pearl! What's up?" I say, all nonchalant.

"You know what's up. You busted up a press conference in Baltimore claiming that a Pulitzer Prize–winning story written by a major network star was stolen from you, like, thirty years ago. Not only did you not give me a heads-up or write something to send me before you busted everything up, but you never mentioned it in all the time we've known each other."

She sounds hurt. I would be, too. "I'm sorry, Pearl. I am. But by the time we met, I had put it behind me."

She scoffs. Black-girl scoffing is bad. "Apparently not."

Fine.

"When I come back, assuming you haven't quit in disgust, we will talk all about why letting a Pulitzer Prize–winning story slip through my fingers isn't my favorite topic of discussion. I am sorry I hurt you. I should have explained what was going on when I found out about the movie, and I'm in my own pocket by not writing something sooner for us. Thank you for getting something up so fast. It makes us look bad not to lead this story, and I own that. I trust you to save me again."

Pearl is silent. Fuming. Righteously. "OK, Dawn," she says. "Walk me through it real quick."

I walk her through it real quick and give her a quote about how I was not going to drop the matter and am pursuing the truth and the exoneration of myself and my late husband. She reads it back to me.

"Anything else?" Pearl says when I've approved it.

"That I'm super sorry?"

"You said that," she says, and hangs up.

Tonya looks at my frown. "That did not go well, I take it."

"It did not," I say, sighing as I pull up to the hotel. We jump out, and I hand the valet the rental car keys and twenty dollars.

"Slow down, big tipper," Tonya says. "Your deputy editor hates you now and might bolt at any minute. I would keep my money."

I ignore her as we make our way down the dark hallway to the lobby.

"Ooh, can we get a drink first before we go upstairs?" Tonya says. "It's probably going to get very unpleasant soon. And you owe me."

Why do I owe everyone all of a sudden? It's not crowded, but Tonya places her purse and decorative scarf on some stools to save them anyway. Nightclub rules die hard. It's all happiness, for about fifteen seconds.

"Hello, Dawn!" says Susan, who is starting to be a problem. Honestly, she's been a problem since we were chugging cheap beer in my car. If this were a club, I'd have paid the bouncer to keep her out. Or kick her out now.

"How did you know where I was?"

"I imagined that you would stay in a nice place, near interstates and with easy access to other parts of the city," Susan says. "Just good journalism."

"You followed us," Tonya says.

"That, too," Susan says.

"Let me say this once, so that you understand this has been stated," I say, getting as close as possible without being accused of physically threatening a reporter. "No comment. I'm not talking to you. That is not going to change. Any further attempts that you make to tail me will be considered harassment. And I'm writing about all of it."

Susan seems confused, like she thought there was some argument she could make. She must not remember me well. "Dawn," she begins.

"No," I say. "Whatever it is, NO. I just want to get along with my day. I imagine it's going to be a busy one."

Suddenly, she's looking past me. I don't like that look.

"I imagine it will be," Susan says, creepy satisfaction in her smile. "Let me know if you change your mind."

She waves. That's weird. "Nice to see you again, Joe," I hear Susan say as she walks away from the bar.

"You too, Susan!" Joe says. "I imagine we'll be talking soon."

"How does everyone in the world know where I'm staying?" I yell. The bartender looks up suspiciously.

"Sorry," I say, yanking a twenty out of my wallet and sliding it toward him. "That's my tip, just for my drink."

"You haven't ordered anything yet," says the bartender, whose name tag says he's Nate.

"Oh, I will, though. A lot."

Nate smiles, pockets the twenty. "What can I get you?" he asks, suddenly no longer bothered by the noise.

"A tequila sunrise?" Joe says. "You still drink those?"

"I do not," I answer. "That's the drink of a little girl who was easily fooled. I'm not her anymore."

"Noted."

Nate seems amused. He's invested now because there's drama and also there are more people ordering expensive drinks. A bartender win-win.

Tonya and Bria James are staring at me like they're watching a gazelle get into a knife fight with a lion. The gazelle will get eaten for sure. But she's doing some fascinating, inspiring nonsense, and it's impossible to look away.

"What can I get you, ma'am?" Nate asks.

"Manhattan. With your most expensive rye."

"Your little website must be more lucrative than I thought," Joe says, settling onto a stool. "Or is it that life insurance money?"

"You evil troll," I say, "you really gotta stop talking about me and my husband. And don't bother sitting. You aren't staying."

Joe acts as if he hasn't heard me. "Nate?" he says. "I'll have what she's having."

"I know you heard me."

"I did. But we must talk. And I think we're both going to need a drink."

My phone beeps. It's a text from Tonya , who has moved to the other side of the bar. You OK down there? Need me to call the cousins? Devonte and Charles are in town for the party, and they'd do this beatdown for free.

Nate hands us both our drinks.

"What should we drink to?" Joe asks.

"You having an allergic reaction to rye?"

Joe chuckles and takes a sip. "You really have changed," he says. "And not just physically."

"You look remarkably the same. Are you in some sort of frequent-facelift program?"

"I'll make sure to send you the information."

"You're an evil, evil man," I say.

"And I'm not sure what you are now. Bitter? Grief-stricken? Regretful? Trapped in an emotional tailspin?"

"I'm tired of being told what a genius you are. I was willing to gut through this weekend, but then you went after me and Dale. What you wrote about him stealing money? You know none of that's true. Why do you need to mess with a dead man?"

"Because the script needed more . . . tension. Creative license. You know how it is."

Nate materializes in front of us. He must have come back to make sure his big tipper isn't about to throw down. "You guys doing all right?"

"Right as rain, my friend," Joe says. "We'll take two more. And some fries."

"*Two* orders of fries, please," I say, handing Nate another twenty-dollar bill. "We aren't sharing. I'm not eating after you, Joe. What do you want?"

"Obviously, I want you to retract your ridiculous statement and say you were having a breakdown—that it was all too much for you with what you've been through this weekend."

"You need to drink more. Or less," I say evenly, "because that's not going to happen."

Joe laughs. "You made a huge accusation; you have no proof, and this is the first time you've said this . . ."

"The truth. I said the truth."

"So you say."

"YOU WERE THERE! You were my friend, and you stabbed me in the back! You stole my story! Did you tell them I wasn't writing the story anymore because you were in over your head at the *Sentinel* and didn't have any good ideas? I bet you even stole my notes! I always thought I was missing a notebook. And then you lied about your mother's party so you could finish the job."

"I don't recall it happening that way."

Nate appears again. He doesn't want violence in his bar. Blood's hard to get out of wood. "You good?" he asks.

"My friend," Joe says, nodding fake-sagely, "I am very good. Which seems to only be a problem for some people."

Nate, who has read the room, wants no part of whatever this is, so he just nods and walks away. Smart. He'll get tipped more.

"Don't involve anybody else in this," I say.

"That's very funny coming from you." Joe laughs. "You involved *everybody* in this, calling me out at my press conference. You started it."

"No, dear. You started it with that script. Honestly, you started it being a thief in 1994. You couldn't just be happy being loved by people who obviously haven't met you. You just had to mess with me and Dale. You had to try to hurt me. I don't know what I ever did to you for you to repeatedly try to ruin my life. But now it's time to expose you."

Joe takes a sip of his Manhattan. "You sound like you're trying to be an investigative reporter at this late date. Admit it: You couldn't hack it. You're better suited for fluff like that band story, and the superior journalist took it where you couldn't. You've had a nice little career, and you need to leave it alone."

"Like I left my notebooks?"

Joe doesn't like this. At all. "Enough!" he says, loud enough to get Nate's attention but not loud enough to get bounced out of here. "I thought you might come to your senses. But you don't know what you've done. You've put a major motion picture production in jeopardy. You've slandered me. You've brought the Pulitzer and *National News*

Now into this. All those entities are within their rights to seek legal action."

Well, there it is. My phone beeps.

Well, there it is, Tonya has texted, still at the end of the bar, now with fries.

"You're threatening to sue me, Joe? When you know I'm telling the truth?"

Joe takes another sip of his drink, this one longer than the last. I hope he chokes. "I don't know any such thing," he says. "I do know that you can't possibly prove any of this or you would've tried already. It's just a stupid scheme orchestrated by you and your silly sister, who, by the way, signed a contract that she's violated."

Oh crap, Tonya texts.

"All you had to do was leave town and go back to being pudgy and stoic covering has-been child stars and the cast of Real Housewives of Hicktown. But you're a bitter hag who couldn't just let me have this."

"My *friend*," I say, imitating the way he said the word to Nate, who is pretending to work on a particularly stubborn spot on the counter, "you tried taking everything. And I'm taking it back."

Joe's face is impenetrable—equal parts attitude and Botox—and I'm curious what's going on in that devious lizard brain. "Good luck to you," he says. "Just remember when you're destroyed and even more pathetic than you already are that you brought all of this on yourself."

He throws down a business card. "Have your lawyer call mine. If you have one."

"She does," says a familiar voice behind me. "Brent Shaffer. If you have anything else to say to my client, don't. We'll be reaching out."

Plot twist! Tonya texts as my brother-in-law reaches across me to pick up the card off the bar and offers Joe his hand to shake.

But Joe is already shook.

Chapter 21

STILL SHOOK

I am uncharacteristically speechless, so Joe uses this distraction to make his exit at the exact moment Nate puts the two orders of fries on the bar. Joe snatches one and walks out. With the plate.

"They're gonna charge that plate to your room," Tonya yells from the other side of the bar.

"Don't sweat it," Nate assures her. "We have plenty. Nobody notices if one or two go missing."

"Why are you here, Brent? I mean . . . thank you. But don't you have people at your house?"

Brent sits down on the stool where Joe had been. I hope he doesn't catch anything. *Not* wishing bad things on Brent is new.

"May I get a Sagamore rye? Neat?" he asks Nate.

"My man, not even going for the mixers!" Tonya yells down the bar.

"It doesn't seem like a time for mixers," Brent says. He's not wrong.

Nate puts the glass of rye in front of Brent, who raises it ceremoniously, brings it to his lips, and shoots it.

"Whoa," I say, impressed and slightly terrified because I've lost the plot. I need CliffsNotes for my own life. Is Brent fun and I missed it? Or is he just losing his mind like me?

I put my hand on his hand and am surprised and pleased he doesn't shrink back. I don't think I've ever touched Brent. I've wanted to shake him occasionally, but I like not being in jail.

"Brent, I am glad to see you. But I need to know why you're here."

He smiles and waves at Tonya and Bria James. "She's a journalist, right?"

"How do you know that?"

Brent grabs his phone and pulls up her website. "'*National News Now* anchor accused of stealing Pulitzer-winning story from former colleague,' by Bria James," he reads. "You introduced her as Bria at the unveiling, and it made sense."

"That's very good," I say, "but the truth remains that you don't even like me. Why would you want to help me?"

Brent suddenly looks sad.

"What's wrong?" I say, realizing that everything is wrong. What am I even talking about?

"I don't dislike you. I just never got to know you. You and Dale left, and you so seldom came back. We know we've had our issues. I . . . just don't know you."

That's fair. It easier to make the other the bad guy. Is that what's been happening this whole time? It's been a terrible day for me, but I've had some victories, as fleeting and petty as some of them may be. This dude basically buried his whole family today. I suck.

"If you are my lawyer," I say, "we will have a chance to get to know each other. Why, though?"

"Because you caused a scene that brought reporters to my brother's service?"

I sense this going badly suddenly. "Are you mad at me?"

"Not mad, per se . . ."

"Are you per se—ing me? I didn't ask you to do this. You should be with the rest of your family at your house and not here rubbing my face in your obvious contempt."

Brent pauses for a moment and then raises his hand to get Nate's attention. "Can I get a menu?"

"What are you doing?" I say, but Brent ignores me and takes the offered menu, giving it a cursory glance.

"The burger, please. And another round."

I'm madder than drunk now. "NO!" I bleat, sounding like a disgruntled goat. "I don't need your help."

"But Dale does."

He's teary now. Oh no.

"Don't cry, man."

"I'm going to cry, and then I'm going to do what I have to do for my brother."

"What's that?"

He reaches into his jacket and puts a thick mass of papers onto the bar. "Diving into Deception," it reads.

"How did you get that script?"

"I called the movie producers and told them I was your lawyer, and they immediately couriered it to me. They're very excited to talk to you because they're probably going to sue you."

That shouldn't be funny, but I laugh because terror can inspire levity. "Well, that's not great."

"No, but it got me in the door . . . Fawn," Brent says.

"It's so bad! Like he forgot how to write."

"Indeed. Dawn, look. I know how much you loved Dale. And for you to do what you did at that press conference, there had to be a reason. Between that and the script, it all made sense. You're taking up for Dale. I respect that. I need to help you."

He's always been matter of fact. This is the first time it's been in my favor. "Thank you, Brent," I say, and I mean it. "What do we do now?"

Brent raises his glass. "First, a toast. To Dale," he says.

"To Dale," I agree. We both take a sip.

"He'd be surprised," Brent says.

"By me making such a mess of things?"

"By us getting along. But pleased. Let's get to work."

I almost tell Brent that this is an Olivia Pope gladiator moment, but I think maybe he wouldn't know what that means, and I don't want to do anything to disturb this fragile alliance. I'm learning to leave things alone. Dale would like that most of all.

Chapter 22

NICE TO MEET YOU, PERSON I'VE BEEN RELATED TO FOR THIRTY YEARS!

After our impromptu happy hour, we all head back to my room to put together a plan. No more cocktails. We have work to do.

As I fumble for my keys, Tonya walks quickly ahead of Bria James and Brent.

"Are you sure you want Bria James in the meetings with your lawyer?" she whispers.

"It's fine," I say. "I'm going to talk to Brent alone. For the moment."

"That's another thing," Tonya whispers. "You've always described Brent as the worst, and suddenly he's here in a part of town he doesn't deal with to give you free legal advice? What's that about?"

"It's good to have him in our corner. He's going to offer a layer of protection between us and anyone wanting to sue, and maybe he'll help me find people who can vouch for me, like Sheila from Permits and . . . maybe even Percy?"

If there had been a record playing, here's when it would have scratched abruptly.

"Never!" Tonya says.

I was hoping this would be easier.

"Do you ever see him?"

"I'll see him in hell!"

"Hey, have a seat," I say loudly as Brent and Bria James come in and settle on the fancy leather couch. "There's a balcony, too."

"These rooms are very expensive," Brent says.

"Got a deal on Priceline," I answer. I want to say "Mind ya business," but we're friends now. Friendly. Not enemies, at least.

"OK," Brent says. Rome wasn't built in a day, and a fractured relationship born of regret, grief, and pettiness can't be, either. We're in the same room, on the same page, with the same goal. That's all I got.

"It's very nice," Brent says, perhaps aware that it's getting crunchy in here. "The balcony is lovely. You want to come out here a minute and talk?"

"Could I listen in?" Bria James asks. She should know it's a no, but she has to ask. My admiration for her is growing, despite myself.

"Not now. Attorney-client privilege and all that," Brent says. Bria nods, because she doesn't really have a choice.

Brent opens the balcony door and, like a gentleman, lets me walk through first. We sit and just look at each other wordlessly for a minute. Someone's going to have to say *something*.

"I'm going to start with a question I always ask my clients," he says finally, breaking the silence.

"Shoot," I answer, "although I imagine that with criminal defendants, you don't want them to mention shooting at all."

Brent smiles. "True. The question is: What do you want out of this?"

"I want to not be sued, or at least not to lose if I am. I want them to not make that movie, or at least not make the version that makes Dale look bad. That script says this fake version of him was stealing money from your father's company, and you know that's not true. He isn't here to defend himself."

Brent, who is taking notes, nods. "He was not doing anything of the sort, obviously. This is all good. What else?"

"Like what?"

"Are you looking for money? Proceeds of Joe's first book? Your name on the Pulitzer?"

"No," I decide out loud. "I don't want money. I didn't write his book, and I didn't write the final stories that ran in the paper that won that prize, even though I should have. And honestly, he wrote them well. What I do want is credit for the original story idea and acknowledgment that he stole it from me. I want to not be written out of the legend anymore, or at least not written in as the villain."

"So you want credit."

"I want Joe to not be able to portray me as some idiot who tried to take something that wasn't mine. And for your brother not to be remembered as a horny thief."

"I want that, too," Brent says. "But you're going to need solid proof. And you must explain why you've waited until now to say anything."

"I have Tonya for proof, and she's solid."

Brent nods. "Any other witnesses?"

"I can give you a list of the people that I interviewed, but it's been decades. They might not even remember all of what happened."

More nodding. "What about Tonya's boyfriend at the time . . . Darcy?"

"Percy. Percy Harris. The worst."

"Do you think he would help?"

"Why would he? He blames me and Tonya for his going to jail when it was all his fault."

"Do you know how to get in touch with him? Would Tonya?"

"I don't think so," I say, recalling she just wished to see him in Hades.

"What about his lawyer?"

I laugh. "Bryce Throckington-West, the guy who advertises on bus stops and during *Judge Judy*. Doesn't he sound like he'd try to kill Batman with a radioactive shark? He didn't keep Percy out of jail, but he became some crusader for justice or whatever." Percy was guilty, and to this day has never given Tonya back her $5,000 or her chicken. Everyone in that camp sucks.

"Do you think he would help?"

"If he thought he could get some publicity, absolutely. Do me a favor and don't mention this to Tonya, OK? Percy is a sore spot."

"Wouldn't it be all right with her if talking to Percy might help you?" Brent asks.

I should say no. But I'm not going to.

"Let's get him on the record before we tell her," I say lightly. "Let her be mad at me after we've avoided being sued into the ground."

Brent stops writing. "I assume you don't have any notes from that time?"

"No, sadly," I say. "That was before cell phones and notes apps. I left town fast and didn't take anything with me. And I was missing a notebook or two anyway. I used to wonder if Joe swiped them or if they just got eaten by my desk. I was . . . not neat."

"That's too bad," Brent agrees. "What about your editors or your coworkers in York? Would they remember that the story was originally yours?"

"They were not the fondest of me. There was one guy I worked with—Eddie, a photographer—who I just found out sent my mom some of my stuff when I left, but there weren't any notebooks or anything. We didn't leave things in the best place."

Brent pauses. "A photographer? A Black guy?"

"Yes, and why do you ask?" I say, not liking his tone.

Brent shakes his head, flustered. "No, no . . . I'm sorry. I just remember one of the few times Dale mentioned you before you two moved to LA. He thought you might have been seeing a Black photographer you worked with. That's just how he described him. He said, 'I don't even know if she likes white guys. She's always with this good-looking Black guy,' or something like that. Wasn't trying to offend you. Anyway, that's the guy?"

"Yes. That's the guy. But we haven't spoken since 1994. At the end of the day, I quit and ran off to LA and left everybody in the lurch. And I let my friend steal a Pulitzer Prize–winning story from me."

Brent whistles. "So that's all a negative."

"Sugarcoat it for me, why don'tcha?"

He laughs. "We've got some work to do. Try to find Eddie. And call the *York Herald*. Also we need to put out a statement that I am representing you so that people come through me directly. Are you ready for this?"

I'm not sure. If I can't prove any of this and I get legally hosed, I'm gonna ruin my reputation and my business. My staff and I won't even be able to afford red Solo cups behind the CVS, burning discarded receipts for fuel. Solo cups cost money.

Silence again. Should I say something to fill it?

"You've never been to this hotel, have you?" I ask, knowing the answer.

"No, we don't get down here much," Brent says.

"I remember. We asked you to come down once when we were at the Admiral Fell," I say, and I see that little dark cloud come over his brow. I must stop clouding this man's face. He's trying to help.

"Yes, that's true," he says, and I can feel him bricking himself back up again.

Change the subject, Dawn.

"Much nicer view," I say quickly. "Glad you're here. You and Sarah ought to staycation here or something."

"Maybe," he says. "We'd have to figure out coverage for our kids."

It's so formal the way he says "our kids," like we are new business associates, which we technically are.

"How old are Emily and Peter now?" I ask. "Wait, let me guess . . . fourteen and seventeen?"

Brent smiles, surprised. "Exactly."

"I wish I knew them better."

"Oh."

Oh?

"I mean that," I say. It makes me sad and angry that he doesn't believe me.

"We can work on that," Brent says, "but I didn't think you were all that interested in my family, to be honest."

"Why would you think that?"

"Because we never see you."

I hate when people are right about things that I don't want them to be right about. "Brent . . . if we are going to work together—and we have to, because I don't have another lawyer and a lot of people want to sue me—we need to clear the air. We have never been close. Your wife says borderline microaggressive stuff to me that she knows isn't cool, hoping I don't hear. Or maybe she is hoping I do hear her. Anyway, you're not helping me because you like me. You're here because we both love Dale. But don't act like this distance is just on my end. It's both of us. Also, I got your kids' ages right, so give me some credit."

I let out the breath I was holding because I feel like I just gave a monologue suitable for an Oscar reel. Brent looks at me thoughtfully. He thinks a lot.

"OK. I have blamed you for Dale being so far away, and that's not fair. But I never knew if you were encouraging the distance from us. My wife doesn't mean anything by the things she says—"

I shake my head. "No, she means all of it. She just doesn't expect me to call her on it. Like her calling journalism a dying industry. She has to know that's hurtful, but she feels comfortable saying it anyway. That's where the microaggressions come in. We are not going to solve this today, and I don't have the time to go over every foul, sneaky thing she ever said to me—like the time she seemed shocked that my parents owned their home, or that I wasn't at Maryland on an athletic scholarship because obviously my grades would not qualify. That kind of thing. I expect it now. But she knows if there was a confrontation, it would be blamed on me."

Brent's chin is resting on his knuckles, like he's thinking hard. As someone who likes to be right, I recognize that look. He's trying hard to hold on to the argument that would get him a win, and he's committed to being, or at least looking, right. He paid for a lot of schooling to hone that skill.

"Thank you, Dawn," he says quietly. "I don't know if I agree with everything you just said. But I thank you for sharing it with me."

So I have to drop this. Brent's here to help me, despite three decades of bad feelings, and it doesn't matter if I win this argument. I need his help. I was right about Sarah, though.

Tonya knocks on the threshold of the balcony. "Your phone," she says, handing it to me.

"Is this the first time it's rung since I've been out here?"

"Of course not. But this one seemed important."

I look at the phone; its ring seems sort of angry. The screen reads *Baltimore Sentinel*. "I bet it's Susan," I say. "Should I answer?"

Brent nods. "Her organization has an interest in controlling the story and may—"

"May want to sue me. Yeah, yeah, get in line," I say, about to answer. But Brent mouths "speaker." I hit the speaker. I get it. We need receipts.

"What's up, Susan?"

"It's not Susan. It's Barbara," says my long-ago boss, who is indeed from the *Baltimore Sentinel*, or at least she was back a thousand years ago when I was an unimpressive intern she didn't hire. Now I'm claiming that her paper's claim to fame was bogus.

"Hello, Dawn. I think we need to talk."

Chapter 23

How Can You Make Peace with Yesterday When It Won't Leave You Alone?

As we rush to the *Sentinel* office in the rental Jeep, I pull up Eddie's Facebook again. I've been avoiding it all day. He hasn't gotten any less attractive than earlier today. I have never tried to friend him, and I don't know if he's going to answer anyone he's not connected to on here. Especially if it's me. Here goes nothing.

"Hey, Eddie!" I type. Is that too casual? "It's Dawn Roberts. I hope you remember me. It's been years and you're looking well. I'm sorry it's taken so long to get back in touch, but I have something important to ask you about. It's very timely. Thank you."

I sound desperate and pathetic. That tracks.

"We're here," Brent says, pulling into the paper's parking lot. The *Sentinel* offices used to remind me of classic TV or movie newsrooms like in *Lou Grant* or *All the President's Men*, with terrible fluorescent lighting, old desks, and the clack-clack of insistent typing. A creaky clubhouse. Not anymore.

"Wow," he says, whistling. "Was it always like this or did they get an upgrade?"

"Worthy of *Queer Eye*!"

There's a buzzer at the door. We press it. A very loud voice barks back, "Yes?" You can tell they spent some money on this whole setup because you can hear her clearly. The receptionist used to sound like Charlie Brown's teacher.

"Dawn Roberts-Shaffer and Brent Shaffer, for Barbara Smith-Pennington?" I like dropping "Shaffer" in there to remind them who they're messing with and what's at stake.

The buzzer buzzes again, and the door does a clicky thing and unlocks. I feel like Alice in Wonderland. The rabbit hole—or door—is open. Eat me. Drink me. Open me. Don't sue me.

Behind the door, there's a foyer with some of the old front pages laminated and hung on the wall. If I had time, I'd try to see if I could find my name on a page somewhere from my intern summer, like I existed. But I don't. There's another door beyond the foyer, which clicks without our having to do anything. On the other side is the woman that, I assume, belongs to the not-Charlie-Brown's-teacher voice. Her desk plate says Dorothy Morrow.

"Hello, Dorothy," I start to say. "I'm Dawn Ro—"

"Yes, you are," Dorothy says. "Please wait here."

Brent and I look at each other, unsure of what to do, which, I think, is the point.

"Dorothy is the bouncer at a club. But they don't have overpriced Long Island iced teas here."

"Were you always funny?" Brent says, trying not to laugh.

"Yes, but not in this bitter and old way. Have you told your wife where you are? I don't even think I asked."

He nods. "I told her it was for Dale."

"Did that matter?"

Brent chuckles. It's a nice chuckle, I have decided. I wish I had known I liked him sooner. "A little."

"I'll take it."

The door next to the receptionist opens, and Barbara, looking thirty years older but as distinguished as she's ever going to get, walks out. "Dawn!" she says, almost convincingly cordial. "It's been forever."

"It certainly has. This is Brent Shaffer, my attorney."

"*Attorney,*" Barbara says, repeating the word as if she's never heard it. "That wasn't necessary. It's just a conversation."

"Sure," I say, "but are *you* going to have an attorney during this conversation?"

Barbara smiles a smile so phony I wonder if even she believes it. "Well, yeah," she says, laughing. Oh my God, they really do think I'm that stupid. "Good thinking. OK, come on. It's going to be fine."

"That's what they tell the baby cows on the way into little, tiny cages where they make them into veal when they can't run."

"Sure," Barbara says, ushering us toward the door. "But unlike the veal, you've apparently been good at running."

Brent's eyes widen. "Buckle up," he whispers.

Barbara leads us into the refurbished newsroom, sparkling and soulless. There are more desks than journalists at this point, which makes me sad because I really thought I'd be working here by now. A younger woman with Taylor Swift bangs looks up from her computer, registering who I am. She gives me a thumbs-up under her desk. I see you, Swiftie! Much appreciated.

"Here we are," Barbara says, opening the door of an office that says "Darlene Hammond, publisher." Seated behind a very large and expensive-looking desk is a fiftysomething blond woman with a brisk Hillary Clinton vibe that I assume is Darlene. There's a kid that I think I saw at the press conference, plus someone named Kevin, who I guess is the lawyer. And . . . is that Jenn?

"Hey, Dawn," says the former copyeditor, now the news editor. She was also my friend before I skipped town. Is she here to be a friendly face?

"Jenn!" I say, stopping myself from hugging her. It's not that kind of visit. It's nice to see her, though.

"Let me give you my card," she says. "I'd love to catch up."

I laugh. "When I come up for air, maybe? There's a lot going on. Obviously." I start to turn to Brent, but Jenn leans over, trying not to look as urgent as she seems to be.

"Why don't you call me on your way back to Baltimore?" she whispers, and those reporting Spidey senses are going wild again.

Barbara clears her throat and makes introductions around the room. I notice that it gets a little quiet when Brent introduces himself as my attorney. Barbara gestures for us to sit.

"So," Darlene says, "it's been a while since you've been here, Dawn."

Are we really doing small talk? We've both got lawyers loaded and ready to fire . . . or aim, or whatever it is you do with a lawyer.

"Yes," I say. "You wanted to see me?"

"We did," Darlene says. "Obviously, we've seen the video of your press conference appearance. Actually, Mark Jackson, our reporter, was there, so we know that you made quite the accusation."

"I did," I say. "And it wasn't just an accusation. It was the truth."

An uncomfortable silence.

"Well," Barbara says, "it's been a very long time, but that's not what I remember."

"What do you remember?" Brent says, edgily cordial.

"I remember Dawn as an intern here. She had a good, normal summer, but she was not hired when she graduated. She went to a smaller paper where she wrote a lot of stories about festivals and features. We knew that she was close to Joseph Perkins from the time that they were interns together. Joe came on staff here and was doing quite well, and it's my understanding that when she was told about the allegations against the city, she gave the tip to Joe, as the scandal was in Baltimore, and he—"

"He what?" I say, leaning forward, and something about the hardness in the "what" makes Brent lightly tap me on the knee. Barbara backs up a little. She heard it, too.

"We don't have any proof that Ms. Roberts-Shaffer did anything more than introduce the whistleblower to Mr. Perkins," Kevin the lawyer says quickly, maybe wanting to stop me beating Barbara down. Although that would certainly help their case. Jenn gives me a subtle look, like "Slow that roll."

"The whistleblower. You mean my sister, who's willing to back me up that this was my idea, and that Joe—Mr. Perkins—started talking to people behind my back and lied to me up to the moment when the story broke and ran without me?" I say. I feel loud.

"Voice not so loud, OK?" Brent whispers.

"Sorry," I say. "But Tonya, my sister, the *whistleblower*, she knows what happened."

Darlene smiles kind of smugly, like the argument is already over and I've lost it.

"Well, Ms. Roberts . . . or is it Roberts-Shaffer? I can't keep track," she says. "After speaking with people like Barbara who were here at the time, there's no proof of this. Also, your sister and the other alleged witnesses have never said anything of the kind for decades. I'm not sure where this is coming from."

"It's coming from the truth, *Darlene*," I say. I knew this was going to be messy, but I wasn't expecting a turnpike-gas-station-bathroom sort of mess.

"Dawn," Jenn whispers.

"Look," Barbara says, not unkindly. "I know that there's a lot going on with you, and you feel rejected by us. Now with the loss of your husband . . . and sorry for your loss—"

"No."

"I'm sorry?"

"I am so sick of people like you, and your columnist Susan, weaponizing apologies against me. Joe was your superstar, and it wouldn't do for people to know that he stole this story from someone you wouldn't even hire. I've done just fine, thank you. Now you've got the Pulitzer, and you aren't going to deviate from anything that doesn't support the initial story. I get it."

"But if you get it," Barbara says, "why now?"

"Because, lady, you're—"

"NO," Brent says, no longer trying to whisper. "We're done. I want this on the record. The paper's official position is that you have no knowledge of Ms. Roberts-Shaffer originating what became the 'Diving into Deception' story. Correct?"

The suits all look at each other to make sure that this is their position. The attorney nods. It is. Officially.

"Great," Brent says. "We're done here."

There's a sigh of relief from the other side of the room, except for Jenn, who looks uncomfortable. Me too, girl!

"Well, that's great," Barbara says. "Dawn, would you mind sitting with Mark for a few minutes and giving him a quote retracting your statement?"

Has she not been following this conversation? Brent reaches over across me like he's my dad blocking me from hurtling forward in the car as he slams on the brakes to avoid a deer. "You misunderstand, ma'am," he says, and big ups to Brent on the passive-aggressive use of the word "ma'am." "We are done with you and with this farce, but not with this subject. Ms. Roberts-Shaffer retracts *nothing*. She stands by her story. We will uphold her recollection of events. And if you back off now, we'll consider not revealing that you tried to bully her into reversing."

I am in serious awe right now. He's good! I hope I'm getting a friends-and-family discount.

The brief relief on the other side of the room is now stunned hostility. Barbara really doesn't remember me well if she thought I was going to fall for this.

"Well then," she says, standing up as Darlene and the attorney do the same; Mark the reporter looks like he wants to disappear into the fancy curtains. "You'll be hearing from us."

"I'm sure we will," Brent says, rising as well. "I'm also pretty sure you'll be updating your Google Alerts."

All I can think as we head for the door is that I hope our snappy exit read every bit as much of a "screw you" as I think Brent meant it. As we leave, Jenn walks by and takes my hand.

"I'm sorry this is how we were reunited," she whispers. "But I believe you."

"Why?"

Jenn smiles. "Because the Dawn I knew took journalism too seriously to make this up. And you should have been taken more seriously here, too."

Interesting.

"What do you mean?"

Before she can answer, Dorothy the receptionist buzzes Brent and me wordlessly away.

"Call me," Jenn mouths as I leave with a self-satisfied-looking Brent. I didn't find anything here satisfying, but I like that he's not mad at me.

"You seem pleased," I say.

"I am. You sure better be able to back this up. I would hate to have to apologize to those cretins."

"Why, Brent Shaffer," I marvel. "That's as close as I've ever heard you come to cursing!"

"Only you can make me mad enough to curse," he says wryly.

I'm not sure if that's a compliment, but I'll take it.

"What did that Jenn woman want?" Brent asks. "She seemed agitated."

I nod, unfolding the business card she pressed into my palm. "She told me to call her. It seemed important."

"That's intriguing," Brent says as I dial before starting to drive. She picks up almost immediately.

"Hi, Dawn." Her voice comes out of the car speaker with an echo that suggests that she's hiding in a bathroom stall or a closet. I bet she ran there as soon as I left because she knew I was going to call.

"Jenn! It seemed really important for me to call you," I say.

She pauses. "I wanted to tell you something I should have told you thirty years ago. It's not proof or anything, but it's something you should know."

"You sound like you're about to confess to murder or something." I laugh, trying to defuse the situation.

"Nothing that bloody, but it is important. Do you remember when you interviewed for the *Sentinel* and didn't get it?"

"That one's hard to forget," I say. "Why?"

She sighs.

"I didn't want to tell you this at the time because you and Joe were such good friends . . . or at least you were supposed to be . . ."

At the mention of that name, I feel my fingers tense up. "I thought we were, too. Apparently not. What happened?"

Jenn sighs again. "We stood outside Barbara's office before your interview, and he told you he was rooting for you, but he didn't."

After all Joe has done to me, this should not be a shock, but this revelation is messing with the official Ballad of Joe and Dawn.

"What do you mean?" I ask, both wanting to know and dreading what I'm about to hear.

"After your interview, Barbara asked Joe what he thought of you working at the *Sentinel*. He was not an editor and his word was not official, but it carried a lot of weight," she explains. "I always kind of thought they also figured that if the young Black superstar gave the prospective young Black hire a bad review, they didn't have to feel bad about not hiring you."

My hair feels like it's on fire.

"So he told them not to hire me? How do you know that?"

"Once you didn't get an offer, I saw Barbara by the coffee machine and told her how sad I was not to be working with you. And she said, 'We really were considering her, but her own best friend had doubts, and we had to consider that.'"

Brent clears his throat. I don't think there are legal issues, but bias and prior contempt is something to argue if arguments have to be made at some point.

"Brent Shaffer here," he says. "So you are saying that Mr. Perkins has been professionally sabotaging Dawn since the 1990s? Why would he do that?"

"Because he's Beelzebub?" I blurt out.

Jenn laughs. "I think he saw how good you are," she answers. "And he didn't want competition. It was better for him not to compete, because you really did have something. I think he stole your story because he wasn't getting what he wanted, and I bet your confidence was shaken enough not being at the big paper that you were easy to manipulate."

Son of a . . .

"Hey!" Jenn whispers. "I have to go before anyone looks for me. Sorry to stir up more stuff, but I wanted you to know."

She hangs up, and Brent and I look at each other.

"Did that help at all?" I ask.

"Maybe," he says. "Anyone call you back?"

"Nobody. I did try."

Brent sighs. "That's not what I wanted to hear. We have Tonya, of course, and I'm still hopeful we can get Percy, but it would be helpful if we had notes, especially if they were dated, or any material that could support your timeline."

"Notes," I repeat. "Notes." Suddenly, something clicks in my head, and I put my right turn signal on.

"Where are you going?" Brent asks.

"To the only place that might still have some proof," I say, turning onto I-83 North. "Of course, it's also the place where I skipped out of town in the middle of the night and maybe fumbled them a Pulitzer."

"I assume it's a long shot?"

I laugh. "Of course," I answer. "But everything is. I'm used to it. Something's got to go my way eventually."

I hope that's true.

Chapter 24

Nice to See Me!

I used to make this drive on I-83 between Baltimore and York so often that I could tell how close I was to home not by the mile markers, but by the familiar slant of a big barn or the shrubs surrounding a farmhouse. Driving it the first time in three decades, nothing is familiar. The barn's still there, but it's so faded it seems to be disappearing, and there are newer houses dotting what was once green space around it. I hope the farmer, or the farmer's kids, got good money.

Brent's still in the passenger seat. It's weirdly quiet now. I'm used to chatting out loud with Ghost Dale while driving, but I can't do that now without looking wackier than Brent already knows I am. I look over at him, and for the first time in the three decades I've known him, I think he and Dale have the same eyes. Huh. Guess it's hard to find a resemblance between the love of your life and a guy you haven't ever loved. Until now, I guess.

"Tell me who we're hoping to talk to again?" he asks.

"Zach, who used to be the news editor. He's the publisher now, which means he probably isn't there all the time. There are a few other people I recognize still on the staff listing online, but he's the one I'll have to get past."

Brent nods. "Did Eddie get back to you yet?" he asks.

"Nope," I answer. I have been pretending not to check my Messenger app every five minutes. What would I even say? *Hey, did you save some notepads off my desk thirty years ago? How's life? Are you still mad at me?* It looks like he hasn't seen it yet, but I feel left on "read" anyway.

"You shouldn't call first?" Brent asks.

"Nah. This seems like a good ambush situation."

"I'll have to take your word for it," he says.

"Yeah, you do. Oh look!" I say, pointing out the window at a dingy row house. "That's my old apartment. I know it's a dump. I was a little baby reporter, and I couldn't afford much more. But it was great at the time, like we were slumming for the truth. It was a badge of honor to live in a dump."

Brent nods. "I lived in a dump or two," he says. "I understand."

This is brand-new information because I always thought of Brent as being to the manor born and not slumming with the poors. The more you know!

I pull into the parking lot of the *York Herald's* newsroom. I haven't been here since I made out with Dale in that spot right over there and promptly fled town. I want to throw up. Nostalgically.

"Surreal?" Brent asks.

"You have no idea." When I was on staff, I'd have just gone up the back steps and swiped my employee card to get in. But I sent it back in the mail when I quit, as if that made up for me ghosting. It probably didn't.

I check my watch. If things are at all like they used to be, there should be someone at the desk. Wonder if it's someone who hates me.

"It's taking you a while to go to the door," Brent says, because he is very observant. "Change your mind?"

"Nope. We came this far. Even if no one wants to help me, I might remember something relevant."

Brent nods. "I tell my clients to do that sometimes. You'd be surprised how much can come back to you."

"It would be helpful if I'd forgotten a notebook magically lodged under a floorboard," I say, finally getting out of the car. The back door of the building opens, and a guy in his early fifties, hair less plentiful and grayer than it used to be, steps out.

"Dawn Roberts! I thought that was you."

That "missed a deadline" feeling comes gurgling back so strong I feel I might barf, run up to where my desk used to be, and try to type out a story.

"Hi, Zach!" I say, perhaps too chipper.

"I would ask you what you're doing here, but I'm in the news business, and I kind of expected it."

I can't tell if that's a good thing. Better to assume it's not. "I guess you know about a certain press conference?" I say.

Zach nods. "We had a reporter there. Silas Mitchell. We would have found out anyway, though. You wanna come in?"

I guess! Zach hits the sensor with his key card and edges the door open with his shoulder. I start walking, and Brent follows. "Brent Shaffer," he says.

"The lawyer," Zach says. "I got an irate call from one of your legal brethren from the *Sentinel* notifying me that they've warned you they're willing to sue for their Pulitzer cred, and that if we had any ideas about causing trouble, it was not going to go well for us."

"Not surprising," Brent says.

"We should go to my office and talk, but I thought you might want to see the upstairs," Zach says as we follow him inside. It's weird how much it's changed—new paint, new carpet—but it still smells faintly like pizza, ancient flasks, and newsprint. You can still sort of see the crack in the stairwell ceiling where someone—I can't recall who—hit their head real hard. There used to be a little bit of hair stuck in it. I'm glad the hair is gone, but in a weird way it's sad. It was part of our rough-and-tumble, working-people, drunken aesthetic. It was gross. *But it was our gross.*

"Who's still here that I would remember?" I ask as Zach opens the door into the main newsroom.

"Not a lot of people. James, the photog. He's the photo editor now. Jamie, who was general assignment like you, is now the news editor. Was Casey Henderson here when you were?"

"The intern? She got here right before I . . . ummm . . . no longer worked here."

Zach laughs. "I was very curious as to how you were going to end that sentence."

It's all there, the fractured sum of a memory I usually work hard not to remember. The desks are new, and the stained glass "City Desk" sign is gone. But all the paint and renovations can't obscure the sights, sounds, and smells in my mind, like the big TV that used to hang on the wall that we watched the local news on when there was a crisis.

When the door opens, the staff looks up to see who's coming in, and none of them know who I am, so they turn back to their screens.

"What's it like being back in this room?" Zach asks.

"Weird."

"DAWN!" I hear behind me, and it's Casey the Intern, only she's no longer the intern so I shouldn't call her that.

"Congratulations," I say. "You stayed!"

"And I see you're still making rash choices!"

I know she's a full-grown woman and not a sophomore from Elizabethtown College anymore, and she probably wears a bra with her white tank tops now, but I still feel some kind of way about letting her clown me. "Well." I shrug. "I go big."

She laughs. A young guy who sort of looks like Lil Nas X if he'd gone to J-school comes up behind her. "Excuse me. Are you Dawn?" he says, sticking out his hand for me to shake. "I'm Silas Mitchell."

"Silas!" I say. "You caught the press conference."

"Yeah, that was cool," he says and then looks at Zach. "Is that OK to say?"

I laugh, because when I was young, we kept it real professional—or as professional as a place with hair stuck in the stairwell could be—and saved our complaining for when we went to Round the Clock Diner at midnight with no bosses around.

Well, until we made out with a source in the parking lot.

"It's fine," Zach says. "He's coming with us to my office. OK, Brent? I don't usually like lawyers, but you kind of look like my husband."

"You got married? I missed that."

He laughs. "What didn't you miss?"

Fine. I deserved that.

We follow Zach to the other staircase, past where my desk was. It's not the same desk, but I feel a familiar panic—the stress of deadlines, and trying to impress everyone, and doing what was expected of me while going for my dreams. Go big or go home.

Spoiler alert! I went home.

We walk down past the empty reception desk. "You remember Evelyn, the receptionist? She passed a few years back."

"Sure do," I say, not adding that Evelyn, who started our relationship refusing to believe I was a reporter, continued being terrible and once offered me up as a suspect in the mystery of who stole the Christmas luncheon ham, even though I didn't eat pork. You never forget your first workplace-based racism.

We head past the downstairs newsroom and the sports department and into Zach's office. I'm proud of him that it's his now. His wedding photo is on the desk, and yes, his husband is a burlier, more rugged Brent.

Zach motions us all to sit as Silas closes the door. "You must be busy, but obviously people are curious about whether you really were working on that story," Zach says. "I have a vague memory of your mentioning wanting to do some enterprise—"

"And that you weren't really into the idea."

"I wasn't, because you were hired to do the cop shift and then the festival feature stuff, and we had other people to do investigations. And the connection to York was legit but tenuous. And I didn't think anything was going to come of it."

"Did you remember it when the story came out in Baltimore?" Brent asks, and Zach looks kind of sheepish.

"Of course. I wondered if you realized that you weren't up to it, had given Perkins the story, and then left town because you were embarrassed. When we discovered you had been involved with a source, you seemed . . . I don't want to say *toxic*—"

"You just did," I say quietly. Ouch. "I shoe-leathered that thing! I did all you wanted me to for my regular beat and then worked my butt off up and down the highway for a story that could have made us. I know I should not have told Joe about it. But he stole it from me!"

"I believe that now," Zach says. "But that's not what I was told."

"What were you told? By who?"

"I asked someone I knew at the *Sentinel* if they had ever heard of you. They told me that you and Joe were friends and that Joe had told everyone that you'd passed the idea on to him, which pissed me off because you had pushed so hard to pursue it, and then you folded, slept with a source, and split. So we moved on and put it behind us. I'm sorry I had the story wrong back then."

That makes sense but it still sucks what I put in motion all those years ago.

"Would you be willing to say that I had worked on that story and that it was my idea before it was Joe's?"

He shrugs again. "I could, but again, Joe isn't disputing that he first heard the tip from you. He's saying that you gave it to him and he ran with it. The way you ran out of here was so sketchy that I didn't know what to think."

That's not helpful.

Brent turns to Silas. "Do you have any questions for my client?"

Silas runs through the basics, clarifying some dates and having me reiterate my claims. He's thorough. I like the kid. I bet he wouldn't get his story stolen.

"I wish I could help more," Zach says. "Did you ever tell anyone else about the story who might remember?"

"I spent so much time running down to the basement on my breaks to organize my notes. I did so much, and now it's all gone."

Zach chuckles. "Boy, it was nasty down there. There was an old couch down there, remember? I heard that the minute it hit the landfill, it caught fire. Smelled like funk and corruption. Eddie took pictures. Made *Inside Edition* and everything."

Wait. Eddie.

"Eddie knew I was working on something. He never said anything?"

Zach blushes. "There was a thing there, right? With the two of you? He never said, but all Dawn talk was strictly forbidden. When you left, he went silent about you, and we followed his lead."

I want to find Young Dawn and shake her real good. "I guess in all the renovations you never found any of my old notebooks? My sister told me Eddie sent my mom some stuff off my desk."

"I think he grabbed that nasty coffee mug you had. There was a family of ants living in it so long, they had squatters' rights."

I choose to ignore that. "About Eddie . . . I haven't talked to him in a while."

Zach whistles. "Like I said. Drama. Carmen What's-her-name, the night editor, said you had a fight down here the night before you left, and we wondered if that's why you went."

I feel my Black-girl blush coming on, the heat of memory and embarrassment. "Not really. But it was not a great scene. Anyway, we used to be friends—"

"That all?"

"DUDE. Look, that was so long ago. You and the *Herald* and I didn't end well, but I'm decades older and I'm a professional. I'm not that girl anymore, and you aren't going to talk to me like that."

Zach pauses. "You're right. I'm sorry. Really. What's your number? I'll send you Eddie's information. If we had been able to do that in 1994, we might not have had this problem. It's like carrying a notepad in your pocket."

"Can we see the basement?" I say as he forwards me Eddie's contact information from his phone.

"Why?"

"Just curious."

We head back down past the former hair crack and into the basement. Somebody changed the light bulb. And it no longer smells prominently of feet!

"What else was down here?" Brent asks.

"Funk and a file cabinet. What happened to it?" I ask Zach.

"We got rid of that. We were afraid it was flammable, too, but we got anything important out before we tossed it. Why?"

"I spent a lot of time down here. I hoped that maybe I'd left something . . ."

"And it was magically still here three decades later?" Zach says.

"Well, yeah," I say sheepishly.

Brent gets a text, something that gives him the face clouds.

"What?"

"I'll tell you in the car," he says, shaking Zach's hand. "We gotta go."

I look around the basement again, desperate to remember something that could help me. Of course, there isn't anything. This is hopeless.

"It's nice to see you, Dawn," Zach says, and we hug, which is not as weird as I thought it might be. "I'm sorry I couldn't think of anything to help. Sorry for all of it, really. I should have paid more attention."

"And I shouldn't have bailed."

Zach and I were never close. But there is something meaningful to be said, and I am reminded that this was never just about me. This was about two news organizations and everyone who worked there, whose ethics were as important as mine. Youth makes you think that you're the only one that counts, and when you're older, you remember everyone else was human, too.

"No, you shouldn't have bailed," Zach says, "but at the end of the day, that was for love, right?"

"Yes," Brent says. "It was for love."

I have to stop myself from sprinting up the steps and potentially smacking my head on the ceiling so nobody sees me cry.

Chapter 25

AM I CHARLIE BROWN, LUCY, OR THE FOOTBALL?

We get to the car, and Brent hands me his phone, paused on the video of a CBS News broadcast with the banner "Joseph Perkins from *National News Now* replies to accusations of plagiarism."

"Uh-oh," I say, hitting "Play."

"I obviously deny the accusations by Ms. Roberts, a former colleague whose recent widowhood has sent her into a desperate spiral triggered by the announcement of the cinematic version of a story she surrendered," Joe is saying. Around him are the actors, including Crystal "Fawn" Dirkins, who looks pissed. If I was the first wife in those Lifetime movies in which she plays the murderous cheerleader babysitter, I'd be scared.

"I am truly sorry for Ms. Roberts's loss but will not allow her to sully my work or the efforts of these many brave people, including her own sister," Joe continues. He's such a good actor, I'm shocked he's not playing himself in this movie. "Rest assured that we will defend ourselves zealously, availing ourselves of all legal recourse."

"Say it with your whole chest, Poindexter!" I yell at the phone.

"Don't break my phone," Brent says. "It's new."

I hand it back to him overly carefully, as if cradling a baby. "Hope I didn't breathe on it too hard."

Brent smiles. "Being the messenger who gets shot is part of the job."

"I can't even think about harming you. You haven't gotten me out of this pickle yet," I say. "Not that I would harm you anyway."

"Lawyers inspire strong emotions," Brent says.

"Not wrong about that," I say, about to drive off, then remember something.

"I have to call Eddie. I've been putting it off, but I'm sort of hoping he miraculously has an old notepad of mine, and I can run to his house, get it, and then hit Joe in the head with it."

"That's a very unlikely scenario," Brent says. "Unlikely, but I admire your resolve."

I take a deep breath. The phone rings. And rings. And rings.

"Not answering."

"Text him," Brent suggests. "Nobody answers their phone."

I leave a voicemail anyway, though no one listens to voicemail. (Well, besides me.) "Hey, Eddie! It's Dawn Roberts!" I say. "Listen, I don't know if you saw that I kinda crashed a press conference about a movie but . . . it's a long story. But I just found out you sent my mom stuff off my desk when I left. I know it's unlikely, but you didn't save anything else, did you? That's weird. OK. Whatever. Can you call me? It's important. I hate asking you for anything important after we haven't talked in thirty years, but . . . you know. Bye!"

Brent shoots me a look that can only be described as "Whoo, child." "You sounded kind of insane," he said.

"Desperate times," I say, pulling onto the highway. "By the way, Attorney, how much is this costing me? You're very good, and I doubt I can afford you."

Brent directs me toward the Leaders Heights exit with the McDonald's drive-through. "Right now, all it's going to cost you is a Big Mac meal and two apple pies. And proof. I hope your friend Eddie calls you back."

"I can do the food," I say, putting my turn signal on. "I hope he calls back, too."

"So there was something unspoken with this Eddie, huh?"

"Too unspoken," I say.

Brent is silent for a beat, and I can tell he's parsing his words during this fragile peace. "All things being equal, if you hadn't had your story stolen the very same moment Dale got his big break, do you think you would have gone with him? Or would you have decided your job was more important, and Dale would have just been some flirty guy you never heard from again?"

I'm gonna need a minute. OK, ready.

"I used to ask myself that all the time. That night was a perfect storm of emotion and weirdness, and I went for it. Without knowing about Joe, I might not have left then. But if I was going to find out about it the next morning anyway, maybe I would have been hoofing it down to the airport hoping to catch Dale. There are so many what-ifs, and I just choose to believe it was meant to be."

"That's what I never got about you guys," Brent says measuredly. "A wing and a prayer is not a plan. It didn't make sense to me."

"*I* didn't make sense to you." Oww. Once you say things like that out loud, they're impossible to retract.

"Right. Part of me will never understand it."

"So why are you still here?" I ask.

"Because you're Dale's wife. And I believe you."

"Thank you, Brent," I say. "You can have all the pie you want."

We order and then wait for our food for what seems like a very long time. I check my phone to see who's looking for me. Pearl tells me she's been fielding calls for TV appearances. Tonya confirms that she's talked to her lawyer, our cousin Bobby, who said to tell me, "Girl, you messed up." And Bria James asks if we can talk later.

"What's her deal?" Brent asks. "Bria."

"She's a young reporter who won't go away, so we're finding her useful. I need to keep her on my side for now. She got me this script, and in her own weird way, she kind of reminds me of a younger, more tech-savvy me."

"Annoying, then."

I giggle from behind my Filet-O-Fish, which doesn't have nearly enough tartar sauce on it. "I am shocked every time you make a joke. I look forward to knowing more about you. And my niece and nephew. And my sister-in-law, too."

"Really?"

"I think so," I answer.

Brent pauses, his fry in midair. That's not a good sign. Those are excellent fries. "Well, maybe."

"Uh-oh. Are you gonna lawyer me about it or tell me the truth?"

Brent clears his throat. Like a lawyer would do. "Dawn," he says, more emphatically enunciated. I am the daughter of a Black woman of the Clair Huxtable generation. I know a hostile, clipped statement when I hear one.

"Sorry," I say sheepishly.

"I don't think you guys are ever going to be close. You aren't each other's sort of people. She's very traditional, and yes, she's snobby sometimes. She's not a fan of the city—"

"Boy, that's a loaded statement."

Somewhere in my brain, Dale has paused the chess game he's having in heaven with my dad and is pounding on my ear. *Stop. You're getting along. Make this point after you've won.*

"He started it," I whisper.

"What did you say?" asks Brent, who, unlike Dale, is alive and physically present in my car.

"Sorry. I was talking to Dale."

The look on Brent's face is hard to discern. Confused? Perplexed? Convinced that I've lost it?

"Hmm?" he says.

"It's a thing I do. He can't talk back to me, obviously," I explain. Can you really explain your own lack of sanity? "When I'm alone in the car, I swear I can hear him. Just now I thought I could."

It's a good sign he hasn't tried to jump out. "And what did he say?"

"To stop talking because I need you, and we can talk about all this after I've won," I say.

Brent pauses. Does he think I'm crazy? "That sounds like him. Ever the diplomat. Such a good businessman. I'm jealous."

"Of Dale being such a good businessman? I've seen your house. You're no slouch, obviously, in the business department."

"No, not of Dale," Brent says. "Of you."

SNAP.

"You're jealous of the odd lady talking to dead people and trying not to get sued because she waited thirty years to admit that she let a Pulitzer slip through her fingers?"

"You're the crazy lady," Brent corrects me, "who got to spend so much time with him, who kept him away from us—"

"I did not."

"But I felt that way. I know Dale loved LA. But I always thought that if you had wanted to come back to the East Coast, he would have."

"My folks thought the same thing about Dale. Our jobs were out there. You can't just blame me for that."

"But I did. I missed my brother. And it was easier to make it your fault. But it's more than that," Brent says. "I talk to him, too, you know? All the time. In my head, in the car. He just doesn't talk back. And I'm jealous of you for that, too."

I want to comfort him, because he's never been this vulnerable with me. I also want to comfort myself, because this is uncomfortable. My therapist, who is probably expecting a call from me if she's watching the news at all, tells me that it's good to sit with your discomfort.

Sit with it, Dale is whispering. Ghosts are annoying.

"Maybe you aren't crazy enough to hear him," I say. I mean that in a good way.

"Maybe."

And just like that, it's OK.

I start driving back toward Baltimore. My phone rings, punctuating the silence.

"Can you see who that is?" I ask, knowing that if I were alone, I'd be looking it up myself because I am not a good driver.

"It's a private number," he says. "Want me to let it go to voicemail? It's probably a scam wanting you to buy a time-share."

I laugh. "Nah, put it on speaker. I know who it is, and I don't think she needs my money."

He does, kind of startled.

"Dawn Roberts speaking." And three, two, one . . .

"DESTINY'S CHILD!"

"What the heck?" Brent mouths.

"Hello, Miss Vivi," I say. "How are you?"

"Better than you, Dusty Springfield. Or so I hear."

"Seriously, who is that?" Brent whispers. I tap him gently on the hand. I hope we're close enough now that he doesn't interpret that as violence.

"What have you heard?" I ask.

"People are out here trying to sue you for claiming what you say is yours."

"It *is* mine."

"Well, as long as you believe it and can back it up and nobody can prove otherwise, it is," Miss Vivi says sagely. "Ask Gwen Stefani about the time we worked together."

"I wasn't aware you knew Gwen Stefani."

"I would tell you about it, but I'd have to pay somebody thirty-seven million dollars, and I know you don't have that kind of cash to pay me back."

"Sadly, true. I wish I could say that I've worked on your story—"

"But you can't because you're out there making trouble for The Man. Or at least *that* man. He's fine. Very distinguished. Much more famous than you."

"That's kind of the point," I say.

"Let me know when you've finished my story, girl," she says. "My eyelash architect is here, and if I talk while they work, my eyes stick together. Don't get sued too bad. You'll need the money. Maybe you have a cousin you could ask for help. Or maybe I do."

And then she hangs up.

"Who was that, and why do I feel like I'm drunk?"

"That's Vivienne St. Claire, the singer. I interviewed her a few days ago before all this happened."

"What was that cousin business?"

I smile. "That's her weird diva riddle for the day, apparently. She seems to have become my own Patti LaBelle Yoda. I am going to ask my mom if any of our cousins know her, although I'm sure this would have come up by now. She's a superfan, apparently."

Brent laughs. "You and Dale had the most fascinating life."

"Why do you make that sound backhanded, like that Chinese curse about living in interesting times?"

Brent digs back into the bag to get the last stray fry. "The side of the hand you get depends on how fast you can duck," he says.

"That is deep."

"Now that sounds backhanded," Brent says.

"Duck faster," I reply, and we both laugh. I like this dude so much better when I don't hate him.

Chapter 26

Who Knows What Weasels Lurk in the Hearts of Men?

I drop Brent off at the Sagamore Pendry to get his car. He promises to let me know if anybody else tries to sue me, as long as I promise not to do anything else that someone wants to sue me for. I get out and wave for the valet. I need to change, as I smell of french fries and bad vibes.

"Hey," says Marcus, the valet. "You're Dawn Robinson?"

"*Roberts.* Roberts-Shaffer, really. Dawn Robinson is from En Vogue," I correct him, handing him a twenty before he can tell me he doesn't know who that is.

"Sorry. Some people were looking for you."

Susan or Joe? I wonder. "What did you tell them?"

"That I hadn't heard of you."

What a nice young man. Funny how I can look at a twenty-one-year-old and think of him as a nice young man I have no interest in dating. I just want to bake him a pie and judge his choices. "I hope you keep not having heard of me."

Marcus beams. "I have done this with real famous people, too. I got you."

He doesn't know he just low-key insulted me. He's lucky I'm in Auntie mode.

"Miss Roberts-Shaffer!" The desk clerk, whose name I think is Lita, is waving at me. At least she remembers my name.

"Hmm?"

"You've gotten a lot of messages today," Lita says. "A few people left voicemails, and . . ."

Those ominous ellipses again.

"And?"

"And some wanted to see you in person," says a person who's suddenly manifested next to me, either from the side reception area or Hades. He sticks out his hand for me to shake, and I wonder if there's a buzzer on it.

"Titus Blaylock," says the former mayor's brother, one of the dudes I sort of sent to jail, indirectly. "You can call me Junior."

I'd really rather not.

"Mr. Blaylock," I say cautiously. "Can I help you?"

"Perhaps," he says. "Have a drink with me."

This is the point when my pushy free lawyer-in-law would yell "No comment!" as he shoved me into the elevator. I shall embody that. "With all due respect," I say calmly to this man who is due no actual respect, "my attorney would not want me to."

"Of course he wouldn't," Junior Blaylock says, gesturing toward the bar. "Lawyers are always in your business. You know I know something about that."

"I do."

"It's interesting that you know a lot about me, but until yesterday, I had never heard of you," he continues, and now he's just walking, and I guess I have to follow him. Once he's far enough ahead of me, I pull my phone out of my pocket and text Brent Something's up. Yes, it's ominous and lacks specificity, but maybe he'll call faster.

We get to the bar, and Junior sits at the corner, motioning for me to sit next to him.

"I really don't have a lot of time," I say, standing awkwardly by the stool. "I'm expected at a family event very soon."

Junior smiles and waves at . . . hey, it's our bartender!

"Hello, Miss Dawn," Nate says. "Can I help you?"

"Hello, young man!" Junior interrupts. "I would like a scotch, neat, and . . ."

"Water," I say.

"You're no fun," Junior says. "Scotch and a boring old water."

Nate gives me a curious look, like he's not sure if this is cool. No, baby, it's not cool. "That all you need, Miss Dawn? Your family's not with you?"

Junior cocks his eyebrow. "Family, like your sister?"

"YES," I say. "You remember her, of course, as the whistleblower and former girlfriend of one of your accomplices. This is getting tedious. If you're going to sue me, get in line."

One of the most unsettling things about stone-cold weasels—and I'm an expert in spotting them in the wild—is their shamelessness. They refuse to be embarrassed when they absolutely should be. Their commitment to their lack of shame would be almost admirable if it wasn't so TERRIBLE. I just told this man I knew he was here about something stupid, and he's still smiling at me, unbothered, like I asked him how his grandma was faring after her hip surgery.

"I'm not planning to sue you, girl," Junior says as if he's my uncle and I've disappointed him by even suggesting any animus. "We have a lot in common!"

"Is it that we should both be somewhere else, having never spoken?"

He laughs. Creepy laugh. "You're a funny one, aren't you? No, it's that both of us have been wronged by Joe Perkins."

"There is a difference. He did me wrong by stealing the story about the crimes you committed. I don't give that guy a lot of credit, but at least he stopped you."

"*Alleged* crimes."

Ooh boy.

"Sir, there was evidence. Lots and lots of it. And I know, because I found a lot of it."

Junior nods sagely, stroking his well-trimmed goatee. I want to pluck it out, salt-and-pepper strand by salt-and-pepper strand. "That's what I wanted to talk to you about," he counters. "I'm wondering if you recall any so-called evidence that would point to . . . a new understanding of the case."

"What new is there to understand? There was audio of you admitting to the scheme! Talking about the condo in Montego Bay you were going to buy! They snapped a series of photos of you mouthing 'I did it!' coming down the log flume at one of the parks! I don't see how any of this matters at this late date. You were found guilty in record time—the jury didn't even take time to slice their lunch pizza. I believe the jury foreman later said you displayed 'a shocking lack of discretion for someone who wants to stay out of jail.'"

Junior waves his hand as if batting away inconvenient facts in the air. "That's not how I remember it. I remember a group of hardworking citizens swayed by the fantastical scribblings of a charming but career-hungry journalist, who we now know stole the whole thing from a lesser—"

"WATCH IT."

"*Lesser-known* writer, who would have no doubt surpassed his glory had he not cruelly lied and stolen the fruits of her hard labor. It's true that I was locked away from my family for a crime I did not commit—"

"Your vanity license plate literally read DIVE IN."

"Allegedly."

I throw up my hands. "Do you even know what that word means? They got you dead to rights. You did it. You went to jail. You got out. It's my understanding that you bought shares in a funeral home chain and you're doing just fine."

He nods. "It's true that I've made some good investments. But things have not been easy for me, as you might imagine, with the stain of false guilt forever attached to my name. Who knows where things would have gone if I hadn't been unfairly impugned?"

"My guess is rich, with the poor education of little Black city children on your hands?"

Junior chuckles. "There's that sense of humor again! No. I would not have had to live with the shame brought upon my family. You know what happened to my brother's career."

"I do. He wrote a book, did a 'It's not my fault' tour, and got reelected because somehow people in Baltimore keep doing that."

"But he could have been governor. President, even. We'll never know—"

"*Because you did illegal things.* Look, man, I don't know what you want from me . . ."

Junior smiles again, and he would almost be handsome if I couldn't imagine horns popping up on top of his immaculately shaved head. My phone beeps. Text from Brent. What's up?

Stupidity. I'm handling it, I type hurriedly and then turn back to Junior. "OK, so what do you want?"

"I'm just wondering if, considering this newly uncovered version of events of Joseph Perkins's malfeasance against you, you might see me as an ally in casting doubt on the initial record of events."

Oh.

"You want me to lie and say that Joe wrote things that can't be proven and make him look bad because you and I both have beef with him?"

Junior dips a fry into a neatly poured pond of ketchup. I didn't even notice the fries arriving. When did he even order them? Is Nate just handing them out to anyone he sees hanging out with me now? Is this like the new version of the bread basket?

"Of course I'd never ask you to *lie*, Ms. Roberts-Shaffer. I simply wonder if there's anything you forgot you remembered."

For a millisecond longer than I'm comfortable admitting, I consider what that would look like. I hate Joe for what he tried to do to Dale's memory and my reputation. I've already made these accusations with my whole chest, thrown that unretractable gauntlet. Why not dirty him up a little more, even if it's to help city hall Terry Crews over here?

But then I take a good, long look at Junior. It's not just that he's obnoxious, or that his tie matches his pocket square, his socks, and his belt like Patrick Bateman in Garanimals. It's that he's a bad guy. Tonya was driven to turn on him and her boyfriend, who she regrettably loved, because her pride as a city school kid couldn't take that he was trying to get rich by ruining public education. Our schools have enough problems without putting a waterslide where the cafeteria used to be.

I straighten my skirt and step toward the door. "Nah," I say. "I don't want anything to do with this. And if you tell anyone that I'm in on whatever stupid move you make next, you'll hear from my lawyer. I've given him so much work this week, he won't notice one more cease and desist."

For the first time, Junior looks less than confident. "I know you dislike Joseph Perkins," he counters with his best cheesy deacon smile. "We could channel that into something mutually beneficial."

"Or you could just slink back to whatever subterranean lair you lurk in and leave me alone. Remember that I'm going to be in the media a lot. Don't think I might not accidentally spill this if you don't go away."

Junior waits a beat to see if I'm serious, confirms in my face that I am, and dismounts from his stool, throwing a wad of bills onto the bar. "This is for you, young man!" he yells to Nate, turning to leave before dramatically pausing and turning back around.

"You're curiously resolute, ma'am. With that kind of fire, I'm shocked you waited this long to drag Joseph Perkins. I think you're missing an opportunity. But it seems that's what you do," he says disappointedly. Like I'm supposed to feel bad! He does a solicitous bow and then leaves.

Nate comes back over and scoops the wad of cash into his apron. "I don't know who that was, but he's a schmuck. You seem to know a lot of those," he says.

"You're not wrong," I say. "I just hope I'm not one of them."

Chapter 27

In Which I Do Something Stupid

When I pull up to my mother's house, she's sitting on the porch with her cordless phone. I start to say hello, but she shushes me.

"Yes, ma'am," she says into the phone, getting up and beckoning me inside. "This Tesla keeps driving by here, and nobody on my block drives one. Of course I'm sure. I've lived here forty-seven years. I know. Yes. Exactly. Oh, you know I will."

"Was that nine-one-one?"

"Three-one-one," she says, shutting the door and locking the dead bolt loudly behind us. "I told them a car keeps circling the block and slowing down when it gets to our door."

"Listen," I say tentatively because I don't want her to call 311 on me, too. "Tonya says one of my coworkers—Eddie, the photographer—sent you some stuff off my desk in York. Do you remember that?"

"Girl, that was a thousand years ago. How am I supposed to remember that?"

"Mommy, it's important! Do you think you still have it?"

"I doubt it. Remember we had a flood in the basement after your daddy died. We lost a lot of boxes and mess down there. You can check, though. Carry something for the party up with you when you go."

Of course she's gonna get some free work out of it. I go in and down into the basement, the 1980s wood-paneled clubhouse of my dreams. The electronics and couch are updated, but if I close my eyes, I can still see the big ancient TV that Tonya and I used to sneak-watch soap operas on before we did our homework. Then we'd try to cool it down so our parents didn't know it had been on.

Tonya and Marcus, carrying folding chairs, come in from the back of the basement, where all the storage, laundry, and the world's grossest bathroom are.

"Sister-in-law!" Marcus says, coming to hug me. I think about this relationship versus the one I've had with my other brother-in-law until very recently. Marcus was great, an upgrade from Percy just by not being Percy. He was also good to Tonya, nice to us, and wasn't involved in massive fraud. All pluses.

Tonya was mad at me for so long. When they met in the late nineties, I wasn't sure Marcus was going to like me. But he picked up her phone when I was blowing it up to no response.

"She might get mad at me for butting in, and I know why she's mad at you, but I can tell she misses you. You can't force it. I just thought you should know that she is going to call you back when she's ready. OK?"

And then he hung up. That is love.

"What are you doing down here?" Tonya asks me. I look behind her, and my heart drops, because my mother is right. All the formerly scattered and stacked boxes are gone, replaced by neat shelves of old dishes and appliances my mother might use one day. What a time for her to stop being a pack rat.

"Fool's errand," I say as we all go back upstairs. I take a chair from Marcus so it looks like I helped. Weedie and my mom are taking fish out of the freezer, which is new. It's been decades since I've lived here, and it's stupid to imagine they'd still have the original appliances. But I feel like everything in my history has been replaced. That sucks.

"Girlie!" Weedie says. "I saw you on the *Today* show!"

"I wasn't on the *Today* show."

"But they were talking about you. I bet they're gonna call you. They didn't call you yet?"

My mother hands me a rag and some Windex. "Dawn has a lawyer who is probably fielding those calls for her. You know, Brent. Dale's brother. Has he gotten a lot of calls for you?"

"I guess. Why are you handing me Windex?" I ask.

"Because I haven't had that many people in here in a long time. Something needs Windexing. Find everything and spray it."

"Even you can handle that!" Tonya says. "Mommy, let me borrow Dawn a minute."

"A short minute," she says. "Those spots aren't going to clean themselves."

Tonya takes me by the arm and pulls me through the kitchen into the postage stamp–size backyard. "What's going on?" she asks when the door is closed.

"Why? Do you know something?"

"No, Paranoia Jones, I don't. But you've been running up and down I-83 and memory lane. Something's up."

I fill her in on everything with both papers and reaching out to Eddie with the long shot (he hasn't called me back yet) and then the call from Miss Vivi.

"Vivienne St. Claire!" she says. "She's your fairy godmother, like Whitney was to Brandy in *Cinderella*."

"Except I can't ever imagine her being that gracious about duetting with me," I say, spritzing some Windex on the glass door. "I think her crazy is a screen to cover how smart she is. She's trying to tell me something. She said something about cousins. This is a weird question, but we don't have any cousins in the music business that might know her, do we?"

"Charles was a rapper for a hot minute. Remember DJ Crabcake? But she wouldn't have heard of him because he was not good. Maybe she's just crazy," Tonya says. "Anyway, you've got more important things to worry about. I called Sherri and George and neither of them are willing to say anything that's going to void their checks. Holly won't even call me back."

"Oh no," I say. "Not even Sheila from Permits?"

"Not even Sheila. And she was the nice one!"

Now I have to ask her something she won't think is so nice. "There's someone we haven't called yet."

Tonya's eyes open wide, as if she's been hit in the back of the head with a softball, and I know what that looks like because I once accidentally hit her in the back of the head with a softball. "I know you aren't talking about Percy."

"I am."

"My God, Dawn!" Tonya throws her cup of whatever she was drinking at me. "I have gone out of my way for you! They're trying to sue me! I was gonna use that consultation money for Ricky's college and maybe a pool table. You remember Ricky, your nephew you've barely asked about? I risked it all for you. Percy went to jail, and he broke my heart, and you're bringing him into this."

"I wouldn't if it wasn't necessary! Tonya, I'm trying to prove that I was right. That *you're* right! You've risked so much, and I can never pay you back for how far you've stuck your neck out for me. Truly. I know I can salvage this somehow. But I need someone to help, and I can get Percy to talk."

She glares at me and goes down into the yard to get the cup she just threw at me. The water leaves an angry splotch on the sidewalk.

"See what you made me do? Mommy is gonna kill me if that doesn't dry by tomorrow," she says, putting her hand up to catch the Windex rag. I toss it, and she starts dabbing forcefully at the wet spot.

"It's concrete," I say. "It'll dry. You look like Lady Macbeth."

"*You* make me murderous," Tonya says. "You know how Percy hurt me."

"Well, Percy hasn't called me back yet," I say, and the words are out of my mouth before I can take them back. Tonya springs up from the walk and sprays the Windex at me hard. A strong stream of chemical mist hits me.

"Tonya!" I scream, covering my face with my hands. "Are you trying to blind me?"

"*Girls!* Whatever's going on out there, stop. I've called the police enough today, and I can't have anybody calling them on us," my mother yells from inside the house.

"You called him and didn't tell me?" Tonya shrieks at me.

"Brent called Percy's lawyer. I tried to tell you! I asked you about him, and you wouldn't help me get in touch with him, so I did it myself."

"Behind my back."

"You turned your back!" I yell.

"I turned my back? On you? What am I even doing then? Do you know what I gave up for you, what I'm giving up for you?" Tonya yells, arms crossed in front of her like a shield.

"I don't mean now," I protest, spinning, because this situation is out of control and I can't get it back. How do I explain why I have to do this without twisting the knife my sister believes is firmly planted in her back? I don't know the right thing to say, but I know there are a million wrong ones. "I mean then. I know it was wrong, but I left, and everything with Joe and the story happened, and you didn't say anything. You knew he stole it from me, and you let him. You were my sister. You were supposed to protect me."

The snarl on Tonya's face is frightening, like her jaw's going to extend to reveal a scarier set of foaming jaws, and she's going to eat me with both of them. "Girl, you really are out of your mind. No wonder you and Miss Vivienne St. Claire get along so well. You both think the rest of the world is your backing band, your support staff. You didn't protect ME! I came to you, and I trusted you to do the story, and I knew that you would handle it, or I thought that you would. But you were so far up Dale's butt you never even noticed Joe was stealing from you."

"It was too late by then," I yell.

"I'm coming out there with the hose!" my mother hisses from behind the door. Or maybe she's upstairs. I don't know. Mothers learn to throw their voices like ventriloquists so they can sneak up on you.

"It might have been too late. But I was scared, Dawn. They were trying to prove I was part of it, and Percy was so mad. I needed you to back me up. I needed my sister, and you checked out. I didn't have anything left, and I went along with it because if you weren't going to defend yourself, I didn't know how to. And . . . you chose Dale over me."

Wait, what? Did I?

Oh, right. I did.

"Tonya . . ."

"You chose Dale when I needed you. I thought you'd figured this out back in the car with Bria James because it felt like you were sorry. But you're not. Or maybe it's like Joe said: You couldn't do the story right, so you ran away," Tonya says. "I'm trying to help you, and you still can't see it."

"Tonya," I say again, frightened by the desperation in my own voice. I don't know how to get us back to where we were a few minutes ago, cordially Windexing. I did choose Dale because I didn't think I had a choice, but we all do. I chose to get on that plane, to stay in LA, and to come home when I felt like it, which was not as often as I should have. I made the choices that were best for my life. And I left everyone else to figure it out.

"I didn't mean to hurt you. But I couldn't think of any other way."

Her gaze is stone. Cold. The kind you can never warm.

"That's your problem, *Dawn*," she says, enunciating my name like she's sharpening the letters into a shiv with her teeth so she can spit it back at me. "You don't think about anyone but yourself."

The imaginary shiv settles somewhere in my heart, or right above it, and I feel like I'm going to bleed out. I run up the steps, throw the door open, and run through the kitchen into the dining room, nearly tripping over one of the folding chairs. I need a break from these people.

I really want to run, jump in the rental Jeep, grab my stuff, and head to BWI for a last-minute flight anywhere that's not here. I can afford it.

But instead of hitting the front porch, I fling open the basement door and head down the steep stairs.

"Where are you going?" Weedie asks as the door slams behind me. "Anita wanted you to Windex the mirrors down here and upstairs. More fingerprints than a crime scene."

"Ask Tonya!" I yell behind me. It is rude to yell at your elders and let doors slam in their faces, one more thing for everyone to be mad about. But I can't help that right now, and I'm not going to fit through the little tiny basement windows, so I'm just going to sit here in the back, with the storage stuff and the new washer and dryer, until I'm ready to come out or someone drags me out.

I hear muffled voices upstairs in the kitchen. I think someone says "Well, what happened now?" and someone else, maybe my mother, says "I'm not getting involved in their mess." I don't blame her. That was not a graceful escape, and now I'm kind of stuck down here.

See what I always told you about having a plan? Dale says in my ear.

"Dude, you are not helping," I say back.

There are steps coming down into the basement, and then across the finished floor before the doorknob to the laundry room turns. And I know who it is by the sound of those Temu pumps.

Chapter 28

In Which I Become a Basement Troll

"Bria James," I say. "What are you doing here?"

She looks slightly sheepish. "You didn't answer your phone so I called the landline again, and your mother promised me fish if I came and helped with the party prep," she says. "I wanted to get an update, and I like fish."

My mother pressing strangers into service doesn't surprise me at all.

"But why are you down here in my mother's basement?"

"Honestly, I asked where you were, and they told me you had some sort of fight with your sister and had locked yourself in the basement," she answers. "I think they wanted me to see if you were OK."

I throw up my hands. "Well, it's obviously not locked, is it?" I retort. "If they care so much, why didn't they come check on me?"

She laughs. "Because the mood is weird, and you're mad, and they probably thought you'd be less likely to beat me up." Bria shrugs. "Do you want to talk about it?"

Her question is weird, because I didn't think we were in a confidante space. I take a good look at her and am reminded, again, that I like mentoring younger reporters and normally I'd be encouraging this connection. But she came at me wrong, and I still don't quite trust her.

"Would that be on or off the record?" I say, maybe a little too gruffly, and she looks a little insulted. Before she can say anything, there are steps coming down the stairs and across the family room floor, and then a knock on the laundry room door. Now they're whispering.

"What should I say?" I hear my cousin Devonte ask someone.

"I don't know," my cousin Charles says. "Ask if there are any tablecloths or something."

"Hey, Dawn!" Devonte says louder, like I didn't hear him whisper. "Your mom wants to know if there are any tablecloths back there!"

Bria James snickers. "They are very bad at this."

"No!" I say. "I don't see any."

"Uh, OK," Devonte says hurriedly as I hear him walk back upstairs.

I let out an exasperated breath. "I wish somebody in my family would not be shady and just use their words and say 'Are you OK?'" I say. "I have half a mind to leave."

Bria James shakes her head.

"You never see your family. You'd actually run away?"

"Sweetie, you have no idea how good I am at running away. Ask my sister and her former boyfriend. Heck, ask my sister's various dolls and broken Etch-A-Sketches," I say. "Something goes wrong, or gets damaged, and I'm in the wind. You're not going to lecture me. You're the one who started this, making me feel bad for looking like a human being getting off a plane. You put this whole thing into motion, and I had to react."

"Look, Dawn," Bria James says, taking a seat on an old chair. "I wanted a story. And then I wanted to help you out because I thought it was badass that you were taking the power back from people who took it from you. But be real. You did some awful stuff. They did some awful stuff. It was all awful. They were worse. Still . . . me and Tonya and your brother-in-law . . . we're all trying to do something for you. You can't keep acting like a victim. You pushed me to get you that script, but you're the one who used it. You did all this."

Let's think about this. Back a thousand years ago in the car, I told Bria James she didn't know Journalism 101. I flew in here as a big-time media founder, but this zygote reporter is schooling me. I've had about thirty years to build a life on another coast without anyone on this one in my face to contradict my version of events. And now I see the truth—my version left out a lot. Everyone made mistakes but I feel like they only want to talk about mine. She's not wrong about some of that, but I don't want to concede that right now.

"Look." I throw up my hands. "I am so sick of being ganged up on. You have not stopped being in my business, and I don't even know anything about you."

All of a sudden, Bria James's expression is gentle.

"You're right," she says. "I'm sorry. What do you want to know?"

If this is a tactic to disarm the angry lady, it's working. I want to hold on to my snit, but I just said I was sick of being beat up on, and she's being nice.

"Everything, I guess," I say, so she quickly runs me through the Bria James basics:

She was raised in the burbs of Bethesda, outside DC. Went to Georgetown for undergrad and then got her master's in journalism at Morgan, did some freelancing for the *Washington Post*, *USA Today*, and the *Washington Blade*, the local LGBTQ+ paper. She bided her time as a stringer for TMZ in DC, mostly following politicians and athletes who were doing something stupid. That gave her a lot of work but not enough money, so she started her own site, initially with a girlfriend who proved to be an unreliable partner both romantically and business-wise, so she ditched her, slapped her initials on the site, and never looked back. Her advertisers and sponsors are decent, and she's making it work.

"You're an entrepreneur," I say, immediately hearing the condescension in my voice.

"Yes, like you," she says. I guess she heard it, too.

"Don't mess this up," Dale says in my ear. *"She's the only person that might like you right now, except me. And I'm dead."*

There is another knock on the door.

"What did y'all forget now?" I yell.

"Your mother wants that cooler back there," my Aunt Weedie says from the other side of the door. Oh, now they've called in the big guns. I sigh, grab the cooler that's in the corner, open the door, and hand it over. I don't know if it's the right one, but it's not like this is a real request.

"Y'all OK in there?" my aunt asks.

"Nobody's bleeding," I answer.

"Well, keep it that way," she says, and closes the door.

Bria James just kind of sits there silently for a minute. There is something more to say, but I don't know what that is. I think we both want to go into reporter mode, because that's where we work best.

"What happened with your sister?" she asks. "She was running out the door as I was coming in."

"Basically, she's mad that I had my brother-in-law get in touch with Percy, her ex, the one that worked for the mayor's brother, because he could vouch that it was my story first," I answer. "I know it's a sensitive subject, but I need him, and she'll have to be OK with it."

Bria James shrugs. "Will she, though?"

"You know what's at stake here!" I say louder than I mean to. "This is my life, my reputation, and my husband's memory on the line, and I'm sorry if it hurts her feelings."

"Are you, though?"

Just as I was beginning to like her.

"What is your problem?" I blurt. "You're judging me while you're trying to benefit from my story . . ."

Bria James holds up her hand. "Oh, come on, Dawn. You literally pulled me into this! You made me a part of this. Ethics, out the window. I don't even know how to square this with my training and the way

I want to do this job. You can't claim to be this Boss Lady and this helpless damsel at the same time. It's irritating."

We've taken a hard turn here, so I'm leaning into it. "I am so sick of hearing about your ethics. You have no idea what I've done or how hard I've worked, and you just sit there and tell me how people my age have done everything wrong," I said. "What are these ethics that you demonstrated by ambushing me, and an urn, at the airport and not even asking me for a quote, like a tabloid hack?"

Bria James shakes her head. "First of all, you want me to worship you as my elder and accept this storied journalistic tradition you guys won't stop talking about, but it's gone. Even you know that! You made the supposed big time and got a parachute to start your own thing. They don't make those anymore. Some of us were born too late to even get our feet in the door, so we started our own thing."

"There are differences. I admit I don't know what it's like to be you in this industry, not only in this sucky place we're in, but as a queer woman on top of being Black," I say.

She puts her hand up again in a "Stop" motion, something we oldies would have called "Talk to the Hand" back before Bria James was born. "Yes, my identity is different than yours. How many queer Black women did you work with when you were my age? You probably did, and you didn't even know. Things have changed, and I can be myself differently and openly now, but that adds one more layer that people can point at and decide if I'm filling a quota. There are few jobs that I don't make for myself, and I'm doing them. I'm not going to get into a pissing contest with you about who had it harder. It's all hard."

I don't say anything. But that Black-girl blush of shame is creeping back.

"Also," Bria James continues, "good job ignoring everything I just said about you and your inability to be honest about yourself. I am so sick of Gen X and your 'We used to stay out till midnight under a broken streetlamp and fight rats in the alley for fun' bravado, wanting to tell everyone how tough you are. You liked fighting rats 'cause you thought it made you cool," she says. "Now you're just older and tired, and you spin your version of events in a way that makes you look good."

"Are you talking about me specifically or my whole generation?" I ask.

"Both."

What's that they say about the student becoming the teacher?

"Look," I say. "You're right."

Bria James is stunned, because in the short time she's known me, she gets I don't say that a lot. "Continue."

"I left all those years ago and lived my life the way I lived it. Joe bamboozled me, and I did the same to everyone else, I guess, but the thing he did to me seemed worse, so I kind of ignored what I'd done," I say. "Tonya was mad, but she was always mad, so I let her just be and went on with my life. And when Dale died, it wasn't polite to be mad at the grieving widow, so they kind of let me off the hook until Joe vomited this all back up. Everybody's caught strays. Even you. And I'm sorry. I'm not sorry I busted up that press conference, but I'm sorry I haven't faced my own stuff."

Wordlessly, Bria James gets up. "This is weird to ask, but can I hug you? It seems like you need a hug."

God, I do. So I just open my arms and hug her, and the instant I feel her close in tight around my shoulders, I feel all my fight leak out of me. I have been in this fight for so long—for Glitter, to keep my job at the *Los Angeles Times* when there was no saving it, to keep Dale alive, and all the way back to that fight for my story in York.

Which I lost because I gave up.

I've done so much fighting that I haven't always thought about the people caught in the fray, like Tonya and Percy and even Dale's family. I have said for thirty years that they were on my mind. But were they really?

"Wow," I say. "I really am terrible."

Bria James laughs, releasing the hug. "You are," she agrees. "But you defend yourself and your family and you don't stop. That's heroic, in a way."

"I don't always feel that way."

She shakes her head. "Well, you know you Gen-X folks. You had to fight rats. You're survivors, even if you're sometimes surviving yourself."

That's profound.

"Thank you, Bria."

"That's the first time you haven't called me by my whole name," she says.

"It's the first time I didn't want to piss you off," I answer, turning my phone on. I've missed a call. Probably spam.

"Do you know what area code 340 is?" I ask. She shakes her head. I check my Facebook Messenger. Nothing from Eddie.

"I really hoped Eddie would have gotten back to me," I say.

"Do you think he has anything helpful?" Bria asks.

"I have no idea. But I can take all the help I can get."

My phone rings again. Brent.

"DAWN," Brent says. "Are you OK? I've been trying to reach you for three hours. Why was your cell phone off? Your mother says you're holding that blogger in her basement?"

"That's absolutely not true," I say. "Never mind. Why are you looking for me?"

"I'm coming to get you early tomorrow from your hotel."

"Where are we going?"

"To Channel 13. They want you on *CBS Mornings*."

"*Does Gayle King want to talk to me?*" I scream.

"I'm not sure," Brent says. "But don't you want to find out?"

I hang up and look at Bria James.

The laundry room doorknob turns and it's my mother. I'm in trouble now.

"Is your tantrum over? Are you ready to come out of this basement and act like an adult?" she says. "You already caused a scene with your sister."

"I didn't cause the scene!" I protest. "She—"

My mother interrupts, shaking her head firmly. "We're not doing all that right now," she says. "Let's not focus on that. Let's focus on me. It's my party."

This is her way of defusing the tension, and I'll take it, I guess.

"*Tomorrow,*" I say, hugging her, since apparently I can't stop hugging people. "Tomorrow is your party."

"Don't you forget it," my mother says. "Why don't you two come out of here, and then you can tell me all about Gayle?"

I crack up. I would ask her how long she's been listening outside the door, but it doesn't really matter. She seems to forgive me for the moment, and I'm really tired of being in this basement. So I follow her upstairs and start thinking about my big interview. Gayle or no Gayle, it's gonna be epic.

Chapter 29

No Comment!

"Don't they usually just do this by Zoom now?" I ask Brent as we wind our way to TV Hill, so-called because it's a high hill in the city where the TV stations are located due to the strong signal. We're driving through Hampden, another Baltimore neighborhood I would not have hung out in back in the day. They blew up a Black family's house when I was in high school. I took that as a hint.

But now it's super trendy and artsy. Maybe if I have any money left after this, I'll take myself to brunch.

"It makes us look more official to do it in person," Brent says. "We still don't have all that proof we need, and you need to be able to talk around that. Percy and his lawyer haven't gotten back to me. Can you ask your sister again?"

At the mention of Percy, my fight with Tonya and all the amends I have to make come into full relief. "I'll work on that," I say. "What do you think they're going to ask me?"

"I imagine they'll recap the story and maybe have some sort of statement from Joe or the movie people. You're a journalist. What would you want to know?"

"I'd want to know why I had never said anything before. I'd want to know if there was any proof of my claims or if I was the sad, bitter widow Joe says I am," I say.

"Do you have good answers for any of that?" Brent asks.

"Maybe?"

"I guess that's what we have to go with, then," Brent answers.

"Do you know who's going to be interviewing me?"

"Someone I've never heard of named Connie Sisson," Brent says. "I looked her up when I was waiting for you in the lobby. She's youngish, been in New York for about six months, mostly doing weekends."

"Oh," I say. It seems stupid to be insulted that I didn't rate Gayle when all I'm trying to do is get out of this without filing for bankruptcy. And Gayle can be tough. I still think about what she did to R. Kelly. Then again, he deserved that. I do not.

"Maybe with this other lady, there's less of a chance of any gotcha moments going viral, not that anyone cares about me," I say.

"They care," he says, "or we wouldn't be here."

We get to the hill and are buzzed in through a mechanical gate that vibrates to life and opens excruciatingly slowly. I watch too many movies and almost expect the gate to reverse when I'm halfway through and impale me through the car door. But we make it through alive, park, and walk to the door, waiting to be buzzed in there. So much buzzing.

"Brent Shaffer with Dawn Roberts," he tells the receptionist, who hits some buttons under her desk. It's an all-button and buzzing operation. In a few moments, a producer comes out and shakes our hands.

"I'm Maurice," he says. "Nice to meet you. And Ms. Roberts, you don't know me, but we went to the same high school."

"Apparently you were there long after my time," I say. "You're gonna make sure I don't look stupid, Maurice?"

"I'll do my best!" he says, and I don't know if he's being earnest or I'm being clowned. He gives us the rundown. They're going to set me up at the desk and mike me, and then I'll be able to hear NotGayle in my ear. This could be a good stopgap measure or a complete disaster. I'm just hoping for no bleeding.

"Is there somewhere to do my makeup?" I ask. I've done segments on local TV in LA, and I figure correctly that a station this size wouldn't have their own makeup artist.

"Yeah, I was going to ask you about that," Brent says.

"Do I look that bad?"

He smiles. "I want you to present yourself in the crispest, most positive and professional light," Brent answers.

"Expert dodge," I say. "Very happy to have you in my corner."

At a certain age, your face is sick of you, and it's done hiding it for you. When I've spackled myself into presentability, I take one last look in the mirror and decide that the airwaves are going to get the face that they get. Maurice takes us over to a glass-walled seating area to wait.

"How are you feeling?" Brent asks.

"As ready as I'm gonna be."

"That's good," he says. "I know you have a big day ahead of you at your mom's."

"I'm not sure how welcome I'm going to be there," I answer.

"Yes," he says. "I didn't tell you because I didn't want to get into your head before the interview, but your mom texted me."

"Why does my mom have your phone number?"

"We've been somewhat related for thirty years. At some point she must have had occasion to have my number."

True. "What did she say?"

"That she wasn't able to reach you, and that there had been what she termed a 'situation' at her house, but she loves you and expects to see you this afternoon."

"She can expect anything she wants. It's a messy scene, and I have a lot to unpack, but I don't want to do that in front of my whole family."

Brent chuckles.

"What?"

"Well, it won't just be your side of the family."

Ruh-roh. "What other canister of snakes is waiting for me?"

"Nothing bad. She invited Sarah and me."

Did not see that coming. "Why?"

"To thank me for helping you. She said it was high time we act like we're related."

"She's messing with me."

"Maybe. But it's nice. And she's right."

"I guess. Are you coming?"

Brent nods. "I remember your mother brought potato salad to a dinner once, and it was delicious. I would enjoy having that again."

"Does Sarah like potato salad enough to come?"

He laughs. "Sarah is eager to be supportive."

"Eager, I imagine, is a stretch. But it's nice."

Maurice knocks on the box. Here goes nothing. Brent gives me a supportive shoulder squeeze, and I head to the desk as Maurice mikes me.

"You're going to look into that camera," Maurice says, pointing, "and you'll hear Connie in your ear and see her on the monitor, although it might not line up exactly. Don't be thrown off. Just answer her as you hear her, OK?"

"Got it," I say.

"You're going to be fine. Just wait for Connie and the other guest. And don't worry about him. I hear he's not as unstoppable as he seems."

"Hmm?" I ask, but Maurice has already given me a thumbs-up and stepped away.

"Hello, Dawn," Connie Sisson says in my ear. "Are you ready?"

"Who is your other guest?" I ask, but I think I already know.

"I hope you are ready, Dawn," Joe says from some remote location that's either another studio or an evil lair. I bet he's got a lair. "We have quite a lot to talk about."

I crane my neck to meet Brent's eyes, which are popping out of his skull.

"He's on here, too?" I hiss, covering the mike with my hand but knowing everyone knows what I said.

"Do you want me to kill it?" Brent mouths.

"Can't back down now," I say. "Not in front of . . . that person."

"Hi!" Joe says.

"I have no words for you unless necessary. This is an ambush."

"You know about ambushes, so I figure you'd be right at home," Joe trills. He's *trilling*. Like this is a variety show and he's doing the high harmony to "End of the Road." I hope it's not the end of *my* road.

"You two gonna be OK?" Connie says. "The countdown is beginning."

"Connie, I seriously doubt it's gonna be OK," I say. "But that's probably going to play better on YouTube anyway."

And we're on!

"Welcome back to *CBS Mornings*. I'm Connie Sisson," she says as the words "Journalism Controversy" appear below our boxes. "Yesterday, a shocker from the world of news. Dawn Roberts-Shaffer, an entertainment writer from the LA-based site Glitter, made a major accusation at a Baltimore press conference set to announce the movie version of the Pulitzer Prize–winning 'Diving into Deception' series by Joseph Perkins of *National News Now*. She asserted that the original story had been hers and that she'd never gotten the credit. Perkins and the *Baltimore Sentinel*, which published the story, dispute that. Now the future of the movie, as well as the official history of this important story, hang in the balance. Joining us, separately, from Baltimore are Dawn Roberts-Shaffer and Joseph Perkins. Welcome to you both."

This would be so much more fun if Maury came out to solemnly tell Joe that he is not the father.

"Thank you, Connie," I say.

"Yes, thank you," Joe says. "Thank you so much for inviting us to address this."

Oh, shut up.

"So, Ms. Roberts-Shaffer—"

"Dawn is fine."

"Dawn, thank you. Tell me what brings us to this moment."

Girl, you do not have the time or the censors for the whole story, I think, but instead I say, "Well, Connie, I was here in Baltimore on an important family matter—"

"Interring your late husband's ashes."

"Yes," I say. "I was not aware of the movie or that Mr. Perkins would also be here in Baltimore. But I heard about it and then obtained a copy of the script, and I knew that I had to speak up."

"Why now?" Connie asks.

"There were details in the script that were not only personally and professionally harmful to me and implied false and actionable things about my late husband, but also reinforced the idea that I was a thief when I wasn't the one doing the thieving."

"If that's true, Dawn, why didn't you say anything until now? I mean, that story was written in the nineteen-nineties. You've had decades to set the story straight."

"Yes, why now, Dawn?" Joe says, low-key taunting me.

"Well, Connie," I say, because I'm not talking to Joe. "Back when I found out that the story had been stolen from me, in a moment of emotion and devastation, I fled to the West Coast. It wasn't a well-thought-out decision, but I was young and felt betrayed and made a big choice. Would I have done that now? I'm not sure. Back then I was willing to leave it all behind, but three decades later, I couldn't have that movie out there cementing this lie. The book doesn't mention me by name at all—it just said someone gave him the tip. But now, this 'Fawn' is all over the script. Even with the barely changed names, it's clear who he's writing about. You know, most people who see a movie or a TV show assume what they're seeing on-screen is the truth."

She nods. "What is the truth?"

"Well, my sister, Tonya, the original whistleblower, came to me with what she knew and asked for my help. I took it to my editor at the *York Herald*, who agreed that I could work on it as enterprise—outside of my usual beat—if it didn't get in the way of the rest of my work. They didn't know how much I'd done on it, which was a lot. The contacts were mine, and those people had confidence in me. I wonder if they would have trusted Joe without me. But then I found out that he was doing interviews with those same people behind my back and lying about it."

"I understand," Connie says. "But why didn't you stay and fight for your credit?"

"I think I can answer that," Demon Johnny Gill says. "Dawn, whose involvement in the story was very minimal apart from the initial referral from her sister, was focusing on some light features, including one about a small local band in the small town she worked in. I believe she became overwhelmed with the story and gave it to me, someone she knew could handle it."

"Lies," I say under my breath.

"What was that, Dawn?" Connie says. She heard me. Oh, we're playing games now. Fine. Deal me in.

"I said that's a dirty lie, Joe's a dirty liar and a thief, and his veneers are freakishly white."

I glance at Brent, whose face is turning purple.

"That's rich coming from a lightweight who slept with a source—Connie, you know that's highly unprofessional—and left town in the middle of the night, like the Baltimore Colts fled our native Baltimore under the cover of darkness a decade earlier," Joe said.

Oh, we're invoking our city's eternal football shame now? How dare he?

"I believe that with the recent loss of her husband—and I truly am sorry for that loss—she's trying to cash in on something that she had nothing to do with," this evil Taye Diggs–looking Muppet continues. "No one from either newspaper has been willing to offer any proof of her claims. I'm at a loss as to why she thinks anyone is going to believe her."

I am trying to keep my composure, and I must make whatever I say next count.

"So, Dawn . . . response?" Connie says.

"He had already started stealing my story before I left, and yes, I did leave town in a moment of betrayal and . . . emotions . . ."

Joe snorts. "Emotions! Is that what we're calling it now?"

"He'd lied to everybody, and the story was coming out the next day," I continue. "And yes, I had started falling in love with the man who became my husband, which is completely separate from Mr. Perkins's outright theft. I wish that I'd stood my ground, that I had kept my notes, and that people were willing to back me up. But I do have my sister, the whistleblower," I say, remembering that the sister of which I speak hates me and maybe I don't have her anymore. But I'm not going to admit that right now. Not with the Vampire LeVert sitting there gloating at me.

"Anything else?"

"If Mr. Perkins wants to talk about my character, I wonder if there are women in various clerks' offices in and around Baltimore City who might have some stories about him, given how easy it was for him to sway them. But that's neither here nor there. My attorney and I are very confident that we will be able to prove our side," I say. "I would not have come forward if I didn't have to stop this movie. It's damaging to myself, to my late husband, and to the truth."

Connie nods. She's no Gayle, but I like her. "You just want to set the story straight?" she asks.

"Yes. I want everyone to know that I'm not a liar. I might not always be a good friend or sister—and Tonya, if you're watching, I'm so sorry—but I am *not* a liar, or a thief, no matter what 'Fawn' in the movie does. And really? Fawn? Joe meant that person to be me, knowing that this could greatly damage the reputation I've worked so hard for."

"Come on, Dawn," Joe says. "The truth of the story has been out there for years."

"No, your version has been out there, ya fake Clark Kent! The movie presents me—sorry, FAWN—as a non-talent trying to take credit for your story because she's evil with a bad wig and doesn't have anything else to do. The truth is that I had a good story, and you took it from me, and I made a bad call that made it easier for you. If you had just left me alone in this script, we would not be here."

"Where does this leave the movie?" Connie asks. Good question, girl! I want to know, too!

"Trust that the producers and I are willing to take legal action to clear this up. We postponed the filming for a few days, resulting in a loss of time and money, and we're trying to best decide how to rectify that. Make no mistake—we will resume, and our truth will be told on the big screen, once and for all."

"With the existing script?" Connie asks. Yes! You keep getting to the bottom of it, lady!

"We see no need to make any changes, although we might have some material for a postscript," Joe says. "But this is going to continue. Mark my words."

"Oh, words are being marked," I say. That seems very "I know you are, but what am I?" but this is where we find ourselves.

Joe does that thing he does when he doesn't have a good argument. He scoffs from the back of his throat, like the very act is a waste of his time and he's insulted to have to bother. He doesn't have anything left to say, so he hopes that I shrivel and die. Or at least shut up.

Never gonna happen.

"Was that a response?" I say, sitting straighter in my chair. The producers in the studio sit up, too, probably happy that they didn't schedule this ambush in person. Or maybe sorry? That would have gotten more clicks on TikTok. Or WorldstarHipHop. Is Worldstar still a thing?

"My response," Joe says, "is that we're going to end this. If you don't have any proof of your scandalous lies, this is over."

"Good luck with that," I say, considering doing that dramatic movie exit where you stand up, rip the mike off, throw it down, and storm off set. But I don't want to look any more unhinged than I already do, plus I remember that I didn't drive.

Connie pauses, waiting for either of us to say anything. We just seethe. "OK!" she says. "There's obviously still a lot here left to talk about, so we'll be following this story very closely. Joe, Dawn, thank you for being with us."

"Thank you, Connie, for your time," he says evilly.

"Yeah, whatever," I say. And just like that, we're done. I hope I'm not done as well.

"OK!" Maurice says, taking my mike off. "That was . . . something."

"How do you think it went?"

"I think it's going to do very well on the website!" he says.

"What did you mean before about Joe not being so unstoppable anymore?"

Maurice shakes his head. "Nothing," he says. "But good luck to you. That guy's kinda sleazy."

You think? I step away from the desk and find Brent. I'm trying to decipher his mood. I fail.

"Let's go," he says.

"What did you think?" I say, following him out of the studio.

"We better hope we get that evidence, any evidence, and you better hope that whatever is happening with your family doesn't mean we lose the one witness you have."

I am very much hoping that, too.

"What about the other thing?"

Brent keeps walking, faster now, so fast I have to double my steps to keep up with him. He opens the door, holds it enough to get me through, and then lets it go, continuing his stride to the car. He opens my door and waits for me, wordlessly, to get in.

"I'm sorry you had to hear your brother's sexual past brought up on national television," I say. "Messy."

Brent clasps his hands together. Takes a breath. "Dawn, I am under no illusions that my brother was a virgin or a saint before you met," he says. "I admit that it was easier to believe you were the driving force in all bad decisions and keeping him from us. You both did some dumb things, but none of it amounts to theft, like Joe. Dale was a real person who made mistakes, and we had our own issues. None of that changes the fact that you loved him enough to stick with him, even now. And even if that's the kind of information I'm glad my mother isn't hearing on TV, it's part of the truth. Messy, like you said."

Relief.

"And in the middle of it all, I let Joe steal this thing from me," I say. "Thanks for helping me fix it."

"Understood. During the interview, I got a cease and desist letter from Joe's people."

"Why did they wait till we were on TV?"

"I think they were waiting to see if you would present evidence during the interview, and when you didn't," he says, "they decided it was time to legally shut you up."

"That's what he meant about it being over?"

"Probably," Brent says. "They are going to sue you if you continue to speak publicly or if you interfere any further in the movie production. They are threatening to hold you financially responsible for any losses incurred."

"Can they do that?"

"They can try."

This keeps getting worse.

"What do I do? There are stories being written about this, including at my own publication."

"I think you start 'no commenting' a lot. Do you think there's any chance of Eddie coming through?"

Speaking of messy stuff from the past.

"I still haven't heard from him . . . wait, let me check." I check my phone, and there's another missed call from that international number.

"I keep getting a call from a weird number in the Caribbean," I say. "I ignored it the first time, because everything is a scam these days. Should I see if it's something important?"

"Can't hurt, I guess. Just don't say hello more than once in case they record you and clone your voice."

One more thing to worry about. I hit "Call" and wait. Ugh. It's an error number. "It didn't go through," I say, dialing again. Same thing.

"It's probably nothing. If it's important, they'll call back," Brent says. "Any chance that Percy will come through?"

Snort. "Percy never came through in any way for anybody that was not Percy, and he blames me for sending him to jail, so . . ."

Brent turns off the car. "I can't believe I never thought of this. Do you have that in writing anywhere?"

"Have what in writing?"

"That he blames you for sending him to jail. That means that he knows you have some part in the story, right?"

Oh, wow.

"I guess! I always assumed he blamed me because he knew that the original tip came from Tonya and that she told me."

"But what if he knew more? What if he had some reason to believe that the story was yours?"

"He might," I say, "but he and his lawyer won't call us back, right? I wish he'd written me letters, or that there had been text messages, but they didn't exist then, and he hasn't even texted me as much as 'You ruined my life.'"

We both look at each other at the same time, because suddenly we have the same thought.

"But maybe he's texted that to Tonya," I say.

"And maybe he mentioned you!"

We are happy about this for about twenty seconds, until the cloud forms over my face.

"Oh no," Brent says. "This is the drama in your family, isn't it? With Tonya."

"About this very thing!" I say. "I'm an idiot. I've messed this up. But that's for me to work out with my sister and my therapist."

Brent shakes his head. "If Tonya knew that talking to Percy was the only thing that would help you, don't you think that she might want to do it?"

"I'm not sure Tonya wants to help me at this point. Especially about this."

"I know something about having issues with your sibling—big issues," Brent answers. "And I know that if I could have saved him a lot of hurt, I would have bitten my tongue and done it."

I sigh. "I wish we could redo all of that," I say.

"We can't," Brent answers. "I can only help you, and Dale, in a way, now. But I do think that your sister would do anything to keep you safe."

"I hope so. Didn't you see me begging on national TV?" I say.

Brent picks up his phone from the console and makes a call. "Yes, this is Brent Shaffer again for Bryce Throckington-West. I'm going to need to be in touch with him and his client, Percy Harris, today. Time is of the essence. Thank you."

He hangs up.

"Do you think that did anything?"

Brent shrugs. "Better than nothing."

Here's hoping!

Chapter 30

PARTY OF THE YEAR!

Brent drops me back at the hotel to change for the party. I look cute enough. I'm just trying not to be dragged to debtors' prison or whatever they call it now. As I wait for my car, I call Tonya. I know she's not going to answer. She might not even listen to it. But here goes, straight to voicemail.

"I don't know if you saw me on TV, but I kinda apologized for being a massive jerk for the whole world to hear," I say. "I'm so sorry about what happened, today and back then. I didn't mean to hurt you by mentioning Percy or by going behind your back. I should have told you I reached out to him and why I had to do it, but I did what worked for me and decided you'd have to deal with it. And that makes me a bad sister. I blew up your life, and I left you, and I'm so sorry, honey. I am. But . . . I'm asking if you ever sent Percy any text messages since he's been out of jail that might have mentioned me and my role in his downfall. Love you. Bye!"

I hope my sister sees past my begging to accept my apology and also help me. Not ideal. I'm terrible. But also . . . you know . . . Help me?

The entire drive to my mom's party, I think about what I'm going to say to everyone. Her big day is not the venue for true confessions. But it's going to be weird if I act like nothing happened. As I pull up, still mulling possible openers in my head, I see Bria James's car is parked out front in the good spot. Why is she here so early?

"Where is Bria James?" I say, throwing the door open. Aunt Weedie and my cousins Devonte and Charles, who are putting up TV trays in the living room, stare at me.

"The cute little blogger girl? She's in the basement on the Wi-Fi filing a story," Weedie says. "You're rude, busting in here like this. You looked cute on TV, though."

"How long has she been here?" I ask.

"She said she had work to do, and she was coming here for the party anyway, so she asked your mom if she could do it from here," Devonte says, unrolling a purple plastic tablecloth. "Did you really invite a reporter to your mother's party?"

"I guess," I say. "Where is Mommy?"

"Right here, TV star," my mother says, hugging me. "You looked really cute."

"I told her!" Weedie says from the living room. "I hope that helps Joe not sue you."

"It won't," I say. "So . . . have you heard from Tonya?"

The royal birthday-ish girl shakes her head. "I have not. All she's texted was that she had things to do and didn't know when she was coming tonight."

"What does that even mean?"

My mother sighs. "I don't know. But remember this isn't all your fault. May I remind you that your sister was involved in a movie being made behind your back with your archnemesis?"

"How dramatic of you."

"It's a very dramatic thing," she says. "I am saying that it's not all on you. We're a family full of loud, powerful women. We have to get better at communicating and saying what we feel, straight up, even at this late date. And now, daughter, I have a party to reign over, and you need a break from trying not to get sued. Ask your cousins what help they need and fix your eyeliner."

Always comes back to that, doesn't it?

Bria James comes up from my mother's basement, laptop under one arm, folding chairs under the other. She's wearing a little plaid skirt, a white Oxford shirt, and a tie.

"Very 'Avril Lavigne' of you," I say approvingly. "Is this what the kids are doing these days?"

She laughs. "I think you've just decided to sound old on purpose."

"Do you mind being put to work?" I ask Bria James, knowing that she's going to say no even if she does, because she seems to be a nice person, and she wants a story and free food.

"Nah," she says. "Your mom is nice, and she's always trying to feed me."

"Nice journalistic ethics you got there," Marcus says, coming in the door with my nephew, Ricky, who I have not seen since I've been here. I need to visit more. He hugs me and runs off to swipe a cookie. "Aren't you writing about Dawn?"

My sister's family is here, but I don't see her. Is Marcus here to make amends, or to represent her, or to murder me in her stead?

"Yes, she is," I say, hugging him. "Man, Ricky got bigger and cuter. Where's your wife? Is she really not going to come?"

"I think she has something to do first," Marcus says.

"Ordering a hit man?"

He hugs me again. "Patience," he says. "Something neither of you is good at."

What?

My mother sweeps by on her way to get more gorgeous, hugging Marcus. "Tonya with you?"

"Not yet," he says.

She starts to ask for more information and decides that's not going to get her wig on any faster. "Here I go to complete my transformation!" she says, and sweeps upstairs. "Weedie!" she says over her shoulder. "I need some help with my hair. I can't lift it by myself."

My aunt nods. "Dawn, make sure the gift bags are all straight," Weedie says.

"Gift bags! That's fancy," I say, impressed.

"I told you we weren't going to cheap out. We saved money. But you won't be able to tell," Weedie says, going upstairs. Bria James comes over holding a BJ's Wholesale Club–size package of paper towels. I was supposed to bring those!

"Seriously, you don't have to do all this," I say.

"They kinda just hand you things and tell you where to put them, and you just do it."

"Welcome to my life," I say. "So we cool?"

"I think so," Bria says. "You're going to be less terrible, and so am I."

"It's like it's a birthday gift for me at my mother's party!" I say.

"Your family is very nice and loud, and they gave me free Wi-Fi and shrimp salad," she says. "I feel right at home. I get to hang out and fold napkins, and they let me add songs to the special Luther Vandross–themed party playlist . . ."

"You know who that is well enough to have input?"

Bria laughs. "I'm not a barbarian."

There's a knock on the door, the kind where the person is just gonna come in anyway but wants you to know in case you need to find a bra or you're still on the toilet.

"Bunny!" I say as my Aunt Bunny and her daughter, Sondra, come in.

"We saw you on the news this morning," Sondra says. "Why didn't you ever try to get credit for that story before now? You could have your own movie and be able to introduce me to Michael B. Jordan."

"Never liked that Joe," Bunny offers. "I remember him from your college graduation. He had a big head. Not just that he's vain. His head is super big. Glad you never got together with him. Y'all woulda had some big-head children."

I have no idea where this conversation is going, but I notice that Sondra is no longer listening. "And who are you?" she says to Bria James, who is rearranging stacks of plastic cups according to color.

"I'm Bria."

"Friend of Dawn's?"

"Sure," Bria James agrees, shaking her hand. "And you?"

I don't have the energy to stand here and watch whatever flirty reality show mess this is, so I'm delighted to see more people come through, including my cousin Natalie, her boyfriend, and, as promised, his cousin. But not Tonya. I step onto the landing and message her again.

Sweetie, I type. Please text me back. I don't even care that much about the Percy thing as much as I care about you.

"Hello, Dawn," a voice says from the doorway. Brent and Sarah are standing awkwardly on my mother's porch.

"Oh, hello! Thanks for coming!" I say, opening the door so they and the present they are holding can fit inside. I hand them a gift bag.

"What a nice house! I've never been over here before," Sarah says.

If we were in a different place, on a different occasion, I would say something like, "Why do you sound surprised that it's nice?" But her husband has been trying to save my reputation, so my trap stays shut. We're hopefully going to be closer as a family soon. Baby steps.

"Thank you," I say. "We're still sort of pulling everything together, but there is punch made already." I point to the table where Bria James is rehanging streamers to make them more symmetrical.

"Wait, I know you," Sarah says. "You were at the cemetery?"

"Yes, I was," Bria says, handing her a cup of punch.

"You were with Tonya, right? Is she here?" Sarah asks, looking around. I recognize that look, of a woman who doesn't want to be at a party and feels so out of place that she's seeking her only acquaintance to point out the exits in case something goes down. I don't know her life, but I imagine Sarah doesn't go to a bunch of "Something's about to go down" parties—though she would be a lot more interesting if she did.

"She's not here yet," I say quickly, "but her husband is. You've met, right? Marcus, these are my in-laws, Brent and Sarah."

"I want to meet him, too," says Herman, my mother-in-law's "friend," stepping inside.

"Herman! What a nice surprise! How did you get here?"

"I drove. I'm not that old."

"No, no," I say. "Why are you here?"

"I called Brent when I saw you on the news and told him it was a shame I hadn't gotten to spend more time with you," Herman explains. "He asked your mother if it was OK if I tagged along."

Of course it is.

"Sorry to interrupt," Brent says, "but I just got an email from Joe's lawyers. They say you have twenty-four hours to respond with proof of your accusations or they are going to proceed with a lawsuit."

"Why would they do this now? Why are they moving up the deadline?"

"My understanding is that the producers want to start filming in two days or the whole production might be halted. They have to deal with you definitively so there's no question."

"And there's nothing we can do?"

"Not really," Brent says solemnly. "Just hoping for a miracle."

Marcus walks by with more cups.

"No Tonya yet?" I ask.

"No," he says. "She needs more time."

"More time for what?"

This is getting bleak. No Percy, no Eddie, no Tonya. It's over. Just as I'm considering retrieving that flask in my purse to perk up this punch, the strains of Luther Vandross's "Stop to Love" fill the living room.

"OK, ladies and gentlemen, put your hands together for the woman of the hour, the birthday girl . . . ," my cousin Charles is saying. It's the return of DJ Crabcake! Where in the world did that strobe light come from?

"I love this family," Marcus says.

"Seventy years of fabulousness in one sequin dress! Your guest of honor, ANITA ROBERTS!"

My mother floats downstairs, Weedie walking behind her, putting every prom entrance I ever had to shame. The wig, as promised, is immaculate. The makeup is expert. Miss Regina, who has done my mother's hair for thirty years, follows her carefully, making sure her masterwork remains pristine. I know she says she did all this since I never come home, but I know she is enjoying it.

"Was Miss Regina up there the whole time?" Devonte asks. "I've been here for hours and never saw her. Did she sleep here?"

"I have learned not to ask questions about the magic of Anita Roberts," I say as my mother circulates around the room to greet her subjects . . . er, guests.

"I guess there's no point in asking her for money when I get sued," I whisper to Marcus. "She's spent my inheritance on this party."

"You really thought there was an inheritance?" Marcus says, sipping his punch. "This tastes too sweet. Where's your flask? I know you have one."

Another knock on the door. Can you tell if someone sucks by the way they knock?

"Hello, Dawn," Susan says.

Yes, you can!

"What are you doing here?" I say, slapping the gift bag that Sondra is about to give her out of her hand. "No bag for her!"

"Dawn," Brent whispers, "be careful."

"I would like to know why you're in my mother's house, at her birthday party you were not invited to, *Susan*," I say, hoping I sound scary instead of scared.

"We were given a tip that you were sent a cease and desist order from Joe Perkins and the company making the movie, and we know that you are leaving town tomorrow—"

"How do you know all that?"

"No matter," Susan says. "I just wanted to get your comment."

"Clearly, there's a cease and desist, so I can't actually comment on anything," I hiss. "God, what is wrong with you?"

"Dawn!" Brent says.

This is unadvisable, but what isn't at this point? Susan is in my mother's house with a camera, trying to start trouble, and I'm not having it. I don't know whose Facebook page she was stalking for this information, but I'm unfollowing all of y'all.

"Dawn!" my mother says, materializing at my elbow. "What's all this?"

"Mrs. Roberts!" Susan says, too sweetly. "Susan McNally, *Baltimore Sentinel*. Happy birthday!"

"I know who you are, Susan," my mother says. "I read your column. I don't think you're staying long, but if you get me on camera, get my good side."

"They're all your good side," she says. I still hate her. "Dawn, I know that you're not able to comment officially, but what's your game plan? If you can't talk about the case, can you talk about your next steps? What does this mean for your career?"

"I'd rather talk about you stepping out of my mother's house," I say. "How did you even know about this party?"

"I told her," Joe says, stepping toward the door.

This episode of *America's Funniest Home Videos* is hot, flaming garbage.

"Joe Perkins!" my mother says, swirling the cape fringe of her dress around her. "Another person not on my guest list. You bring me a gift?"

"Miss Anita," Joe says, leaning over to kiss her on the cheek. "You look beautiful."

"Of course I do." My mother laughs. "So no gift, then?"

"What do you want?" I say. "We got your cease and desist."

"I know," Joe says, nodding at Brent. "I just wanted to make sure that you considered the implications."

I should ask one of my larger cousins to quietly escort him out. But that's going to be another lawsuit.

"You just can't let it alone," I say. "Fine. Let's do this."

Joe laughs. "After all this time, you think I'm the one who can't leave things alone? You had to come to that press conference to ruin my movie."

"You mean that scandalous pack of lies you created to bury me and my dead husband so far under your garbage that no one would ever believe me about anything and you could go on lying?"

Joe snorts. "That part's all true, your lack of ethics, and fleeing because you couldn't hack the work. You got put in your place by one of your betters. I carried you ever since you couldn't figure out how to save a story on what was essentially a Fisher-Price play computer, and even with my help, you couldn't do what I did."

"Wait, what happened?" Weedie whispers.

"I'll tell you all about it later," my mother whispers back. "You can't pay for this sort of party entertainment."

"Dale and I are none of your business," I say. "But you were already stealing from me, taking things away from me. You were a lousy friend! We were supposed to look out for each other, being the only two Black kids there. I get it if you thought there was only one slot for an up-and-comer. But you didn't have to do that to me. There was room for us both."

Joe pauses for a moment, and for a minute I see my friend, who looked out for me, who said he had my back. Did he make a terrible split-second decision and then just decide to follow it through? He looks like he wants to speak. But he doesn't.

"You keep talking about my leaving town, but that only helped you. I don't know what I did to you to make you turn on me like that. You played like you were this big shot with all the talent, and you sabotaged me. Don't think I don't know you told them not to hire me at the *Sentinel*."

The room goes quiet.

"If true, is that actionable?" whispers Sarah, who has been married to a lawyer for a very long time. I like the way she thinks. At least at the moment.

Joe's eyes widen. "Are you serious?" he yells. "Really? I didn't need to sabotage you, Dawn. You did a good job doing that yourself. Barbara asked me about whether you could handle a paper that size, and I told her I had questions."

"Was your question whether you could handle competition, so you got rid of it?"

Joe's face is hot. "Competition? You got lucky! You answered one phone call because you lost your wallet and suddenly you're reporter of the year?"

Wait.

"Are you talking about Stewie the dog?" I yell. "Did you try to mess with my career because I got more attention than you? Did you really not believe in me?"

"I remember that story!" Aunt Weedie whispers to my mother. "That bar put a picture of him on the wall, like they do with Frank Sinatra at Italian restaurants."

"It wasn't about the dog," Joe says. "There was just so much fuss about that stupid story, that anybody could have done, and I just asked Barbara if, maybe, you were talented but not ready for the big leagues. If they had really wanted to have hired you, they would have. I think they knew you belonged in the bush leagues!"

Suddenly I don't care if I'm getting sued.

"Keep going," I say, looking him square in the eye.

"You were up in Pennsylvania writing about stolen pumpkins while I was killing myself at the *Sentinel*, chasing every lead, following every thread, looking for the story that was going to be my big break. And it came to *you*! You! It should have been mine! So I—"

"So you what?" I ask because this sounds like he's about to say something he will regret.

Joe seems to realize that and looks like he's trying to rewind his tongue. "I wrote the story of the century," he spits. "Too bad you couldn't."

"I didn't think that was what he was going to say," Sondra whispers.

"Joe, you know what happened!" I say, anger giving way to tears. It's all slipping away, and I can feel it. "You wrote the actual story, which was good. That part was yours. The Pulitzer is yours. I don't want money or any of it! I just want you to admit that you stole it from me. Just say that, please."

His smirk is cruel. "It's not true," Joe says. "There's no way to prove otherwise, is there?"

Suddenly the door swings open, and a massive cape, even bigger than my mother's, unfurls like a million productions of *Dreamgirls* into the living room.

"Did somebody say there was a birthday girl here?" booms Vivienne St. Claire. "Anita Roberts! Where you at, girl?"

"Dawn, what did you do?" my mother squeals, gliding over to hug Miss Vivi, who is now holding the mike like it was automatically attracted to her hand like Thor's hammer. "This is amazing! Are you here to sing to me?"

"Yes, girl!" Miss Vivi says, handing a CD to Charles. "I'm your birthday present. And I've got a present for you, too, Dawn. Everybody, this is my cousin! Ain't he fine?"

Into my mother's living room steps an incredibly handsome man in his fifties holding a large manila envelope. There are specks of attractive gray at his temples, and he has a well-manicured beard and a shy smile that highlights little lines around his eyes.

Eddie always had pretty eyes.

"OK, now I'm really confused," I say. I'm trying to make sense of everything that's happened, running through the events of the last thirty years and the last three days in my head like a glitching VHS tape.

Wait . . . did Miss Vivi say "cousin?"

"What are you doing here?" Joe asks, trying not to sound nervous.

"Eddie's your cousin?" I ask. "Eddie, you told me you worked for Miss Vivi but not that you were related!"

"Yes! C'est moi," Miss Vivi explains. "He was sixteen and making noise like he was going to quit school and be an uneducated little baby drummer. I didn't win all that money in that strip poker game with The Isley Brothers for his college fund to let that happen. So I fired him."

The crab cakes are going to get cold, but nobody seems to care. That's when you know you've captured a Baltimore audience.

"I told you I knew who you were, Dawn," Miss Vivi says, swirling a bangled hand in the air. "All is revealed in time!"

"Ooh! That reminds me of that DeBarge song! Do you know it?" my mother says excitedly.

"I do!" she says. "But let's get through this part first, shall we?" She motions to Eddie, who hands me the envelope.

"Did you get my messages? Plural?"

He nods. "I'm so sorry. I was shooting a wedding in the Virgin Islands when I got them. My phone was dying, so I called you from the room. The connection was spotty, so I don't know if it went through. But I was able to get to Vivi on WhatsApp, and she filled me in."

"He called her from a landline. That's expensive," Weedie whispers to my mom. "He must still like her."

"Yes," my mother whispers back. "I sure hope someone's recording this. All those heifers at church I didn't invite are going to die!"

"What is this?" I ask Eddie, looking at the envelope.

"Open it. You look good, kid."

This is not the time to blush.

"It was a bad scene when I left," I say softly. "I'm sorry."

"I appreciate that. I'm sorry, too, and sorry about Dale, by the way. I hope this makes up for all of that, at least a little."

I open the envelope and slide out two ancient reporter's notebooks. My chicken scratch in black Paper Mate ink on the covers reads "Water Park Story."

"Oh wow," I say.

"Oh *no*," Joe says.

"How did you get these?" I ask Eddie, who is now holding a cup of punch. That was fast.

"When you left and they were tossing your desk, I took the mug and some things to send to your mother, and these were shoved into the back of a drawer. I recognized the name of the story, obviously. I thought about trying to find you, or telling Zach and other editors, because I was sure that the big story in Baltimore was what you were working on. But I didn't know whether you'd really given it to Joe Perkins, and I didn't exactly know how to find you."

"Why didn't you send them to me with the mug and stuff?"

He shrugs. "I guess I hoped you might come back for them and take what was yours. But when you didn't and years went by, I knew I couldn't let them go," Eddie explains. "I wasn't in town when this all went down, but Vivienne flew to the island in her jet and demanded I come back and find them."

"I even had them play the theme from *Apocalypse Now*," Miss Vivi confirms. "I am very clever."

"But if you knew I knew your cousin, why did you blow me off all these years for an interview?"

Miss Vivi smiles. "All I knew of you is that you were a woman who had some past with my cousin, and it didn't seem good, and I don't have to talk to anyone I don't want to," she trills. "But when we planned this tour, I was over it. Eddie finally told me what happened, and that he knew you had worked on that story before Mr. Perkins with the good hair here. Also, you're a boss as a journalist. I knew I had to be interviewed by you. This movie just happened to happen at the same time."

"How do we even know these notebooks are real?" Joe says evenly. "Are they dated?"

I riffle through them with my thumb, and it's all there—the first interview with Tonya, the notes I made of every name of every person in the office she thought would talk to me. I think I'm missing one, though. "There are dates," I say. "And they're all before the story broke."

Joe's face is a study in defiance and anger.

"By itself, this doesn't prove anything," he says, still even and crisp. The wobble seems to have been corrected. "They are old notebooks that this guy says he found from thirty years ago. What's that they say about the chain of evidence? Who knows where they really came from? And I still say you gave the story to me."

The door opens again. "She has a witness," Tonya says, coming inside. "You remember Percy?"

Percy Harris, my sister's ex and the man I kind of helped send to jail in a roundabout way, comes in behind her.

"This is like at the end of every episode of *Death in Paradise* when the inspector calls all the murder suspects together and tells everyone who did it," Weedie says.

"I love that show," Miss Vivi says. "I died on an episode."

"I saw that!" my mother says. "You were a famous American diva murdered in her dressing room by the sound guy who was secretly her son. You were beautiful, even dead."

"Shut up!" Joe yells, and everyone does. Nobody likes him, but it's all going down and they don't want to miss it. I guess Sarah finally got to go to one of those types of parties!

"You might want to calm down, my guy," Percy says.

"I don't have to do anything of the sort," Joe says. "You're a felon. Who would believe anything you have to say?"

Percy smiles and looks past him. "Miss Vivienne St. Claire, the goddess," he says, kissing her hand. "May I borrow this microphone, ma'am?"

"Yes, young man, you may," she says, handing it to him.

Percy takes his phone out of his pocket. "This is from June 21, 2021," he says, "when I got out of jail."

"Jail did not dim your light, young man," Miss Vivi purrs. He smiles and hits "Play."

"Tonya! I know you're not going to call me back, and I don't blame you. But I saw that Dawn's husband died, and I'm so sorry," Percy's voice says from the phone.

"Aww!" I say softly. "Thank you."

"SHHH!"

"I know she was never a fan of mine, and she was right, honestly, and I blamed her and you for so long. I know she only started looking into that story because she wanted to back you up and because she wanted to say something important, and then Joe got ahold of it. I don't know how, because she called Junior's office the night before she left. That's why I was extra mad at you both, because she wouldn't let it go. And I wasn't in the mood to defend either one of you. It all started with her, and I was so mad. But I forgive her. I forgive you. I'm so sorry. I don't even know why she didn't write it. I know all the ladies in the office said she talked to them first and she kept calling, but they didn't call her back because Joe told them not to."

The room is completely quiet, which I can tell you never happens in a room full of people that are related to me. I open my mouth, hoping that a voice comes out.

"I never listened to this message," Tonya says, filling in the space, "until yesterday. Dawn, I was so mad at you, but I had to know what it said."

"Brent, is that enough evidence?"

My brother-in-law nods. "I would say so." He turns to Joe. "Mr. Perkins, I believe that my client now has enough people on the record . . ." He looks up at Eddie and Percy and Tonya. "We are all on the record, yes?"

They all nod.

"I'm going to need that microphone back," Miss Vivi says. "Diva's rights!"

"I know what we are able to prove now," Brent says, "and I assume that when you talk to your lawyers, you are going to find out it negates this cease and desist."

"You can go now," my mother says. "*Don't* take a gift bag."

Joe folds his arms like a petulant child who's just seen a video of himself breaking into the pantry for extra cookies but still refuses to concede. "None of this proves you didn't hand the story over to me," he says. "I didn't steal anything."

The door opens again, and an older lady with a short natural steps in. "Yes, you did," she says. "Is this the Roberts house?"

Wait.

"Miss Sheila? From Permits?" I ask.

"Yes," she says. "Tonya asked me to come. Can I still help?"

Tonya hugs her and brings her to the center of the room. "Miss Vivi, may I borrow the mike?"

The diva smiles and presents it to Tonya, who gives it to Sheila from Permits. "Yes. And I don't ever hand the mike over to just anybody!"

"Just ask Michael McDonald," Weedie whispers. "It's in her book."

Sheila from Permits clears her throat. "I didn't think that Dawn was still working on the story, but then she called me the night before it came out, except I know now she didn't know it was coming out because she was like, 'Can we talk again?'" she says. "Joe had told me she had given him the story when he and I had been talking, so I gave him all the proof. But when she called, I didn't know what to think."

"I don't remember it that way," Joe sputters.

"You don't remember leaving this at my house?" she says, pulling something out of her bag. Written on the cover in that familiar scrawly scratch is "Water Park Story #3."

And there it is.

"Where did you get this?" I say, taking it out of her hand.

"Like I said, Joe was . . . at my house once," Sheila says, looking sheepish. "You know . . ."

"Miss Sheila," I say. "I thought you had a girlfriend."

"I have a wife now," she says. "But back then I was into whatever was cute."

"Dawn, you weren't the only one sleeping with sources!" Tonya says brightly. "It's a moral victory!"

"Thank you, Miss Sheila," I say, giving her a reassuring hug. I am so glad she came, but I think we should lock the door now.

"I have a question," Bria James says. "May I?"

"Well, don't start asking for permission now," I say.

"Mr. Perkins," she says to Joe, who seems to be trying to shed his well-moisturized skin and slither away. "We know what you did. There's evidence. But why did you change the script all of a sudden? Why did you double down on making it so nasty to Dawn, like you were scorching earth?"

Brent clears his throat. "I can answer that. Remember at the TV station when the producer made the comment about Joe's not being unstoppable? I called him—Maurice—back and asked him on behalf of you, his fellow City College alumni, to elaborate," he says. "And he told me that the rumor around the business was that Joe's tenure on *National News Now* was not going so well lately. Writer's block or something."

"That's a pattern," I say.

"Anyway, the word is that he was worried about his job and wanted to make sure that this script was salacious enough to be a hit while muddying the waters and ruining your name so badly that the court of public opinion would never believe you."

Son of a . . .

"Whatever you're thinking, don't say it," my mother whispers.

"Dawn, do you have a comment?" asks Susan, who I had forgotten existed. You gotta hand it to her. She doesn't give up.

"Still no, Susan!" I say, turning to Bria James, who has been recording the whole thing. "You got that?"

"I do. We'll share credit."

Joe is still standing here, vibrating with anger. You can almost see the velvet blazer start to spontaneously combust. "This is ridiculous— libelous—and my lawyers will be in touch," he says.

"We're counting on that," Brent says.

Joe seems suddenly small. Smaller than he ever has been. I almost feel sorry for him . . . Nah.

"You know what? You take a gift bag anyway," I say. "I imagine you'll need a snack."

He takes the bag and silently leaves. Didn't even have to drop a house on him.

"That was not a pleasant young man," Miss Vivi says. "But his skin is lovely."

The music comes back on, and she starts singing the chorus of Stevie Wonder's "Happy Birthday."

"Schmevie Schmonder," I say, and laugh.

"What?" my sister says.

"I'll explain later," I say, and grab and hug her. "Tonya! I'm so sorry. For everything."

"I know," she says. "I saw the TV. I was only watching to make fun of you later and be mad some more, but then I realized I was wrong, too. So I had to find Percy."

"You saved the day."

"I did, didn't I?" she says.

"Again, I messed up . . . ," I start, but Tonya puts her hand up to stop me.

"Stop," she says. "You and I can hash it all out later. But I couldn't leave you hanging."

"And you got Percy to come! How did you do that?"

She laughs. "He's changed a lot," she says. "And he even gave me this." Tonya hands me a check.

"Fifteen thousand dollars?"

She nods. "It's that five thousand I loaned him that time. With interest."

Well, the worm has turned. And done cartwheels.

"Did he ever tell you what he did with it? It was hookers, right?"

Tonya shakes her head. "He was going to buy a pit beef truck, but he lost the money in Atlantic City. He was always a bad gambler."

"Maybe," I say. "But he had the winning hand this time."

"That's by far the corniest thing you've ever said," my mother says, dancing by in an impromptu conga line with Miss Vivi, who is now singing "Sweet Child o' Mine" by Guns N' Roses.

"Is anyone going to believe this?" I say. "I barely believe it myself."

"They're all going to believe you now," Tonya says.

"Thanks to you."

"True," my sister says, and plants a big, sloppy kiss on my forehead. "I guess I'm gonna have a bigger part in the sequel."

"What sequel?" I ask. I'm confused, and I haven't even had any punch.

"The one you're gonna write," Tonya says. "To your own story."

And that seems like a really good idea. I'll even give her credit.

Epilogue

The Big Finish

"DAWN!" my mother is yelling from the living room of Suite Two in the ultra-swanky Ivy Hotel, another luxury resort in the City of Baltimore, because we seem to be getting a lot of those here. "They're bringing the car around, and you don't have your shoes on!"

"These are not shoes you put on before you have to," I shout back from the bedroom as Miss Regina puts my last lash on.

"Hold still," she says. "You Roberts girls are so wiggly. Don't you dare mess up this face. This is my first Hollywood premiere, and I need this to look good on Instagram."

Miss Regina has been honing her craft as Miss Vivi's new on-call eyelash architect. I'm shocked we could book her.

"Do it faster," my mother says. "We can't be late to the Senator Theater. There will be cameras."

Tonya comes out of the bathroom, looking immaculate. "It's Dawn's movie. As long as she's waited for this moment, don't rush her."

The heroine of the day. My sister hasn't always liked me, but she loves me.

"Do you think they're going to ask me any questions on the red carpet?" Tonya says. "I have things to say."

"Of course," I say, and hug her carefully so that no one's makeup is mussed. "None of this would be happening without you."

So much has transpired in the two years since my mother's big *Death in Paradise / Columbo* party reveal. The movie people, and Joe's lawyers, immediately wanted to play ball, because it's not a good look to have their golden goose laying bad eggs. They not only dropped all plans to sue, they called Brent immediately to see what arrangements we could make to keep their movie going while not looking stupid.

We agreed that I would rewrite the script, including everything shady about Fawn, except now her name is Dawn. Just Dawn. And Chip's name is Dale, and they fell in love with each other and left to be together. Love is stupid. And Joe is a hotshot who overshot and made the decision to cut me out, but in the movie he is an excellent writer that turns out an amazing story that he runs with. An antihero. People love that stuff. Joe took a break from *National News Now* for some "self-reflection," but now he's back, chastened as much as an ego like that can be. They know a story when they see it.

It's messy and nonlinear, like the truth usually is—all of the hurt and betrayal and punking out that happened. The identities of the good and bad guys depend on who you ask. We are all of those things. But this time, I am not a thirsty mess, and Fawn/Dawn's wig is solid. Crystal Dirkins is a revelation. There's Oscar buzz. I hope she remembers to thank me.

It didn't take me a long time to make that script less terrible. Joe agreed to it because he didn't really have a choice. We have joint credit as screenwriters, which was financially beneficial. Brent asked if I wanted to pursue a defamation suit, but I needed it done with, so I said no. The money for the script was awesome, and I negotiated a percentage of the earnings of the movie on the back end. I put a lot of that into Glitter, which now has an East Coast bureau I lead. Pearl is handling LA. Her stories remain solidly on time. George Michael and Andrew Wham! are still being haters but now in Baltimore.

That's not the end of it—I got a book deal for my memoir, *Into the Deep End: The True Story Behind "Diving into Deception" and One Woman's Crusade for the Truth*, an instant *New York Times* bestseller. It also upped my previously semi-decent speaker's fee to $25,000 a pop, which should go even higher once the movie comes out.

As for the Pulitzer, I didn't sweat it. I did not write the story, and it seemed weird to claim otherwise. But I am listed now as a contributor. The weirdest thing is that Joe and I are OK, as much as we can be. We will never be friends again. I will not forgive him for attempting to bury that guilt under slander about my husband and me. But I look at him sometimes and remember when we were going to be Black Woodward and Bernstein. In a way, we are. Just not like we thought.

And I got this check.

So tonight, Joe and I will both be on the red carpet at Baltimore's legendary Senator Theater for the world premiere of *Diving into Deception*. We will be civil and then go back to our lives, he with Holly Jarvis, the former day care director who is his new, surprisingly age-appropriate girlfriend, and me with . . . you'll never guess.

Fine, you'll guess. Eddie.

"I'm glad I got to make things right in the end," he said to me the night of my mother's party.

I remember smiling in the glow of my victory. It made me super brave. "I'm going to be in town more often," I said. "I'm pretty sure we'll catch up. But I have a question. Do you remember what you wanted to tell me at that Christmas party a thousand years ago?"

Eddie smiled to himself. "You were working that dress," he said. "And for a moment I wanted to tell you how much I liked you, but it wasn't right to go into that, with Sabra and all."

"Whatever happened to her?" I asked.

"We broke up the next day," Eddie said. "I wasn't being fair to her, when I was into someone else."

And again with the blush!

I asked him again why he never sent the notepads. "You had moved on and were happy. After a while, it felt disrespectful to intrude. And we'd not left things on the most positive note. I admit that I kept tabs, right? But it never came up that you were claiming credit, so I left it alone. Is that OK?"

It was. And that was that. I respected that he respected me. It started slow, and then he asked me to come with him to DC to watch him play the drums for a set behind Miss Vivi on her "I'm Still Here!" tour.

"This is my cousin, Eddie! Ain't he cute?" she asked the crowd. "And look down at the front row, everyone, and say hello to his girlfriend, Dawn! I bought her that dress! I have good taste."

"Girlfriend?" I mouthed to Eddie, who smiled.

"Well, if she says so," he mouthed back.

Now I'm back on the East Coast with him, and my family. All of them. Including Brent, Sarah, and their kids, who I see all the time. They seem to like me. They'll all be at the premiere, as will Bria James, whose site rode the traffic to big advertisers. She even has a few staffers. She's also dating my cousin Sondra. They're doing great, and we haven't yelled at each other since the basement.

I wasn't looking for any of this, the movies and premieres. But I like it. I'm telling the truth and being acknowledged for it. I like that I am home with my family. And I love that I can do that in my own way, in my own time, in my own truth. And it's great.

Did I mention the checks?

"Dawn!" my mother says. "Stop monologuing. The car is here."

I grab my tiny purse that Christian Siriano made to match this dress, because he went to school here in Baltimore and he likes a queen of size, then head into the living room.

"Look at you!" my mother says. "I honestly can't say anything bad about how you look."

"Thank you, Mommy," I say, kissing the top of her head.

"I have to tell you something," she says, smoothing her hair. "I don't say this lightly. Dale would be proud of you. He knew that you were talented, and he believed in you. He would be so happy that you told the truth. You did it, girl."

I did, didn't I? For me and for my Dale. He would be proud of me and proud of the truth, and maybe he would have even enjoyed the drama. And I don't need to hear his voice.

I know.

The End. And the Beginning.

ACKNOWLEDGMENTS

Dawn Roberts and her dramatic life are a work of fiction, although there are some things we have in common, like widowhood and a tendency to talk too much. Mostly, we share a deep love of journalism, burnished by a lifelong respect for its truths and responsibilities. So it seemed like a good time to thank all of the people that shaped my own newsroom journey. I'm sure I'm going to forget someone, so forgive me in advance:

Allen Rosskopf, my high school newspaper adviser at Baltimore City College and the first person who made me believe this was a real job. None of this would be possible without you.

Olive Reid, my former associate dean at what is now Philip Merrill College of Journalism at University of Maryland, who provided a shoulder to cry on and her office couch to whine on for classes, jobs, and meaning-of-life stuff.

Every editor who ever hired me: Mohamed Hamaludin, the *Miami Times*; Deena Gross and Stan Hough, the *York Dispatch / Sunday News*; Jan Tuckwood and Nicole Piscopo Neal with thanks to Larry Aydlette for wrangling me, the *Palm Beach Post*; and Kimi Yoshino and Andrea McDaniels, the *Baltimore Banner*.

Special shout-out to all the female journalists who ever mentored me, showed me what was possible in this business even when it got hard, and repeatedly stopped me from quitting to go work at The Gap, including Liz Evans Scolforo, Lauri Lebo, Lynn Kalber, Carol Rose, Liz Balmaseda, Carolyn DiPaolo, and Laura Lippman. Special shout-out to Dara Dixon Kluger for saying "I don't hear clicking!" so I'd stop socializing in the newsroom and sit down and finish my articles every single week.

Besides my journalism friends, I'd like to thank everyone that supported me in writing this book: including my mom, Tina Smith; my bestie, Melanie Hood-Wilson, for hanging out with my kid so I could get pages in; my sister, Lynne Childress, for picking up the phone every time I called to read her something; all of the folks who read earlier versions, including Jon Mattingly, Lauri Lebo, and Nina Metz; Rissa Miller Creative for my beautiful author photo; James Patterson for always telling me the truth; Alex Glass at Glass Literary Management for fighting for me; Charlotte Herscher for the insightful edits; and Selena James at Amazon Publishing for believing in this project in all its iterations. (You said I didn't have to thank you, but I did it anyway.)

Last but not least, I have to thank my son, Brooks, for being so understanding about all those times when Mommy was furiously typing away for days on end and wasn't any fun. This is all for you. I hope you know how much I love you, which you should because I'll never stop saying it.

ABOUT THE AUTHOR

Photo © 2024 Rissa Miller Creative

Leslie Gray Streeter is an award-winning journalist and columnist for the *Baltimore Banner*. She is the author of the memoir *Black Widow: A Sad-Funny Journey Through Grief for People Who Normally Avoid Books with Words Like "Journey" in the Title*, the cohost of the podcast *Fine Beats and Cheeses*, and a frequent speaker on grief. She is also a slow runner, an amateur vegan cook, and a fan of *Law & Order*. Leslie lives in Baltimore, Maryland, with her son, Brooks. For more information, visit www.lesliegraystreeter.com.